gen:LOCK™

STORM

WARNING

gen:LOCK™

STORM WARNING

BY
MELISSA SCOTT

BASED ON THE SERIES CREATED BY
GRAY G. HADDOCK

SCHOLASTIC INC.

ROOSTER 🐓 TEETH

© 2020 Rooster Teeth Productions, LLC

All rights reserved. Published by Scholastic Inc., *Publishers since 1920.*
SCHOLASTIC and associated logos are trademarks and/or registered trademarks of
Scholastic Inc.

The publisher does not have any control over and does not assume any responsibility for
author or third-party websites or their content.

No part of this publication may be reproduced, stored in a retrieval system, or transmitted
in any form or by any means, electronic, mechanical, photocopying, recording,
or otherwise, without written permission of the publisher. For information regarding
permission, write to Scholastic Inc., Attention: Permissions Department, 557 Broadway,
New York, NY 10012.

This book is a work of fiction. Names, characters, places, and incidents are either the
product of the author's imagination or are used fictitiously, and any resemblance to
actual persons, living or dead, business establishments, events, or locales is entirely
coincidental.

Library of Congress Cataloging-in-Publication Data available

ISBN 978-1-338-60107-7

10 9 8 7 6 5 4 3 2 1   20 21 22 23 24

Printed in the U.S.A.   23

First printing 2020

Book design by Betsy Peterschmidt

TO JO AND AMY, WITH LOVE

1

From thirty thousand feet, the distant wall of cloud looked almost beautiful, the swelling towers gleaming in the sunlight, the sky a rich, deep blue above them. The satellite feed painted a far uglier picture, a broad curve of cloud reaching inland from the Gulf of Mexico, and when Cammie looked from it to the image beside the communications console, only the faint glow of blue eyes indicated that Julian Chase was mixing in to *Renegade*'s cabin and not actually standing there.

"Say again, Lieutenant?" Chase said. "I'm not sure I follow you."

"I think you do." Miranda Worth's projection gave a wry grin and reached to one side, dragging a map into existence and flattening it to show the terrain under the storm. "We had word that a group of refugees was making their way along the back roads network, and we'd already assigned a Vanguard unit to meet and collect them once they crossed into the delta."

Chase looked faintly skeptical, and Cammie couldn't blame

him. That was a fairly typical mission, not one that required the gen:LOCK team.

"However," Miranda said, and behind her avatar, Cammie saw Kazu Iida roll his eyes.

"Here it comes." The spoken words were in Japanese; the translation flickered across Cammie's field of vision, and she grinned. Kazu generally said what he was thinking, and this time you couldn't really argue with him.

Miranda ignored the comment. "Since we made that arrangement, the group contacted us again to say they had linked up with a second group of refugees who claimed to be carrying information vital to the Polity. The refugee leader is a member of the underground; she couldn't vouch for its accuracy, but the new group said it had something to do with stolen brains, or maybe stolen minds. You see why that caught our attention."

"Yeah." Chase lifted one hand to his head, though everyone knew he couldn't actually scratch his scalp. "Okay, I see why you—why we—would be interested . . ."

"We have a Vanguard unit on the way to the rendezvous point," Miranda cut in. A beacon flared on the map. "We've now received intel that Union forces are moving to intercept them. If they've got anything on the Union's use of the gen:LOCK technology—we want it. We need it, Chase."

Chase looked over his shoulder. "Cammie?"

Cammie touched keys and hooked her fingers into the projection that appeared, stretching and turning it so that it matched Miranda's map. She gave it a push, and it settled over the image, hiding the details under the ugly bands of cloud. She frowned and moved a virtual slider so that the angry reds and yellows and greens faded enough to see the terrain through it. A lot of it was flat and open, the kind of terrain where they could land and upload to the Holons, but all of it was under the shifting color that marked the outer bands of the incoming hurricane.

Chase gave her a quick smile of thanks, but his eyes were on the map. "Where—" he began, and a new beacon appeared on Miranda's map. "Got it. What's the Vanguard's ETA?"

"The rendezvous is set for 1450," Miranda said. "Crews report that they're on schedule in spite of the weather."

Chase sketched a course across the map, then looked over his shoulder. "Yaz?"

Yasamin Madrani didn't look away from *Renegade*'s controls, the map repeated on her heads-up display. "We can just do it. If the weather holds."

Chase nodded. "It'll be tight, Captain, but we can get there."

"Good. Back up Vanguard and help them get the refugees to the base at De Soto. And find out what it is they know."

"Roger that," Chase said. Miranda's projection vanished, but the map remained, and Chase poked at it, stretching and shifting it to examine the terrain. Kazu pushed himself up out of his seat and came to join him.

"That's the rendezvous? Looks like it could flood."

Chase nodded. "We'll need to get in and out before the rivers rise."

Cammie looked at the map. The rendezvous point lay between two rivers, the land flat and empty. She pulled up the latest satellite data, but nothing had changed since the last time she'd seen it. She looked back at the rest of the team. "Ahem. I cannae believe I'm even asking this, but isn't that an actual hurricane? Right there, where we're going?"

"Yep." Chase gave her a quick smile.

Cammie swallowed the word that rose to her lips. She was trying to work on her cursing, as Dr. Weller had put it, and had agreed to forfeit Ether credit for every time she swore out loud. On the other hand, she thought the situation warranted a curse or two. Hurricane Pam was coming ashore right on the 88th meridian, the dividing line between the territory taken by the Union and the part still held by the Polity, and that was only going to add to the chaos along that contested border.

Four years ago, the Union had swarmed ashore in New York City, capturing the city and pushing west. It was only in the last year or so that the Polity had been able to establish a new border along the 88th, and the Polity was still reeling from those losses. gen:LOCK had done its part to hold that border, but the Union had made more than one incursion deep into Polity territory. It was worrying to think about what

4

the Union might be hiding behind the swelling storm. The clouds in the image looked more menacing than ever.

"Another thing for which I did not sign up," Valentina Romanyszyn murmured. She didn't move from where she was sitting, one leg cocked over the arm of the seat.

Cammie shot her a glance and decided that she wasn't going to help. "But I mean—" Everyone was looking at her now, except Yaz, who was flying, and she swiveled the "ears" on her headband for emphasis. "*Can* we fly into it? It's a hurricane!"

"It's within *Renegade*'s tolerances," Yaz said.

"Yaz is right," Chase confirmed. "The Hornbills are designed to take worse than this."

"Though of course that has not been tested," Valentina said.

Chase dropped his head to look at her. "Seriously?"

She spread her hands. "What? I'm not saying we shouldn't go, but—"

"It'll be fine," Yaz said through gritted teeth.

Kazu shrugged. "Eh, if the Vanguard needs our help, I say we help them. It's only weather."

Cammie nodded agreement. gen:LOCK was intended to work with the Vanguard, to fight alongside its more conventional units. Despite Dr. Weller's best efforts, the five of them were the only people who could safely use the gen:LOCK technology, uploading their consciousness into the Mindframes that controlled the giant mechanical Holons.

Well, there *had* been six of them, once, but the man they'd known as Rob Sinclair had turned out to be a Union spy and nearly brought the program down before it even got started. Dr. Weller had worked closely with the Vanguard to develop gen:LOCK and the Holons. After his death during the Battle of the Anvil, gen:LOCK had continued to work closely with Vanguard's command. They'd done everything from combat support to hit-and-run rescues. Helping refugees was certainly something they'd done before.

Valentina sat up, calling a screen of her own to swipe through a series of datasets. "The latest intel says the Union only has a few Spider Tank units in the area. That might be trouble for the Vanguard, but less so for us."

"We should be there in an hour and forty-five minutes," Yaz said. "All systems are green."

The carrier rocked, banking onto its new course, the tower clouds now centered in the windshield. "Better strap in," Chase said. His avatar was standing between Yaz's seat and Miguel Garza in the copilot's chair. Migas wasn't a pilot himself, but he knew *Renegade*'s systems better than anyone else on the team. He also looked after the Holons, of course, but Cammie was learning right along with him. Everyone had liked her first unit mods; she had some more thoughts about that, the next time they had a bit of a break.

If we ever get a break, a treacherous voice whispered in the back of her mind. As always, the memory of Nemesis made her stomach lurch. Nemesis had been the Union's answer to the gen:LOCK team—had been created from gen:LOCK technology, from the Mindframe, the "brain" the Union had retrieved when it captured Chase's first Holon. Union scientists had taken Chase's cyberbrain, twisted him, and placed that consciousness into a terrifying, four-armed monster as powerful as any of their own Holons. She could still remember her first encounter with it, a shadow looming out of the night that leaped on her before she could fight back.

Before she even really knew *how* to fight back.

With a vicious lurch, Nemesis had her pinned, three of its massive hands digging into her armor while she pawed frantically at its arms and chest and empty air, and its fourth hand ripped off her Holon's head. She was blind then, panicked, hearing only the frantic cries of her fellow recruits rushing to her aid while Nemesis tore into her core, clawing through the machine in pursuit of her eBrain. It had been the barest luck that the others had arrived in time to rescue her. But Nemesis was dead, dead and destroyed, and the Vanguard swore there were no other copies. She refused to give it any additional attention. Anyway, gen:LOCK had been more or less flat out since Nemesis was defeated, helping the Vanguard here, running errands for RTASA (Rogue Technology Aeronautics & Space Administration, an underground organization that is sponsored by Marc Holcroft and led by Dr. Fatima Jha) there, even delivering parts and supplies when no other units could get through. It hadn't left much time to think about anything but keeping the Holons running, and there was a part of her that was glad of it. All that work meant she was too tired to dream.

Renegade dropped suddenly, and she clutched at her seat, swallowing hard. She still wasn't entirely used to flying, and the Hornbills seemed to bounce around a lot more than the civilian transports.

"Cammie," Chase called. "Strap in."

"Right, yeah." She pulled the belt across her lap and clicked in the shoulder straps as *Renegade* gave another sickening jerk. "Is it going to be like this all the way in?"

"Probably worse," Valentina said.

"Not too much worse." Chase smiled. "It looks like we can slide in between two of the heavy bands. Get in, back up the Vanguard, and get out before things get worse."

"Will we be able to land?" Kazu asked. "I've been through typhoons before, when I was a kid. This storm is going to push the water right up the bay."

"We should be far enough north of the actual coast," Chase said.

Cammie reached for the latest weather forecasts and satellite feeds and everything else she could find, hung them one on top of the other, and added Miranda's map as an underlay. "According to our weather center, the eye of the storm is going to come right up Mobile Bay," she said. "They're predicting a twenty-foot storm surge along the coast, and a fifteen-foot well up into the rivers." *About six meters, then*, she translated, *and four and a half meters inland.* That was a lot of water.

"When is it supposed to hit?" Chase asked, and Cammie frowned at her displays, trying to sort out the information.

"Working on it." The rendezvous point was about twenty miles inland, depending on where you decided the actual coastline was—there was a deep bay, maybe twenty-five miles from north to south, before you hit the river mouth—but that didn't actually make things better. If she was reading the forecasts correctly, the storm would just drive the ocean up that narrowing space and keep funneling it into the rivers. That might be why there weren't any settlements there. She frowned at the numbers. "Okay, high tide isn't for another eight hours; that's when the flooding's likely to start. And the water will just keep rising as the storm comes onshore."

"How fast is it coming?" Kazu asked.

Cammie checked the latest satellite download. "Seven kilometers an hour—sorry, a little over four knots, I make it."

"That gives us a little time," Chase said. He waved his hand to copy the map to the air in front of every team member except Yaz. A white line crossed the empty green between the rivers, and a red star marked a point just east of one of the wider branches. "That's the rendezvous point, and the line is what's left of Highway 65. It looks like they've picked a point before it crosses the Tensaw—that bridge used to be intact, but maybe they're worried about crossing it in this weather."

"I would worry about that," Valentina said. "Also about Union forces. The Spider Tanks will not be bothered by rain and wind. We can expect air cover as well, though possibly not as much."

"That's all open ground," Chase said. "The weather is going to turn it to mud. They're likely to have more trouble with it than we are."

Renegade bounced again, and Cammie dug her nails into the arm of her seat. They were going to be fine, she trusted Yaz's piloting completely, but it wasn't going to be a lot of fun. The cloud towers loomed closer in the windshield, tops catching the sunlight, the thickening bases hidden in gloom. Yaz glanced at something on her displays and banked *Renegade* gently to the east, threading a path between two of the smaller towers. In the distance, Cammie thought she saw a flash of lightning, and she ducked her head to focus on her own displays. She'd look for a safe place to land, someplace close enough to the rendezvous but on higher ground. If there was any. She scowled at her own pessimism, and went looking for more data.

Yaz threaded her way between the bands of clouds, her hands firm on the controls but not tight, just as she had been taught. *Renegade* bumped and jostled in the unsteady air,

not as bad as it could be, but enough to make her appreciate the harness that held her in her seat. To the south, the
clouds were taller and thicker, columns and towers rising like
distant cities, deceptively beautiful against the bright sky at
altitude. She had seen ruins like that in the desert, piled
stone so ancient only the archaeologists could say for sure
who built them, the once-sharp lines of cut stone worn blunt
and blurred by the centuries. *Towers of Mazandaran*, she
thought. A perilous border to be avoided at all costs.

As if to emphasize the thought, *Renegade* hit an air
pocket and bounced, dropping three hundred feet before
she could catch it. She corrected, grim-faced, and Chase
mixed in between the pilot and copilot's seats, his legs jittering with static where they impinged on the consoles. "How're
we doing?" he asked.

"On course and on schedule," Yaz answered automatically.
The heads-up display still showed them firmly in the corridor
between the two bands of heavier cloud, though that corridor was narrowing sharply as they made their way farther east.
Unfortunately, the rendezvous point was farther south, neces-
sitating a turn into the heavy winds and rain of the banded
clouds. She was still trying to decide if it would be better to
stay out of them as long as possible, and risk a steep descent
into crosswinds, or turn south sooner, and have the wind at
their tail. *Probably the latter*, she thought, and risked a quick
glance at Chase. "We'll need to turn south fairly soon. Migas,
can you put up the course?"

"Right." Migas reached for his console, and the secondary screen widened and brightened in the windshield.

Chase leaned forward slightly, as though that would help him to see. "You think we're better off coming in from the west? That's going to be pretty rough."

"I think it's better than the crosswinds," Yaz answered. She toggled to the alternate course. "That's pushing our tolerances more than we need to."

"Yeah." Chase flicked back to the original screen. "I see your point. How's Vanguard doing? Do we know?"

"I've been monitoring," Migas said. "So far, so good, though the satellites say they're going to hit some heavier weather in the next half hour. They say they'll make the rendezvous on time, but I'll keep checking with them."

"Good."

The radar pinged, Renegade's systems highlighting a blotch of yellow with a rapidly reddening center that was creeping uncomfortably close to their course. In the distance, Yaz picked out an even more solid-looking mass of cloud: no fairy-tale tower this, but a gray-shadowed wall. Lightning flickered in its depths, and she adjusted her course, watching the change cascade through the range of variables displayed beneath the radar image. Fuel consumption, time to target, range and return time, and the rest: All of them looked good, and she nodded. "Do we have a landing site?"

"Cammie's looking for one," Chase said.

Yaz felt herself stiffen for a fraction of a second, made

herself shift against the restraining harness. Cammie knew as much about finding a landing site as either Kazu or Valentina—it wasn't like either one of them had had anything to do with air support—but this was more about hacking the satellite systems. Here on the edge of Union territory, that was an important factor, and she nodded. "Any luck?"

"Nothing yet." Cammie's voice floated forward from her station in the middle seats. "The good news is that it's all open terrain, no towns or anything like that to worry about."

"And the bad news?" That, predictably, was Valentina, and Yaz suppressed a sigh.

"It looks like it's open because it's flat and muddy and floods in bad weather," Cammie answered. "Which is pretty much what we've got. I can pick a lot of places, but I'm having trouble telling if they'll stay secure."

"High ground?" Yaz suggested, and could almost hear Cammie roll her eyes.

"Yeah, I'd thought of that. There isn't much, but I'm still looking."

"Keep on it," Chase said.

"Hey, boss," Migas called. "Transmission from Vanguard, De Soto Team Baker."

That was the group tasked with the extraction, and Yaz frowned. They ought to be maintaining radio silence to avoid drawing Union attention. Chase didn't look pleased either. "Put 'em through, Migas. Let's keep this short."

"Short and sweet as we can, gen:LOCK," a woman's voice

said, and Yaz realized Migas had opened the mics before Chase had finished speaking. "Nguyen here, commanding the drop squad. We're running into heavier weather than anticipated, winds seven to ten knots above satellite prediction in very heavy rain. Thought you should know."

"Can you make the rendezvous on time?" Chase asked.

"Still planning on it," Nguyen answered. "We'll update if that changes."

"Any word from the refugees?"

"Their last transmission reported them on schedule," Nguyen said. "But this weather's going to slow them down, too."

And probably worse than us, Yaz thought. It would be no fun at all to try to push through the wind and flooding rain in whatever motley collection of vehicles the refugees had managed to collect.

"Right." Chase made a face, but his voice was as relaxed as ever. "Let us know if you hear anything more. gen:LOCK out."

"Roger that," Nguyen answered. "Team Baker out."

Chase looked over his shoulder. "Any luck, Cammie?"

"Depends. I'm not having much luck finding high ground—I don't think there really is any; it's all flat and marshy. But—"

Light flared on Yaz's console, showing the ground around the rendezvous site, the line of the old highway cutting across the empty green.

"I know it's a risk and all," Cammie said, "but what if we landed on the highway? It's up on pylons, at least here, by where we're going. And that'll make it easier for us to deploy."

"There's no sign of Union air cover yet," Migas said. "But landing on an elevated highway, in this wind?"

Yaz considered, letting their plans unspool in her mind. Yes, there would be more risk, more wind even a few feet off the ground, and you never knew what shape the old roads would be in. On the other hand, once they were uploaded to the Holons, they could use the road to get to the rendezvous that much more quickly . . . "Maybe not on an elevated section," she said aloud, "but otherwise that's a good idea, Cammie."

"I can find a flat spot," Cammie said. "Yeah, here we go. It's maybe half a mile farther west, but it's not up in the air."

The image on the console shifted, displaying a different stretch of highway, six lanes of cracked concrete and a flat, empty median on a level with the roadway. "Yes," Yaz said, and felt Chase looking at her.

"You good?"

"Yes," Yaz said again. "Good call, Cammie."

"Putting a pin in it for you," Cammie said, and an instant later a beacon flared on the heads-up display, signaling the direction.

"Thanks." Yaz checked her course, running the numbers in her head. Even with the stronger winds, they were within *Renegade*'s tolerances, though lifting again with the weight of the Holons could get tricky. Still, it was nothing she couldn't handle, and she toggled the radar again, looking for the best path through the storm. Conditions were getting worse, but there was still a looping path that would bring them around the area where the rain and lightning were heaviest. "Beginning descent to fifteen thousand feet. This will be a little bumpy."

Cammie clung to her seat as *Renegade* bore through the storm, the harness digging into her shoulders and thighs. Nugget, her four-legged robot "pet," squirmed inside her jacket, protesting, and she tucked him more tightly against her ribs. The last thing anyone needed was the distraction of her robotic pet running loose, or being thrown around the cabin. Maybe she should have left him back at RTASA with Henry Wu, but there hadn't seemed to be any risk in bringing Nugget along this time. When she glanced up from her screens, she could see Chase's avatar standing between the pilots' seats, one hand resting on Yaz's chair as though he could feel it. The image was fizzy with static, the edges blurred and jittering: It was taking most of *Renegade*'s computer power to keep the aircraft on course. Not that Chase needed to be there; since the last terrible fight with Nemesis, he was permanently part of the Mindframe and could receive all of *Renegade*'s data directly, but she suspected he thought they found it encouraging to see him there. She wasn't sure how she felt about it. On the one hand, Chase had been one of the Vanguard's top pilots, so he knew as much as anyone about getting them through this storm. On the other . . . Chase had been one of the casualties of the Battle of New York, saved because he was gen:LOCK compatible. When Cammie joined gen:LOCK, what was left of his body had been suspended in a tank, ineligible for regeneration because of the Union nanotech infesting it. He had given that up in the fight with Nemesis, deliberately exceeding his uptime, allowing his mind to become incompatible with his body. His avatar was a constant reminder of the risks they all ran, the price they might have to pay.

They had reached the last stage of the descent, the windshield full of gray and running with rain, the heads-up display glowing brighter than ever and Chase's avatar balanced between the pilot's and copilot's seats as though *Renegade* wasn't lurching up and sideways before dropping like a stone. Yaz seemed as calm as ever, her hands steady on the controls, eyes fixed on her displays, and Cammie couldn't resist a quick glance across the cabin. Kazu was hunched in his chair, arms folded across his chest, legs braced against the decking. Valentina looked bored, but her hands were closed tight on the arms of her chair. That wasn't something she would want anyone else to see, Cammie knew, and she looked quickly back at her own console.

The line of the highway showed bright on her map, cutting across wetlands and marsh; the satellite display showed darker patches where the concrete had been broken and not replaced since the 88th meridian became the border between the Polity and the Union, but there were long stretches where the roadway was still intact. Yaz had confirmed they could land there. Cammie swallowed a yelp as *Renegade* lurched again. *Yaz said it would be all right.*

The clouds beyond the windshield looked darker than ever, the rain sheeting across the treated Perspex. There was a flicker of something—a shape, a shadow—and then it was gone again.

"One thousand feet," Yaz said. "Ten miles west of the rendezvous."

Cammie looked back at her own displays, the flashing X that indicated the proposed landing creeping closer. To the north, four lights in a diamond formation marked the Vanguard team on its way in. She ran her fingers over the controls, and the computer spit back an answer: Vanguard was landing in fifteen minutes, conditions more or less the same for them as they were for *Renegade*. "Still no sign of the Union," she said, and saw Valentina stir.

"Let us be grateful for small favors."

The windshield flickered again, shadows and more solid images showing at the base of the windshield, and then they were out of the clouds, skimming just below them while the delta stretched out green and gray beneath. The rain smeared the crisp shapes of the satellite display into blurred oblongs. Yaz flicked a switch to bleed air from the compressors, clearing the canopy, and the view steadied, the highway coming into focus as Yaz banked to put the wind behind them.

"The bridge looks intact," she said. "I'll put us down on this side."

"Looks good," Chase said.

"Vanguard is landing." Cammie watched the lights stop and change color. "So far, so good."

"How far are they from the rendezvous?" Chase asked.

"Right on top of it," Cammie answered. Her display flipped to green, and Migas pressed one hand to his earphone.

"Vanguard Team Baker says they're down and safe. No sign of the refugees yet, but they're early."

Chase nodded. "Put us down, Yaz. Whenever you're ready."

Renegade was dropping lower and lower, details of the rain-lashed ground growing ever more distinct. Yaz had them at a slight angle to the highway, crabbing against the wind; the twin lines of pavement appeared cracked and empty, the painted lines faded to nothing. Between them, there was a gap that hadn't shown on the map, the road rising on pylons above turgid water. To the north, the bank rose gently toward a line of trees.

"On the bank or the road?" Yaz asked.

"The road if you can do it," Chase answered.

They were coming closer to the concrete, close enough to see the tops of the trees bending in the wind. The lanes were empty, open, and then *Renegade* jerked upward and a pylon with the remains of a bright green sign flashed past beneath them. Cammie suppressed another yelp and saw the ground drop away ahead of them, the highway a single thread spanning a churning expanse of brown. *Renegade*'s engines roared, the entire machine jostling and slowing as Yaz shifted modes. The great engines rotated to provide downward force, and *Renegade* settled to a lurching halt a dozen yards shy of the bridge. Even through the rain, it was obvious that the other span had collapsed, but their section stretched securely to the far side.

"I don't know about that," Migas said, not quite under his breath, and Chase put a hand against his shoulder.

"From what Miranda said, refugees have been taking their machines across without a problem."

"They don't weigh what a Holon does," Migas said.

"I can put us down on the other side," Yaz suggested.

Kazu unbuckled his harness and came to look over Migas's shoulder. "We can wade across if we have to. We're safer on this side."

"Team Baker says they have the refugees in sight," Migas said.

Chase nodded. "Tell them to expect us." He turned to the team. "Let's suit up. Migas, you and Caliban set the electronic countermeasures and keep an eye on things here."

Cammie unfastened herself from her harness and followed the others to the middle compartment, where the gen:LOCK technology had been installed. As always, she felt a little silly about it, as though she was stepping into some anime she'd watched when she was little, but at the same time, she knew all too well that this wasn't a fantasy. They were the only people in the world who were gen:LOCK compatible, just the five of them against everything the Union could throw at them. And they'd made a difference, though at a cost she wasn't going to think about, not when she was ready to upload.

She sat on the edge of the pod long enough to dislodge Nugget from his place in her jacket, then stretched out on the now-familiar cushions. Nugget leaped out of the pod and onto Caliban's shoulder, and Chase's avatar gave her a quick grin as Caliban lowered the cover into place. She wondered what it would be like to be permanently uploaded, like Chase was, and shoved that thought away before it could settle. That was not something she wanted to be thinking about, not when it was something that could happen if she wasn't careful—

And she wouldn't think about *that*, either. She wriggled herself more comfortably into the padding, hearing the distant whine of the other capsules closing, and shut her eyes, deliberately slowing her breathing. She felt the first prickle of contact, a skittering on her skin, static on her brain, and then the sense of pressure, of a rising pulse that threatened to drive her under, a thudding against the bones of her skull. And then she was in, uploaded, surrounded by the

Mindscape controls, and a heartbeat later settled into the familiar embrace of her Holon.

She was folded up to fit into *Renegade*'s rear hold, arms wrapped around her knees, and controlled the instinctive desire to move as Caliban lowered the rear hatch. The wind shrieked in, the first gust strong enough to move even the mass of the Holons, and she held on more tightly as the system jerked into motion, ferrying them each toward the door. She was the last out, got her feet down in time but staggered as she missed the edge of the pavement and her metal foot sank into the soft ground. A gust of wind hit her, and Kazu caught her arm.

"Careful."

"Ugh." Cammie pulled her foot out of the mud and stepped hastily up onto the pavement. She dragged her other foot after her, shaking it to free the clinging slop, which Kazu barely managed to dodge. A fan of mud spread across *Renegade*'s side, and Migas's face appeared in the windshield.

"Everything okay?"

"Yeah, sorry," Cammie said. "That was me." She was glad there was no way a Holon could blush.

"Vanguard Team Baker, this is gen:LOCK," Chase said. "We're down and on our way to your position. What's your status?"

"gen:LOCK, Team Baker." The voice in Cammie's ears was a woman's, distorted by static, but clear enough to understand.

"We have the refugees in range and are moving to make our pickup."

"We should go on foot," Yaz said. "We're not far, and this weather . . ."

Chase nodded, and voices exploded in their comm.

Incoming! Incoming!

Bogies! Spider Tanks, coming from the river, a whole pack of them—

Strider Four, cover the truck—

"Better fly," Chase said. "Yaz, with me. The rest of you, move in as fast as you can." He angled his wings and leaped into the air, wobbling for an instant before he adjusted to the turbulence. Yaz rose after him, and Kazu crouched, extruding the wheels hidden in his feet.

"What are we waiting for?" he demanded, and started down the highway, his stride lengthening as he fell into a skater's rhythm.

"What, indeed?" Val murmured, but followed, his cannon clutched close to his chest.

2

CAMMIE EXTRUDED HER own wheels and skated after, the wind sending her skidding sideways over the concrete until she figured out how to crouch low enough to present less of a target. The heads-up display said the wind was steady at forty miles an hour, which she wouldn't have thought was enough to shift the Holon's mass, but adding motion changed the equation. Chase and Yaz had already vanished into the rain, were just dots on her heads-up display, arrowing in on the flashing beacons that were the Vanguard Striders and the approaching Spider Tanks, and she poured on the speed to catch up with Kazu and Val.

One at a time on the bridge, Val ordered over the gen:LOCK network, and slid to a stop. *Kazu first.*

I'm lighter, Cammie said, skidding in at his side. The wind hit her again, and she put a hand to the pavement to steady herself. *I should go.*

If it will hold him, it will hold each of us, Val said, and Kazu's heavy head bent in agreement. Cammie opened her mouth to object. She was the lightest, and she wasn't some kid who needed to be protected, but she'd learned not to argue with Val when he used that tone.

Kazu started out onto the bridge, stepping carefully at first, then picking up speed as he grew more confident of his footing. At the middle of the span, he wavered in a gust of wind, then caught himself, and crossed the rest of the way without incident. He turned back, waving. *Come on.*

I will cover you, Val said.

Cammie felt a flick of anger, but suppressed it. Val was the marksman. Covering fire was his job; he didn't need to announce it. Cammie took a deep breath and scooted forward. The concrete showed cracks in places, and there were gaps in the side of the road where the metal drain covers had rusted away. The barriers that were once meant to keep cars from going off the edge barely reached the Holon's ankles, and she struggled to keep in the center of the roadway. Below the bridge, the Tensaw River rushed past, brown and angry, knots of debris poking out of the flood. And then she was across, and Val was following, his Holon's cape pulled tight to keep from catching the wind.

"Twelve Spider Tanks, coming from the south," Chase said on the general frequency, and there confused acknowledgment from Team Baker.

The rain was letting up a little, and Cammie could see the flash of ground fire not a half mile away, three Striders in a V formation across the roadway. There was a Hornbill on the median just short of the river's edge, rear door lowered, and a string of motorcycles was racing toward it, an eight-wheeled cargo hauler lumbering after them. A second Hornbill disgorged another string of Striders, fanning out to protect them, and the third Hornbill had lifted off again, hovering, cannons spitting fire at the line of Spider Tanks emerging from the rain.

Chase swooped down out of the clouds, Yaz a blur of yellow on his tail, bright against the gray as they laid down a barrage in front of the oncoming tanks. The Striders were moving forward, firing, while the motorcycles swerved and dodged, but the river curved around, blocking them to the north, and it was obvious that the Spider Tanks were trying to push them back against it. Rockets fired, and a Strider went to one knee; a second struck among the motorcycles. The lead bike shattered, and the bike behind it toppled and skidded, shedding its rider and a trail of machinery. A third bike couldn't avoid a piece of fairing and went down, too, its rider rolling over and over to lie in a boneless heap.

Yaz. Bank right, Chase said, and flicked to his left. The wind caught and tumbled him, and then he cupped wings and powered fans and came upright with his energy rifle cradled in his hands. He picked off the tail-end Spider Tank, and another exploded under the blast of Yaz's energy beams.

Kazu lowered his head and charged in, leaping off the pavement without breaking stride to grab the first Spider

Tank by its lifted leg. He swept it off the ground, slammed it into another tank, and stepped up onto the wreckage to launch himself at the next pair of tanks. Val dropped to one knee behind the line of Striders, cradling his rifle as he looked for the perfect shot. He fired once; a tank tipped sideways, and Kazu overturned it with a shout of pure glee.

Cammie launched her targeting drones, but instead, a red light washed across her displays: The wind was too strong for her to use them. She swore at the numbers and took a couple of shots anyway, swearing again when she missed. She wasn't going to be much good in the fight, not without her drones, and she looked around, extending her sensors as she did so. There was nothing in range except their knot of fighting, no sign of Union fighters, and she shunted that information into Mindscape for the others, firing unsuccessfully at the line of Spider Tanks.

Out of the corner of her eye, she could see the cargo hauler wallowing back onto the pavement, trying to make it to the Hornbill that still waited on the road. They were on the northern section of the highway, and Cammie pushed off down the southern section, trying to put herself between the hauler and the Spider Tanks, and she felt automatic fire rattle across her legs. Another rocket flashed past her. It missed the hauler but struck the roadway ahead of it, just where the pavement rose to join the bridge where the Hornbill was waiting. Half the lane crumpled away, and the hauler skidded to a stop, one wheel almost over the edge.

Cammie fired both her pistols at the nearest tank, then turned and ran for the hauler, catching the rear frame and holding it steady until she felt the wheels churn and the hauler reverse onto more solid ground. The bridge was in bad shape, with half the inside lane chewed away and more chunks of concrete falling as the water gnawed at the pylons and the mud bank. The main support beam was still intact, though, and if she could just get under it . . .

She slid down into the water before she could change her mind. The Holon's sensors registered that it was cold, the bottom soft and slippery, but the water barely came up to the Holon's calf. She felt more bullets rattle against her skin, and then the flash and sting as a rocket exploded a few yards to her left. She ignored them both, feeling for solid footing in the murky water, and reached for the sagging support beam. It wobbled under her touch, but she could see that both ends were still secure. She turned and braced her shoulders under it, shifting to the Vanguard frequency.

"Go on, I've got it." She craned her head to see if the hauler's driver had heard her, caught a glimpse of gray hair and a grim face behind beating windshield wipers. The hauler slewed and straightened, driving forward onto the roadway. Cammie grunted, feeling its weight as the Holon's servos engaged, and another rocket exploded overhead, shrapnel raining down on them. The hauler lurched forward, and she felt the soft riverbed give way beneath her. Then the hauler was past, rolling onto solid pavement, and

Cammie slipped sideways, the beam falling with a huge splash. She straightened, the muddy water dripping off of her, and turned back to the fight just in time to see Chase dive on a fleeing Spider Tank and blast it to smoking ruin. Kazu had another tank by two legs and slammed it to the ground, then jumped on it with both feet, flattening the armor.

That was fun, he said. *Too bad that's the last of them.*

Anyone pick up further sign of Union fighters? Chase asked, circling back, and Yaz came to a graceful landing beside a damaged Strider.

Cammie didn't find anything.

Keep looking, Chase said.

Right. Cammie hauled herself back up onto the bank, her fingers gouging yard-long ditches in the soft earth, and extended her sensors again. *Still nothing.*

Chase switched to the general frequency. "Team Baker. Better button up and get moving."

"Thanks for the help," the woman's voice answered, "but I'm worried about fighters—"

"We're not spotting any, ma'am," Chase said. "We'll be glad to provide you with air escort back to your base."

Chase, if we go with them, there's a good chance we won't be able to leave until the storm's over, Yaz said.

We can't abandon them, Chase returned, and switched back to the general frequency. "Though you'll probably be stuck with us for a while."

"Glad to have you," the captain answered. "Plenty of room at De Soto Base."

Cammie picked out a Strider, the one hanging back while the others recovered damaged machines and got themselves and anything salvageable back on board the Hornbill. The third Hornbill had landed next to the first and was getting Striders on board as well. Cammie looked over her shoulder to see the hauler stopped at the foot of the Hornbill's ramp. A motley crowd of refugees milled below, the people helping one another into safety, pushing four-wheelers piled high with bags and boxes, one woman even pulling a wheeled suitcase. The last of them vanished into the Hornbill, and the ramp began to lift.

"Glad to oblige," Chase said, touching two fingers to his forehead in salute as the leader's Strider finally turned back toward her Hornbill. *Yaz, get everybody back to* Renegade *and let's get moving.*

What about you? Yaz asked.

The Holons had no facial expressions, but Cammie could feel Chase's grin. *Air cover.*

Do you think that's wise?

They've got a load of refugees, Chase answered. *If the Union does show up, they'll need all the help they can get.*

The wind had picked up again, blasting them sideways as they made their way back to *Renegade,* and Cammie was glad to fold herself up and let Caliban bring her Holon on board. The lid lifted from her capsule, and she sat up, swinging her legs over the edge as Nugget leaped for her shoulder to balance like a cat. Yaz was already out and moving, heading for the cockpit with Valentina on her heels. Kazu looked back over his shoulder.

"Nice work with the bridge."

"Thanks." Cammie felt heat rising in her face and wished for the millionth time she didn't have skin that showed every shift of emotion. She hadn't been much use in the fight. No matter how much she practiced, she still couldn't hit anything without her targeting drones, and they'd turned out to be useless in the high winds. Though she could probably figure out a way to fix that, or at least to build herself a foul-weather drone—

"Cammie!" Yaz called from the pilot's chair. "Strap in!"

Hastily, Cammie pulled the straps into place, and *Renegade* lurched into the air. They seemed to rise forever, engines rotated fully downward and power at full blast, before Yaz switched flight modes. The wings extended and *Renegade* pitched down and sideways as the control surfaces caught, and Yaz brought them back around in a smooth curve to follow the others west toward De Soto Base.

Cammie looked at her own displays, tugging and adjusting the overlays until she had both the satellite weather and *Renegade*'s sensor display in the main window, with the tactical radar, Vanguard's map routine, and a weather overview in the secondaries. The map said they were eighty-three miles from the base—not far even in this weather—and it looked as though they'd be flying out of the heavy rain in only a few minutes. The other Hornbills were ahead of them, three bright blue dots flying just under the cloud layer, and Yaz matched their altitude. A fourth dot flickered in and out at the tail of the Hornbills' formation, and Cammie looked up to see a distant flash of blue through the driving rain. Chase's Holon was still airborne.

"Will Chase be all right in the storm?" Kazu asked, echoing Cammie's thoughts. "This weather—"

"He'll be fine," Yaz said, a little too loudly. "Right, Migas?"

The engineer shrugged. "Sure, yeah, I think—you know, I'm not sure if the Holons have been tested in these conditions. It's possible Dr. Weller did some test runs."

"The Hornbills have," Yaz said. "And where they can fly, we can fly."

Cammie opened her mouth to point out that the Holons' flight dynamics were seriously different from the Hornbills', and then thought better of it. Chase and Yaz had managed just fine in the fight; this wouldn't be any worse. And, most of all, if she was wrong, there wasn't anything she could do about it. She caught Migas looking over his shoulder at her, and self-consciously swiveled the ears of her headband to their most confident position. Whether he believed her or not, he turned back to his consoles, and Cammie let the ears flatten again. Through the windshield, she caught another flash of blue, the sharp edges smeared by the rain. It swelled, growing closer, and suddenly, Chase pulled up, sliding off to the left, the blue and white vivid against the lowering clouds. His voice crackled in *Renegade*'s speakers.

"Coming up on the base in about ten minutes. I'm still not picking up any Union presence."

"Neither are we," Yaz answered. "No fighters, and nothing on the ground."

"Roger that," Chase answered, and rolled away into the murk. Cammie caught a quick glimpse of blue as he flashed in and out of the cloud deck, and then he was just a dot on her screen.

"Well, that's good," she said. "Isn't it?"

Valentina gave her a sideways smile. "Depends on why, doesn't it?"

"The weather is terrible," Kazu said. "That's reason enough."

The weather is indeed terrible, Cammie thought, and it was getting worse, the clouds forcing them lower and lower. Luckily, De Soto Base was only a few miles ahead, and the Vanguard Hornbills were already configuring for the descent. More lights flared on her screen as the base spotted them and turned on local navigation, and she looked up quickly.

"De Soto Base has turned on their beacons."

"I see them," Yaz said. "Locking on."

"*Renegade*, this is De Soto Base." The voice in the speakers was reassuringly relaxed. "We show you on approach. Baker Three, you are cleared to land. Baker One, report when you've locked to the outer beacon."

"Roger that," Yaz answered, and the Vanguard Hornbills echoed her. There was nothing to be seen through the windshield except cloud and rain and the occasional glimpse of trees as *Renegade* banked for the approach. Cammie saw Baker Three appear on De Soto's approach monitor, slowing and flaring as its pilot lined it up for the landing. It touched, skidded sideways in a heavy gust, and settled. Two minutes later, Baker One touched down behind them.

Through the windshield, Cammie could see the sudden opening in the forest, the slash of tarmac that was the landing zone and the pop-up turrets that held the guide beacons fully deployed. There was one Hornbill still ahead of them, Baker Two slowing and banking to make the transition to vertical flight, a low building rising at the end of the runway, hangar door gaping wide. The first two Hornbills were already almost inside, support vehicles dashing alongside, throwing up great fans of water.

"De Soto Base, *Renegade*," Yaz said. "On the outer beacon. Permission to land?"

"*Renegade*, De Soto Base," the calm voice said, and ahead of them the Hornbill lurched sideways in a sudden gust. The engines weren't fully rotated, and the machine tipped sideways, falling out of the sky to skid along the runway, shedding parts.

"Go around, *Renegade*," De Soto Base said sharply.

"Negative, De Soto, we're committed," Yaz answered.

A streak of blue flashed across the windshield, and Chase

skidded to a flailing landing ahead of them, but recovered his balance and leaned hard against the crumpled Hornbill. It stuck and then shifted sideways, and Chase leaned out of their way as *Renegade* slowed, jets roaring. And then they were down, bouncing over rough concrete and debris, and a support car veered out from behind a bunker to lead them to the hangar doors.

"*Renegade*, De Soto Base. Please proceed to Bay Seventeen."

"Stand by, De Soto Base," Yaz said. She switched to the gen:LOCK frequency. "Chase, if we leave now, we can just fly out of this."

Cammie made a noise of protest in spite of herself.

Chase's voice filled the cabin. "You saw what just happened, Yaz. I don't think we should risk it."

"*Renegade* handles better than that," Yaz argued, but Chase interrupted.

"And you're a better pilot, too. But you see how far the weather's spread. Not to mention that we're at our limits."

"I'm fine," Yaz said, but she didn't sound convincing.

"Yaz."

She heaved a sigh. "All right. But this means we'll be stuck here for days."

"It's better than having to put down in the middle of nowhere," Chase answered. *Renegade*'s hull vibrated, and suddenly, Chase's Holon was looking in the windshield. "Besides, I meant it when I said I was beat."

"You're right." Yaz sighed again and switched channels. "De Soto Base, *Renegade*. Proceeding to Bay Seventeen."

It didn't take long to get *Renegade* parked and for Caliban to bring Chase's Holon aboard. Chase mixed in to the cabin to find Migas shaking his head at Yaz.

"No, no, I'm staying right here. I need to check over the Holons; you know that's the first priority."

"Colonel Varden wants to meet us before we're assigned barracks space," Yaz said, and Chase lifted his hand.

"Colonel Varden?"

"He's in charge here," Yaz said. "He's sent Major Rountree to escort us."

Migas was persistent. "I should stay on the ship. Somebody needs to."

"Besides me?" Caliban asked, his voice deceptively mild, and Migas rolled his eyes.

"Yeah, besides you. Better if there's two of us."

"You sure?" Chase asked, and Migas nodded.

"Yeah."

"Okay." Chase looked around to the rest of the group. "Grab your gear, and let's see what Colonel Varden can do for us."

Major Rountree was a stocky woman with dark skin and tight-curled hair cut close to her scalp. She had a round face and a ready smile, but Chase could see the strain lurking in her eyes. It was the same expression you saw everywhere in the Vanguard, and he looked away before she could see it in him, too. She introduced herself as the colonel's second-in-command, and led them through a maze of corridors that were at once new and entirely familiar. De Soto Base was laid out on the Vanguard's common plan, and the downloaded map looked like half a dozen other bases Chase had visited.

Varden's office was just like all the other CO quarters: a horseshoe desk with screens that wrapped around the back and one of the sides. More than a dozen images were playing as the gen:LOCK team entered, shot after shot of wind-tossed trees and churning water, and a fuzzy holographic model floating above a litter of data plaques and tattered slips of paper. A skinny young man stood to one side, tablet in hand, and an older man bent over the model, frowning.

"Lieutenant Chase and the gen:LOCK team, Colonel," Rountree said, and stood aside to let them file in. She closed the door behind them, her back against it, and clasped her hands behind her.

The older man straightened—the model was De Soto Base itself, Chase realized, plus what looked like more distant outposts—and Chase saw the moment that Varden remembered why Chase was mixing in rather than being present in person. "Welcome to De Soto Base," he said, "and thank you for your assistance earlier. You've met Major Rountree. This is Captain Herrera, our security chief."

"Our pleasure," Chase answered. He introduced the team,

aware of Varden's lifted eyebrow when he saw Cammie's ears, and finished, "I think you know why we're here."

Varden nodded. "This message from the refugee party, something about stolen brains? Stolen minds?"

"That's right." Chase picked his words carefully, not wanting to say too much. "If there is any information, it would be of interest to us, and to RTASA."

"We have a standard debrief routine for refugee groups," Rountree said. "We get a lot of them . . . we're the first big southern base once you cross the Eighty-Eighth. We've prepared some questions about this stolen-brains idea, but if they've got something, the refugees are usually pretty happy to trade information."

"Didn't Vanguard say that the group leader was part of the underground?" Yaz asked.

"One group was," Herrera said. "We'd been expecting them. But they hooked up with a second group. It's not yet clear which had the information in the first place."

"Major Rountree will sort that out for us, I'm sure," Varden said.

"Sir."

"In the meantime," Varden went on, "you're welcome here. Captain Herrera has authorized you for most sections of the base, and assigned you quarters on the main floor. That's well away from the refugees, by the way. We keep them in their own section until they're fully vetted."

Chase felt the information click home on his maps, brief

warmth along the artificial synapses as secondary systems parsed and stored the data. "Thank you, sir. Is there any update on how long the storm will last?"

Varden flicked a finger, and Chase felt another packet of data slot home. "I've sent you the latest forecast, and links to our satellites, but the short version is, probably another thirty or forty hours. This is a big one." He glanced back at the model floating above his desk. "We're already seeing flooding in our low-lying areas, and it's just getting started. There are a few civilian settlements in the forest here that we'll need to keep an eye on." He stopped, shaking his head. "But that's my problem, not yours. Captain Herrera will escort you to your quarters, and see to anything else you need. If you hadn't been there, we'd have suffered a lot more damage, and we appreciate the help."

"Thank you, sir," Chase said. "And if there's anything more we can do—"

"I appreciate the offer," Varden said with a faint smile, and Herrera pushed open the door.

The guest quarters were very nearly identical to the barracks room the team had shared at their original base at the Vanguard's stronghold of, the Anvil, with a line of neatly made bunks in one room and a set of foam-square sofas and armchairs in an outer room along with a table large enough to seat the entire team.

"I can have a meal cart sent over from the mess hall," Herrera offered.

Chase thanked him, and the door closed behind him. Chase looked around the space they'd been given. Valentina and Kazu had already claimed their bunks by virtue of tossing their carryalls onto their choice: the same bunks they had occupied at the Anvil, Chase noticed with some amusement, and sure enough, Yaz chose her usual bunk as well. Cammie had dropped her carryall beside one of the foam chairs and was sitting cross-legged on it, a virtual keyboard and display pulled up in front of her. Nugget was curled on her shoulder, apparently asleep, but twitched one ear as Chase drifted over.

The ears on Cammie's headband twitched, too, and she looked up from what seemed to be a drone schematic. "Yeah, my targeting drones weren't any good in this weather. But I've got some ideas how to fix that."

"That's cool," Chase said, "but what I wanted to say was you did great with the bridge. You saved some lives there."

She looked up at him, unsmiling, though her ears flicked upright, swiveling to face him. "I could have done better. What if there had been more tanks? Or air support?"

"But there wasn't," Chase said. "Cammie, you did exactly what we needed you to do."

"Okay." This time she did smile. "But I'm still going to work on the drones."

"You do that," Chase said, relieved, and turned away. *She's a good kid*, he thought. *And maybe not so much of a kid anymore, either.* Nemesis had shaken her badly—almost as badly as it shook Chase himself—but she'd pulled through.

He turned away, and Valentina caught his eye. "A word, please?"

"Sure." Chase let her edge him away from the others, though they were both well aware that between Cammie's ears and the gen:LOCK network, nothing ever stayed private for long. She leaned one shoulder languidly against the wall, but her eyes were hard.

"Did anything strike you as unusual about this little jaunt?"

"Besides the lack of air cover?" Chase waited.

Valentina smiled. "That, yes. Don't you think this was perhaps just a little easy?"

Chase sighed. She wasn't wrong; he just wished that once in a while the team could get something easy. "Maybe. Yeah, I was surprised there weren't fighters."

"Yaz says the Union fighters can't handle this weather," Valentina said, with the air of someone being scrupulously fair, "and perhaps I have not seen anything quite as bad as this. But I have seen the Union take on more risk than this."

"So what are you suggesting?" Chase asked, and Valentina spread her hands.

"I don't know. I just . . . don't trust this, somehow."

Chase suppressed another sigh. "Colonel Varden said they had a standard debrief routine and that the refugees are kept under supervision until they've been checked out. What else would you suggest?"

"I don't know," Valentina said again. "I'm not even sure what it is I think I'm worried about. It just feels wrong."

"I'll remind Colonel Varden about the air cover," Chase said. "Beyond that, I'm not sure what we can do. He's got a program in place; they deal with refugees all the time."

"Yes. That's true." Valentina nodded as though she was trying to convince herself. "What would be the point, anyway? We have whatever information there was."

"Yeah."

Valentina pushed herself away from the wall, shrugging one shoulder. "In that case, I will see how I can amuse myself until our food arrives."

Chase watched her go, then made his way to Yaz's side. She was sitting on one of the couches, carefully adjusting a pair of the goggles used to access the Ether, the global virtual reality network, but she looked up as Chase folded his avatar to sit beside her.

"Valentina talked to you about air cover?" It was barely a question.

Chase nodded. "So what do you think? Should there have been fighters?"

It was always tricky bringing up her former service with the Union, back before gen:LOCK when she'd been on their side, but this time there was no more than a slight paleness to her cheeks. Her voice was steady as she answered. "We never liked to fly in winds this high. Of course, we didn't see them very often where I was, and the

Polity didn't fly in them either. And I don't see any reason to be chasing these refugees specially. If they'd known about this intel, they'd have sent a bigger force to stop them. So . . . no, I don't think it's something we ought to worry about."

Chase nodded again. He trusted Yaz as a fellow pilot and as the first person to follow him into the gen:LOCK program; he trusted Valentina, too, he told himself, but she'd been special operations, a sniper, not from line troops. It was only to be expected that she'd see shadows everywhere.

The door buzzed and then slid open to reveal a couple of Vanguard support staff pushing a meal cart. The others greeted it with glad cries, and Chase was abruptly overcome with longing. He wasn't hungry, he *couldn't* be hungry, but memory supplied the hollow stomach, the watering mouth, the savory smell of the perfectly ordinary hamburgers and hot dogs being revealed as the servers folded back the covers. Sensors picked up the chemical traces, translated them into unfairly accurate smells, onions and pickles and mustard along with the grilled meat.

"No beer," Kazu grumbled, piling his plate full, and Chase was flooded with memory: smoke in the city, the smell of asphalt and charcoal and burned hot dogs, because his father had *always* burned the hot dogs and his mother had never been able to bear having cookouts afterward . . .

"I'm going to talk to the colonel," he said, to no one in particular, and mixed out, because the thing he was truly hungry for wasn't the food.

Cammie picked at the last few chips left on her plate, but finally pushed it away with a sigh. One thing you could count on the Vanguard cooks for was good fried potatoes, hot and salty and greasy, and if she had preferred a nice slab of fried haddock in place of the burger, she was honest enough to admit that was partly homesickness. She couldn't count the number of times her grandmother had sent her down to the chippy to pick up a fish supper, or a sausage supper for her mother when she was home. She'd always hurried back by the shortcuts, down the alley beside Anderson's and then through the fence into the Barbers' allotment and across to the kitchen door. And then they'd unwrap everything on the kitchen table, piling all the chips together into a single shareable mountain while her grand-mother poured mugs of tea and her father wheeled himself about collecting the salt and the vinegar and the sauce that he liked because he'd come from Edinburgh . . .

"A penny for your thoughts," Yaz said, and Cammie shook herself.

"Just thinking, there was a place when I was a kid where you could get deep-fried Mars bars. I could go for one right now."

"A deep-fried chocolate bar?" Kazu cut in, sounding deeply skeptical.

"It's not any weirder than not cooking your fish," Cammie answered.

"That's normal," Kazu said, but he was grinning.

"There is cake," Valentina said, and Cammie reached for a slice.

There wasn't much to say once they'd finished the cake. It took extra calories to fuel their bodies after a session, and now that they'd eaten, she wasn't surprised to catch herself yawning. The others were yawning, too, and Kazu stretched elaborately.

"Bedtime for me," he said, and no one tried to argue.

They retreated to their bunks, Cammie carrying her tablet and her Ether goggles and her charging pad so that Nugget could get comfortable. Valentina had her goggles on, too, already vanished onto the Ether, and Yaz paused at the foot of Cammie's bunk.

"Aren't you tired? I certainly am."

Cammie shrugged one shoulder, sitting cross-legged to connect power cords while Nugget nudged her elbow. "I had some things I wanted to look up."

"You should rest while you can," Yaz said, and settled onto her own bunk.

"Right, yeah," Cammie said, suppressing her annoyance. There was no need for Yaz to act like her mother. The charging pad was ready, and Nugget circled it twice before settling down, curling up like a cat, one foot against her shoulder as she lay back against her pillows. She pulled up the drone specs again, dissecting the virtual machine with deft gestures, looking for ways to make it more durable in heavy weather. They should have thought of that, she supposed, though no one really expected to have to fight in the middle of a hurricane.

She yawned and kept working, even as the others' lights went down around her, didn't stop until she found herself trying to put the left thruster onto the right lifting surface. That was too much; if she was going to make mistakes like that, she was surely tired enough to sleep, without any of the dreams that had plagued her after combat—

She cut off that line of thought, closing down her work spaces, made herself think instead of Gran and fish suppers and hot milky tea with lots of sugar. Her mother hadn't been home often for those; she'd been off working, a part of the teams decommissioning the North Sea rigs, and mostly it had been Gran and Dad. She'd learned to use power tools at Gran's side, helping to build the ramps that let Dad get around the narrow house, and she'd figured out how to get the inside lift to work so that Dad could get to the second floor again. He'd helped her program Nugget, the first version, and she fell asleep smiling at the memory.

In her dream, she was back at the rendezvous point, the battered highway crumbling under her feet. There was no sign of the rest of the team, or of the Vanguard, just the refugee hauler struggling through the rain. The gen:LOCK team was ahead, over the bridge, and all she had to do was get the hauler across and then she could join them . . . But the hauler was barely making headway, and when she tried to push it faster, the metal crumpled under her touch, the refugees screaming in terror from within the damaged vehicle. She stepped into the water to lift the broken beam, and the hauler finally edged forward onto it, but then the beam dissolved in her hands as though it had been attacked by Union nanites. The hauler plunged into the water and disappeared, and she flailed after it. She caught a corner, flung her weight back to lift it, but the metal tore again, spilling people into the muddy current. She reached for them, fingers spread wide, but her feet had no purchase and she went down into the water, rolling and tumbling in the blind dark.

When she dragged herself to her feet again, bruised and shaken, the bridge had vanished. She stood on the river's edge, her back to a line of trees bent nearly double by the wind. Night was falling, or maybe the storm was just getting worse, and she could feel the water creeping up the Holon's legs. The rest of the team was out there somewhere, surely, but when she tried the gen:LOCK network, there was no answer, and when she accessed the Mindscape, it was blank and empty. She called for them, calmly at first, then more frantic, abandoning call signs for names, and still no one answered.

She dropped back into her Holon, staggering in the blasting wind, and ahead of her the muddy water churned and bubbled. Nemesis rose before her—enormous, jet-black, massive pauldrons cutting the air. Its eyes glowed scarlet as it tipped its head to one side. Then all four arms came up, every finger tipped with scything claws, and it leaped for her, laughing, as she screamed and woke.

AS aLwaуs, cammiе didn't know if she'd actually managed to scream. She lay frozen in the half dark, the light of
Nugget's charging pad enough to prove to her that she was in
the De Soto barracks. She concentrated on controlling her
breathing and listened hard to see if she'd woken anyone else.
There was only silence, the distant sound of the others' breathing, someone shifting and snorting, and the rustle of blankets as
someone else turned over. Nemesis was dead; she knew that,
she'd seen him destroyed. Vanguard's analysts were certain
there were no surviving copies, but it didn't seem to make any
difference to her unconscious brain. Gradually, her heart rate
slowed, but she had no desire to sleep again.

She couldn't bear the idea of working on the drone specs
again, told herself that it was better not to risk making a mistake,
and instead, she reached for her Ether goggles, launching herself before she could change her mind. De Soto Base had its
systems gated off, of course, but it was the same system the

Anvil used, and she'd figured out how to bypass that within twenty-four hours of arriving at the Anvil. Not that there was any real reason to avoid base surveillance—she wasn't planning on going anywhere sensitive, or doing anything more dangerous than looking for someone to game with—but old habits died hard. She called a subroutine to neutralize the gatekeeper, and slipped out without a trace.

It was quiet on the Ether, all her favorite spaces more subdued, as though the storm had cut down on the number of people accessing them. And maybe it had: It certainly seemed as though the news volumes were at or above their usual load, and when she ran a basic status query, there were outages across the Gulf Coast. Those would be power outages rather than the Ether nodes themselves, she guessed, but it didn't matter. The people who had power wouldn't be spending it on social sites; they'd be following the storm.

Maybe that was what she should do: Go see what was happening outside De Soto Base. But the base was perfectly safe, tucked securely underground out of harm's way, and the Vanguard would wake them if there were any emergencies. She loped along a main access path instead, her favorite rabbit avatar, drawing no attention as she looked for anything to catch her interest. This stretch of Ether was boring, though, with only the fairground icons of a chanceteria, and a row of pseudo-clubs offering different kinds of music. She didn't recognize any of the performers, and none of the samples she snatched out of the air were particularly appealing. For a minute, she considered trying to break the chanceteria's rigged games—that had been one of her first exploits, back when she was a kid, developing tools that would let her win endless time and prize tickets, and she was sure she could still do it, even on the fly. But that was the sort of thing that Polity Cybersecurity frowned on (even while they admitted that the chanceterias were themselves cheating), and there was no point in drawing any extra attention. They were already not entirely happy that she was no longer working out her sentence in their service but in the ESU's.

The sentence was the result of what had been, she admitted, kind of a stupid mistake. The job had come from someone reliable—someone she trusted—but that was no excuse for not probing a little more deeply. She had been working the black-hat spaces for three years then, since her father died, and she'd known you couldn't really trust anyone. But everyone was talking about Pacific Technologies. The products it allowed out onto the open market were elegant and clever and priced out of most people's reach, and everyone was speculating about what else might be hidden behind the Research and Development firewalls. When XPNSV had offered to set her up with a job that promised her a working password and a security workaround, she'd leaped at the chance. She hadn't pushed for more details, or done any checking; she'd just picked up the code packet and made her run. It had been a Polity Cybersecurity trap, the whole thing, and they'd tracked her back to her home nets. She could still remember the look of shock changing to resignation as Gran realized exactly what she'd been doing to earn the money that had bought all her expensive gear. Cammie had apologized, and Gran had forgiven her, spent her savings on a good solicitor, but Cammie had never shaken that look of disappointment.

But this wasn't something she wanted to think about. She was on the Ether and she was going to enjoy it. She let herself drift along the popular thoroughfares, brushing away advertising bubbles before they could burst and connect with her avatar. The only one that looked even remotely interesting carried the bitter chill of malware, and she crushed it without a second thought. There were other copies floating in the middle distance, and she called up a stinger from her tool kit, turned it loose on the program. There was a hiss and a satisfying series of pops as her stinger cleared the local volume, but there was no pushback from the program's owner.

If things were going to be this quiet, maybe she ought to steal a chance to contact Gran, not through the secured and closely monitored Vanguard networks but through the environment she and her father had built years ago. Technically, it wasn't all that secure—they'd never locked it down in any serious way—but the Vanguard didn't know about it, and she intended to keep it that way. She checked herself for trackers, found none, and let herself drop from the main levels through to the specialty spaces.

The portal was exactly where she remembered it, still candy-colored pink and green and cream, and she went through, offering the system her magic key. It had been a while since she'd accessed the site, but the password was still good. The air in front of her swirled and twisted, and she stepped through into a gray corridor that held a single barred gate. She frowned. That was the default, and she'd replaced that long ago, but even as she watched, it shifted, became the piled stones and weathered wood of her custom creation. Beyond it, she could see grass and trees and pale sky, the familiar high-summer light she'd set the last time she'd been here. She produced the second key, and let herself inside.

The gate vanished behind her, replaced by a wooden stile that crossed the stone wall. She stood now at the bottom of a gentle slope that rose to a low hill crowned by a tree covered with heart-shaped leaves. They were just edged with gold, their color changing with the seasons in the outer world. She started up the hill. That was the message tree where she'd built her own post office app, though there were only a few tattered flecks of white among the leaves. None of them were new. She reached for one, and the message fizzed against her fingers, unfolding only reluctantly to reveal a scratchy heart and her grandmother's favorite font: *Nice one, Bunny, keep it up.* The embedded date meant it belonged to her last year in school, just before she dropped out to pursue her hacking, but she couldn't for the life of her remember what Gran was congratulating her for.

She hung it back on the tree, the signal for the system to keep the message, but the image broke into static and a new message appeared: *system update required*. Cammie swore under her breath, and flicked the warning away. That wasn't really a surprise; the companies that hosted the private environments were always adding new features and securing their systems against hackers, but she hadn't had time to tend to any of this for . . . far too long.

Now that she looked more closely, she could see other signs of neglect. The message tree's bark had reverted to a generic rather than the carefully crafted fractal she and Dad had made together, and the grass was a mown carpet, not the special file she'd imported to make it look like the hills outside her home. Worst of all, there were no flowers, not the Alice-in-Wonderland roses she had planted on the hill's far side, with the suite of mice that popped out to paint them in any color she chose, not the feather-seeds that were supposed to drift through the air and shower the grass with glitter, and most of all, there was not a single cushiony "comfy plant" poking up through the shorn grass. Dad had written them for her, explaining that they were a pun, that there was a real plant called comfrey, but these were *comfy*, like Gran's old settee.

She'd barely been old enough to type then, but she'd gone up on her knees on the bench beside the family console, leaning close while he explained how the strings of code defined a flower. He'd let her write the "seed" and "scatter" routines, taking her in to install them and helping her debug when they didn't work or did something completely unexpected, like when it turned the sky and the grass purple. They'd both burst out laughing, and Mam had come in from the kitchen, carrying her tablet, to see what they were on about. Dad had looked up at her, still laughing, saying *Look, Billie, it's Grape World!* and Mam had leaned down to take a look and started laughing, too. She'd brushed a kiss on Cammie's head, and looked lovingly at Dad, and he'd reached up to take her free hand for a quick kiss. Gran had come out then to see what was going on, and they'd ended up making a whole flock of grape-shaped birds before Gran made them finish the dishes. She'd kept Grape World for a solid month, too, though Dad had helped her figure out where she'd gone wrong.

There was so much work to do. She opened a maintenance window and watched the update list scroll past. The local system needed an update . . . well, *several* updates; she needed to pull fresh files that were compatible with the current system, and there was a whole list of patches and options that she ought to review. She flicked it closed again and sat down hard on the ugly grass. It was a lot—she hadn't been in the garden since before the incident that landed her in trouble, and she hadn't had much time to spend on it while she was working for Polity Cybersecurity or gen:LOCK. And even if she'd had the time, she didn't exactly want the Polity to know about this place. The gardens were for kids;

the last thing she wanted was for anyone to know she still maintained one.

And yet. She and Dad had spent years building it. It had been their secret space, where Dad could run, *really run*, and where their playtime wasn't limited by what was and wasn't accessible to him. After Mam disappeared in a Union attack on the offshore platforms, they'd built the lookout, where if you climbed to the top of the tower, you could look through a magic telescope and see her avatar waving to you. At least the tower was still standing, though she couldn't bear to find out if the avatar was still visible. *Some other night*, she told herself, just like it would be some other night when she went looking to make sure Dad's avatar was available.

She shoved herself to her feet and made her way back to the stile, the steps transforming into a gate as she waved her key at it. She let herself back out again, and found a quick-link to take her to the nearest Storm Center. It was crowded there, hundreds of icons hanging over the edges of the big display where Hurricane Pam churned in an endless loop. She joined them, waving away the menu—latest stats, short-range forecasts, long-range forecasts, regional options and data—to stare down at the towering clouds.

She dropped off the Ether sometime around dawn, barely enough time to snatch a couple of hours' uneasy sleep before Kazu grabbed her foot and shook her awake. She sat up, suppressing a groan, and glanced hastily at the others, trying to tell if they'd heard her nightmare. They seemed focused on the breakfast cart, not on her, and Cammie dragged herself out of her bunk.

She felt more awake after a shower, and joined the others around the table. Someone had thought to order a pot of strong tea, and she poured herself a mug, piling in sugar and a dash of milk. There were chopsticks for Kazu, too, and he flipped an extra fried egg onto her plate to join the rashers of streaky bacon and sliced tomatoes.

"I can serve myself," she groaned, and Kazu shrugged.

"If you're going to stay up all night gaming, you ought to at least eat."

"And were you up all night?" Valentina asked. She was drinking black coffee and picking at some sort of sweet roll.

"I'm fine," Cammie said, scowling. At least she could assume she hadn't woken anyone with her nightmare, but it was seriously annoying that they all assumed she'd stayed up gaming like some kid.

"We've talked about this before," Yaz began, then shook her head. "No, never mind, I'm not your mother. But the team needs you sharp."

"Yeah, I know," Cammie mumbled. "I'm fine."

Chase mixed in at that moment, his avatar solidifying out of thin air, and Cammie grabbed a big bite of the fried potatoes, hoping to avoid more questions.

"Is there news?' Valentina asked, wrapping both hands around her cup.

"Let's see." Chase settled himself on one of the padded benches, his image fuzzing only slightly where it touched solid surfaces. "The storm has continued to strengthen overnight; that's pretty much what the forecast said it would do, and it's done it. Colonel Varden suspended all live patrols at 0300 this morning."

"What about drones?" Yaz asked.

"Drones will be up as long as they can stay airborne, and there are robot ground patrols still out; they should be able to go longer," Chase said. "Plus, there are the fixed systems. They're only minimally affected."

"So you're saying the perimeters should be secure," Kazu said.

Chase nodded. "They should be. I mean, yeah, they're going to have to bring in the drones pretty soon, but everything else is functioning. And the Union will be getting hit just as hard."

Cammie looked from one to the other. "That's a good thing, right?"

"Or do you mean to say that someone else is uneasy about our situation?" Valentina asked.

"Not that I know of," Chase said. "Look, I talked to Colonel Varden again, and he said he'd put the refugees through an extra round of screening just to be on the safe side, but he thinks the Union didn't want to risk their fighters in this weather." He paused. "Right now, I agree."

Valentina shrugged, and leaned back in her chair, extending her legs with insolent grace.

"How long are we likely to be stuck here?" Yaz asked.

"At least another day," Chase said. "Maybe two."

Cammie put her head down, concentrating on her food. She didn't really mind staying another day. It wasn't that much different from any other Vanguard base, or from their quarters at RTASA; she had Ether access and plenty of things she could be doing. Her targeting drones, for one—she was determined to make them usable in heavy weather—and then she should probably help Caliban check over the Holons. Both of those were things she could do just as easily here as back at RTASA, though it would be easier to fabricate new parts once they got back to base.

The air between the table and the door fizzed and filled with color, an avatar taking shape as Colonel Varden mixed in. "Lieutenant. I'm sorry to disturb you, but we have a situation, and I hope you can help us."

"Whatever we can do, Colonel. What's happening?"

"We've gotten a mayday from one of our outposts, Red Wolf, about eight miles south and east of here. They're a designated shelter for a couple of towns, New Janice and St. John's, and they lost the roof off the main building last night. They managed to get everyone into the secondary buildings, but those aren't built to withstand this weather. Captain Mendez says she can't fit everyone into what safe space she's got. She's putting the refugees into crawlers and they're going to try to make it here, while she and a skeleton crew try to keep Red Wolf open."

Chase nodded. "Is there a road?"

"There's an old forest service track," Varden answered. "And that's where gen:LOCK can help. That's all woodland, and we know there are trees down. Your team can clear the road a lot faster than anything we have, and you're in better shape to handle the weather. If you're willing."

"We can't take *Renegade*," Yaz said. "We'll have to go the whole way on foot. In the Holons. You know what I mean."

Chase nodded. "How far did you say it was, Colonel?"

"It's about eight miles to Red Wolf," Varden answered. "But the crawlers will be making time toward us, too."

"We'll need to allow for clearing the road," Chase said, "but we should still have plenty of uptime. Can you give us backup?"

"I can send a Strider squad," Varden answered, "and a spare personnel carrier in case the refugees need it." He gestured, and a three-dimensional map unrolled in front of his avatar. "This is the area, and the old road." A line of light flared among a tangle of trees, ending at a flashing triangle. "That's Red Wolf. And this . . ." Another light popped into existence, this one bright orange. "This is the bridge over Cypress Creek. Normally, it wouldn't be a problem, but with the rain . . ." He shook his head. "The flood gauge washed away, so all we can say is that the water was eight feet and rising. The bridge is supposed to be built to withstand this, but we don't know if it's intact."

"That could be a problem," Valentina said. She had risen to her feet, and came forward to examine the map. "There is no other way?"

"If you miss Cypress Creek, you have to cross Joe Creek," Varden said, "and there isn't a bridge there, just the road on top of a culvert. It definitely won't hold up to this weather."

"I don't see why it would be so bad," Kazu said. "If they send an armored personnel carrier, worse comes to worst, we carry the people across and the APC brings them back here."

That would probably work, Cammie thought, though she hoped she wouldn't be the one who had to carry people over the flooded stream. It was too easy to imagine someone slipping through the Holon's fingers, or grabbing too hard and hurting someone . . . She shoved the thought away and drained the last of her tea.

"I agree," Chase said. "When do you want us, Colonel?"

"As soon as you can be ready," Varden answered. "And thank you."

His avatar vanished, and Chase looked around the room. "All right. You heard the man. Everyone ready?"

For a second, Cammie thought he was talking directly to her, but then his gaze slid past, taking in the entire team. She heaved a sigh of relief, and pushed herself back from the table. "What are we waiting for?"

By the time they'd returned to *Renegade*, the Strider

squad was lined up by the hangar door, a twelve-wheeled APC idling behind them. Cammie settled herself into her chamber, listening with half an ear as Chase gave Migas and Caliban a rundown of the situation. Then the lid descended and she closed her eyes, letting the connection wash over her.

She was still hanging in the rack, and it took a second to remember not to move as the conveyor jerked into motion, shifting the Holons to the door of the cargo bay. She was last out, and got her legs down at just the right moment to convert the conveyor's momentum to her own forward motion so that she strode smoothly after the others. After her not-so-graceful deployment last time, she wished the team had seen that, but it was obvious their attention was on the team from De Soto Base. It was led by a Strider with a bright yellow diamond painted on the top and sides of its cabin, driven by a sharp-faced man who lifted a hand in salute as the Holons approached.

"gen:LOCK, thanks for the help. We're De Soto Rescue One, Luke Griffin, commanding. We've got a heavy lift on the APC, but we're very glad to have you all along."

I hope they are armed, and not just rescue, Val said on the gen:LOCK network.

I'm more worried about the weather than an attack, Yaz answered.

Perhaps so, but better to be prepared, surely. Val checked his energy rifle, automatically running the diagnostics, and

Cammie saw the data flash past as it was uploaded to Mindscape. She looked at the Striders, turning her own sensors on them, and saw that the missile pods were full, shoulder and waist guns fully armed. And that ought to be enough, as far behind the border as they were. Even the Union couldn't attack in the teeth of a hurricane.

"Move 'em out!" someone called, and the hangar door began to slide back, the mechanism rumbling under the concrete floor. The wind shrieked in, carrying a vicious slap of rain, and Cammie hunched lower, glad she'd rebuilt her Holon with a lower center of gravity.

"Rescue One heading out," Griffin said, and the Striders lurched into motion, passing one by one through the gap and out onto the landing pad. The APC followed, and the hangar door slid back another few yards to let the Holons through. Even expecting it, Cammie was rocked back on her heels by the wind; she swore under her breath and steadied herself, ducking her head to protect her vision from the pounding rain. Her rear-facing camera showed the hangar door already closing behind them, and she looked around, trying to find the road Varden had mentioned.

So where exactly are we going?

Follow the leader, Kazu said, far more cheerfully than she thought the weather warranted. She fell into step behind him.

The road was little more than a lane of asphalt, patched and crumbling, and in places the surface vanished altogether in a welter of mud and gravel. The Holons and the

Striders negotiated those patches without difficulty, but the APC had to gear down and take extra care to keep from getting stuck. The farther they went, the closer the trees pressed to the road, their tops thrashing in the steady wind. Cammie hunched her shoulder against the stinging branches and swore as the others slowed ahead of her, a tangle of trees blocking their way.

"Let me handle that," Kazu said, and stooped to heave the first trunk up and sideways, sending it tumbling end over end into another, smaller tree. That tree cracked and split, but most of it fell away from the road. "Ah. Sorry."

Chase stooped to move the second tree, dragging it more carefully to one side, and the column plodded on. Yaz and Chase took turns leading, with Kazu right behind to help move any fallen debris. The Striders and the APC came next, with Val and Cammie following. The rain lashed at them, working its way into any seams in the Holons' armor. Cammie's sensors translated the infiltration as needles of cold, and she ramped up heaters to dry her internal mechanisms. There was no point in worrying about weapons, not in this weather; even Val had slung his cannon over his shoulder and tucked his cloak tight around him to keep it from knocking over a Strider. The rain cut visibility to a few hundred yards, and Cammie caught a glimpse of the clouds sagging toward the treetops, a heavy mass of gray. And then the rain closed in again, and she tipped her head downward to shed the water as best she could. When they got back to RTASA, she should figure out a way to keep the camera ports clear, give herself a fighting chance to see more than the smears of color that were the rest of gen:LOCK. She switched on her Infrared settings instead, the machines now standing out stark and bright against the thrashing trees, and picked her way along the crumbling pavement.

"How much farther?" Chase asked, and in the same moment Cammie realized that the trees were getting thinner. She risked visual again, saw rain and a swirl of leaves whirling up as another tree fell, and then a flash of red as Kazu put himself between a Strider and a precariously leaning tree. He pushed the tree back in the other direction, and the Strider sidled past, its driver lifting a hand in salute.

"We're almost there," Griffin answered. "Less than half a mile; look, you can see the bridge."

Cammie switched back to Infrared, found nothing, and switched to mixed mode. In that, she could just pick out a faint, boxy shape blocking the road ahead. To either side, the trees thinned further and then stopped, and when she switched to external audio, she could hear a new sound above the roar of the wind.

"Copy that," Chase said, sounding grim.

"gen:LOCK, we've made contact with the group from Red Wolf. They say their outriders are at the bridge, but they don't think it's safe to cross."

"Copy," Chase said again, and switched to gen:LOCK. *Yaz, what do you think?*

The river is very high, Yaz answered, *and there's a lot of debris in the water. A lot. Cammie, can you take a look?*

Sure. Cammie picked her way through the waiting Striders, the boxy shape she had seen in her sensors resolving as she came closer to the remains of a gateway. A wooden guard-house had collapsed into a pile of boards, and the stub of a crossing arm pointed at the sky. A pair of stoplights hung from the gate's center span, but even as she watched, one ripped free, tumbling into the roiling water. She pulled the other one loose as well, not wanting it to blow back on the waiting Striders, and let it fall into the river as she bent to examine the bridge.

It was an old-fashioned trestle bridge, mostly metal, but a lot of debris had collected against the upstream side. Even as she watched, a small tree hurtled around the bend and slammed hard against the trestles closer to her end of the bridge. The sound reverberated, a dull boom louder than thunder, but the metal held. The water pinned the tree against the trestles, and the tree began to turn slowly on its axis, the trunk and roots sinking, the limbs rising as the water built up behind it.

Anything? Chase called, and she made herself look beyond the tree. In the center of the span, it looked as though there were some gaps, places where support beams had broken free, but it was hard to tell how many were missing.

I can see some damage in the middle, she said, *and there's a—* She remembered her bargain and rejected the first words that rose to her lips, substituting something more polite. *There's a lot of debris in the water. I can see why they're worried.*

Do you need a hand? Kazu asked, extending his arm as he spoke, and Cammie wrapped her Holon's fingers around his wrist.

Yeah, that's a help, thanks. She leaned out over the edge, feeling Kazu's weight shift to balance her, and flashed a light from her fingers, letting it play over the structure. There were more breaks than she'd seen the first time, mostly among the smaller supports. In a couple of places, all but the main legs had been torn away and the water was frothing through the gaps. She let Kazu pull her back, flicking off the light, and glanced across to the other side. The rain made it hard to see, but she thought she could make out three small haulers, with a couple of armored six-wheelers for escort. *There are two big breaks, and a bunch of little ones,* she reported. *It looks okay right now, but there's a lot of stuff coming downstream, and it's just going to get worse.*

As if to punctuate her words, part of a roof swirled past and struck the bridge with a dull clang. The wood splintered, shedding bits of asphalt tile, and then collapsed into a tangle of wood and sodden insulation. The current whisked it away before she could be sure of what she'd seen.

Across the river, someone climbed out of one of the six-wheelers and waved a flashlight in their direction. Cammie ran a quick scan of the Vanguard frequencies and caught the end of the transmission.

"—try it now that you're here."

"Say again, Red Wolf?" Griffin asked, and the person waved the flashlight again.

"We're willing to try a six-wheeler now that you're here to fish us out."

"Roger that," Griffin said.

"Hang on," Chase broke in. "I've got a better idea. Let's see if we can dam up the stream, divert the water or hold it back long enough for Red Wolf to cross without having to worry about the bridge getting knocked out from under them. Kazu, you and Cammie can deal with the bridge while we do that."

"Are we sure we can handle the current?" Val said, but he was already holding out a hand to Kazu. He took it, bracing himself as he stepped cautiously into the water. It rose well above his knees, and he swayed dangerously, but caught himself. "I can manage. But it will be easier with more of us."

"Agreed," Yaz said, and took Kazu's hand to lower herself in. She and Val linked arms, and Chase stepped down to join them, then turned to steady Kazu.

"Any time, Cammie."

"Right." Cammie felt as though all the Holon's joints were frozen, leaving her rooted to the spot. The way the water churned sent her plummeting into last night's horrible dream, and she couldn't help but imagine Nemesis bursting from the dark water as he'd done before.

70

Get a grip, she told herself. *You just did this yesterday. And nobody's shooting at you now. Nemesis is dead. He's not going to get you again.*

She grabbed Kazu's wrist, and half stepped, half slid down the muddy bank. The water was a shock to the system, not just the cold but the weight of it, pushing her back toward the bridge. She wobbled, caught herself on Kazu's shoulder, and stepped down hard, driving her feet into the muddy bottom.

That's right, Kazu said. *Got it?*

She nodded, nearly overbalanced, and bent her knees to lower her center of gravity. The shock of the water and her purchase on the river bottom were slowly bringing her out of bad memories and back to the matter at hand.

That tree, Yaz said, wading toward a splintered trunk caught on something upstream.

And I'll take this one, Val said, plucking up the tree that had been pinned against the bridge.

Like baseball, Kazu said, and Cammie could have sworn he was laughing. *Swing, batter! And drive everything off.*

Make sure the bridge is safe, Chase said, and waded upstream after the others. *We won't be able to hold this forever.* He switched to the Vanguard frequency. "Okay, Red Wolf, why don't you send over your lightest vehicle?"

"Roger that," a tense voice answered, and a second six-wheeler pulled out around the first.

Ready? Kazu said, and Cammie nodded firmly.

Ready.

The six-wheeler inched out onto the span, moving slowly in the gusty wind. Cammie gave the supports a quick glance, but they looked solid. There was less water coming through, too, and the six-wheeler began to pick up speed, rumbling across and up onto the far side.

"Nice work," Chase said. "Send a hauler next?"

"Agreed," Griffin said, and the person on the far bank waved their flashlight in acknowledgment.

Kazu looked at Cammie, and she nodded back, trying to project more confidence than she felt. If the bridge went, she wasn't sure she could catch a hauler before it went off the edge. But she wouldn't have to, she told herself, she'd just have to hold up the bridge, and she'd done that the day before. It would be fine. She risked a quick glance upstream and saw that the others had formed a makeshift dam that was definitely easing the pressure of the water against her legs. "Go!"

The hauler eased onto the bridge. It swayed, and Cammie caught her breath, checking the supports, but it was just the wind. The hauler steadied, accelerated as the driver picked up confidence, and then it was across.

"Hurry up," Chase called. "We can't keep this going much longer."

"Next!" Cammie waved to the remaining haulers, and one rumbled forward, taking the bridge at a faster pace. Cammie winced, but the supports held firm, and the third hauler made its way across. That left the last six-wheeler, and she began to think they might pull this off.

"Look out!" Yaz shouted, and there was a tremendous crash from upstream. Half a house surged over the makeshift barrier, knocking Val off his feet and sending Yaz and Chase stumbling sideways, logs and brush and more bits of buildings battering them. Something about the horrible sound, the frantic tone of Yaz's voice, took her back to that day, the reality behind the nightmare. When Nemesis tore her head from her Holon body, searching for her cyberbrain while she screamed, flailing in the dark . . .

"Go! Go!" Kazu yelled, planting himself in front of the bridge, arms outstretched to block the wall of debris. Cammie heard the six-wheeler accelerate, knew what she needed to do, but she couldn't breathe. She was caught in her nightmare, waiting for Nemesis to surge up out of the water, unable to move.

Cammie!

She jumped then, planting herself against Kazu's side, her Holon between the bridge's end and the oncoming debris. Kazu dipped one shoulder, shrugging the house off and past him; it hit the bridge hard, and then the entire structure ripped away, metal shrieking louder than the wind. Things thudded against Cammie's legs, hard enough to jolt her backward, but she managed to stay upright.

Kazu?

They made it, he said, and she let out a sigh of relief.

73

Val was on his feet again, swearing and furious, and Yaz spread her wings for balance as Chase lifted out of the water. He landed on the bank, hand outstretched, and first Yaz, then Val pulled themselves out after him.

"Everybody all right?" he asked.

"All good here," Griffin said. "Nice work."

"Very nice," Red Wolf said. "We wouldn't have made it without your help."

"Yeah, well, sorry about the bridge," Chase said.

"We can rebuild," Griffin said. "Once the water goes down."

Cammie clawed her way out of the water, wishing she could sink into the mud. What had gotten into her lately? She'd *frozen*. She hadn't frozen since the last time they saw Nemesis, and Nemesis was dead, dead, dead—

You all right? Kazu asked quietly, for her ears only, and she made herself move as normally as she could manage.

I'm fine, she said, and willed it to be true.

———

It was a tough road back to De Soto Base. *Maybe worse than going out*, Kazu thought, hunching his heavy body to present less of a flat surface to the wind. It was stronger, with fewer gusts but a steady pressure from the southeast, almost as solid as a wall. Chase and Yaz had moved up to take point, and Kazu fell back behind the haulers and the APC, looking over the treetops for any sign of trouble. There was nothing but thrashing leaves and the occasional white flash of a freshly broken branch, that and the rain that drove hard against his lenses and ran in sheets down his scarlet armor. His sensors were empty, too, nothing hiding in the clouds or behind the line of sight—not that he'd really expected anything. Yaz was right that the Union wasn't going to risk their machines in this mess.

At least they had found the locals and gotten them across before the bridge collapsed. They'd be better off waiting out the storm inside De Soto Base: There was definitely plenty of room, and it was well protected. Even this hurricane wasn't going to batter its way through the defenses.

Of course, that assumed they got there. The old road surface was disintegrating in the rain, and the haulers were having a hard time where there was only mud and gravel. Even as he thought that, one of them skidded, and Val caught it, holding it up and steady until the other wheels caught. He felt him look his way, and hoped he could feel his smile in return. They were still learning what the network carried besides deliberate words.

Though with Cammie . . . He let his eyes slide sideways to the white-and-green Holon leaning into the lashing rain. Her ears were pinned back, and she picked her way cautiously over the puddles and mud, looking for all the world like a wet cat he'd seen once, trying to cross its yard to get inside. With Cammie, you didn't need the network to know what she was feeling: If her face didn't betray her, the ears gave it all away.

Right now, she was miserable, and he would have laughed, except that he thought it was more than the storm. It wasn't like her to freeze; yes, at the beginning she'd been less than stellar in a fight, but she'd picked herself up and made herself learn even when it scared her. Even after Nemesis had . . . She'd done well to bounce back from that, he thought, and as though she'd picked up the echo of his attention, she turned her head to look at him. Her ears came up with an effort as deliberate as a smile, and Kazu stopped himself from shaking his head in admiration. She was one tough kid, and he'd be stupid to forget it. She was great yesterday, and she'd been quick to recover today.

His Holon beeped at him, and he saw one of the haulers slowing, wheels thrashing in the mud where the road had washed away.

Hey, Cammie. Help me with this hauler?

Yeah, sure.

Take the right side, keep them going straight. Kazu stepped off the roadway, working his feet until he was sure he had decent purchase, then bent to lift and push the hauler. The front wheel sent a spray of mud and gravel across his armor, but then the tires caught and he and Cammie steered it back onto solid ground.

"Thanks, gen:LOCK," the driver called, and Kazu saw a lifted hand inside the driver's compartment.

Nice work, he said to Cammie, and saw her ears flip up again. *Are you all right?*

One ear twitched, just a fraction, then steadied, cheer as fake as Cammie's smile this morning. *I don't like this weather*, she said, and started off after the hauler.

Who does? Kazu asked, but got no answer.

Val came up beside him as Cammie trudged away.

She shouldn't stay up so late, Kazu said.

I'm not sure that's the problem, Val said in his ear, and Kazu shot him a wary glance.

Kazu began to form a response, then shrugged, letting the gen:LOCK network carry his uncertainty. *But not my business, eh?*

Nor mine, Val said firmly, and they turned their attention to the road.

4

CAMMIE SAT UP as the lid of her capsule lifted, rubbing her hands along her arms. She felt cold and wet and windblown, though she knew she was perfectly dry. Sometimes the physical effects of the upload lingered in the nervous system, so that what she had "felt" in the Holon was transferred to her skin, but knowing that didn't ease the chill. *A nice hot cuppa*, she thought, but there wasn't much chance she'd get that anytime soon. And the Americans didn't really make good tea. She allowed herself a sigh at the thought of Gran's kitchen and the chipped china pot huddled beneath the faded cozy, the tea it held always thick and strong and nearly as dark as coffee. *My mum called it "strong enough to trot a mouse on,"* Dad had said, and Gran had laughed, and that Christmas she and Gran had found him a mug with running mice painted around the rim.

She shook that thought away and followed the others into the main compartment, listening with half an ear as Chase led the quick debrief, saying they'd done well. Through the windshield, she could see the people from Red Wolf unloading themselves from the hauler, knots of two and three and four carrying bags and bundles. They'd definitely be safer here, but she wondered what was happening to their homes.

". . . and it sounds like the rest of Red Wolf outpost is holding up," Chase finished. "All the locals who evacuated there are accounted for, and there aren't even minor injuries. Good job."

"What happens to the evacuees?" Valentina asked.

"They'll be housed with the refugees," Chase answered. "And go back home after the storm's over."

"After the bridge is fixed," Kazu added, and Chase nodded.

"That, too."

Cammie looked away, not wanting to meet his eyes. She knew she'd frozen, and at the worst possible time; he was probably trying to be kind, not mentioning it, but it hurt to sit here waiting for the other shoe to drop. She wriggled, trying not to look too impatient, and Chase went on.

"We've got nothing more on schedule today. It's possible we'll get another emergency call, so stay ready, but otherwise—make yourselves at home. Local systems will warn you about any off-limits areas."

"I vote for lunch," Kazu said with a grin, and Valentina rolled her eyes.

Cammie slipped from her seat and scooted out the side

hatch before anyone could call her back. She headed for the shadowy corner at the rear of the hangar—there would be workshops and tool lockers there, a good excuse—but as she ducked past a grounded Hornbill, the air sparked and Chase mixed in in front of her.

"You're in a hurry."

She shrugged one shoulder and deliberately moved her ears to a more perky position. "I thought I'd see what sort of gear they had here. So I can help Migas."

Chase nodded. "I expect he'd be glad of the help."

"Yeah. So I ought—"

"I saw you hesitate," Chase added quietly. "Not much, and it didn't make any difference, you did what you needed to do . . . but I just wanted to ask, are you okay?"

"Fine. Super." Cammie forced a smile, and then dropped it, afraid it looked fake. "No, really, I'm fine."

"You know, it's okay not to be fine," Chase said. "We've all been through a lot."

Not compared to you, Cammie thought. The idea of complaining about nightmares to Chase, who'd lost half his body in the Battle of New York, and then been driven out of even that—no, had *chosen* to exceed his uptime limits and become an Ether ghost in order to defeat Nemesis. That was bad enough, but when you considered that Nemesis was the corrupted original of Julian Chase's cyberbrain, and the Chase they all knew was a copy created without his knowledge or permission . . .

"I slipped on a rock," she said, forcing her ears into a neutral position. "That's all."

"Okay," Chase said. "But, you know, if you need someone to talk to, I'm here. We all are."

I know, Cammie thought. *That's the problem: You're all always there. And you've all seen real combat, dealt with this kind of thing already. I can't even pretend to compete with what you all have been through, and I can't bother you with it. Not when it's just bad dreams.*

She said, "Yeah, thanks. I do appreciate it. But I'm fine."

"Okay," Chase said, and mixed out again.

Cammie scowled at the spot where he'd been, then glanced over her shoulder toward *Renegade*. A flash of purple disappeared past its tail, and she guessed the others were on their way to the mess hall. Migas was probably still with the ship, looking over the Holons, and she made her way back to the now-open rear hatch. Caliban looked down at her from the opening, the controls of the storage rack in his hands, and a moment later Migas craned to see past him.

"Oh, hey, Cammie," he called. "Everybody else has gone on to the mess hall."

"I'm not hungry," Cammie said, and started up the ramp. "Need a hand with the Holons?"

"Only if you want to," Migas said.

Caliban's head swiveled. "I think what he means is that your help would be appreciated but is not required."

"That's what I said," Migas grumbled.

82

Cammie reached for the nearest tool belt. "For f—" She bit off the next words, and said instead, "Let's get on with it, then."

"You still watching your language?" Migas asked cautiously, and motioned for Caliban to lower Yaz's Holon into an accessible position.

"Yeah. Chase said it was bothering people." Cammie slid back the first access panel, high in the Holon's "calf," and found the proper probe.

"Some people are fussy like that." Migas examined one of the "feet," then used a coated scraper to work mud and unidentifiable plant bits out of the ankle joint.

"Chase said Americans don't swear like Scots do." Cammie gave him a sidelong glance and saw him shrug.

"You're the first Scottish person I've ever known. Well, except maybe on the Ether, but you can't necessarily tell there."

"It isn't that one group swears more than the other," Caliban said, "but that the ranges of words used in Scotland and America are different, and are considered disproportionately offensive. Certain terms that are common and merely intensive in Scotland are profoundly offensive in the United States. And, I believe, vice versa."

"Thanks, Caliban." Cammie rolled her eyes at Migas, who grinned. "Anyway, Dr. Weller brought it up first, said he didn't think people would take me seriously if I swore so much. So I've been trying to cut down."

"He was probably right about that," Migas said. "The doc was a brilliant man."

"Yeah. Only I'm not sure how good *he* was with people."

"He was right about that, at least," Caliban said. "Studies have determined—"

"Oh, shut it," Cammie said, and frowned at Migas. "What?"

"Nothing. Hand me that driver, will you?"

Cammie found the screwdriver and passed it across, then returned her attention to the diagnostics. It was soothing to watch the numbers flicker across her vision, virtual screens sliding in and out of existence, each system broken down to schematics and numbers and then built back up again to the elegant models. The Holons had made it through the storm without suffering more than a few scratches, despite the heavy wind and the time they'd spent immersed in the flooding stream. Mostly, it was a matter of clearing dirt and gravel out of the lower joints, and Cammie cheerfully mixed solvents for the pressure wand and watched Migas blast away the bits of debris. A gasket in Kazu's knee was showing early signs of wear, but that was the worst they found.

"Replace it while we can," Migas said, and Cammie nodded. With Caliban's help, they wrestled the leg into a more accessible position, found the fraying gasket, and fitted a new one into place. Cammie closed the last panel and stepped back to let Caliban fold up the Holon and slide it inside.

"That's everything checked out," Migas said. "Though,

hey, I just thought, you've probably missed lunch, I'm sorry—"

"There's always sandwiches in the mess hall," Cammie said. "I'm not really hungry."

"Well, I am," Migas said. "Come on, you need a break."

Cammie sighed. "All right."

"And you'll leave me to mind the store?" Caliban asked.

"That's right," Cammie answered cheerfully, and followed Migas down the rear ramp. She heard it whine shut again behind her, but her eyes were on a group of Vanguard technicians in one of the maintenance bays. They had a motorcycle up on a stand, its engine disassembled, and there were three more waiting off to the side. "Are those the ones the refugees were riding?"

She hadn't meant to be heard, but one of the technicians looked up. "That's right. Say, are you with gen:LOCK?"

"Yeah." Cammie nodded. "What are you doing?"

Another technician straightened. She was older than the others, with a sergeant's stripes on her sleeve. "If any of the refugees are able to bring transport with them, we try to fix them up. Makes it easier to get them where they're going, and easier for them once they get there, too."

"Need a hand?" Cammie asked, and Migas groaned.

"I need lunch."

"We're just about done," the first technician answered; he had a cheerful, open face. "But you're welcome to take a look."

"Absolutely," the sergeant agreed. "I don't suppose there's any chance we could get a look at your mecha."

Cammie glanced at Migas, who shrugged. "Security," he said. "But we can ask."

"Thanks." The sergeant stepped back, wiping her hands on a rag, and Cammie moved closer. Her father had been a motorcycle racer, before the crash that had damaged his spine and put him in a chair for life, and she hadn't been able to help learning about the machines. These were long-haul bikes, not the stripped-down, over-powered racing models, but the basics were familiar enough.

"Converted to biofuel?" she asked.

The third technician lifted his head from the gear he was cleaning. He was heavily freckled, as though he'd spent way too much time in the sun. "Lots of folks do that, both sides of the Eighty-Eighth. It's easier to get hold of than other fuels."

"That's because you and your cousins brew your own," the other young man said, and the freckled one grinned.

"Ain't like it's hard."

"That's something I don't need to hear, Taggert," the sergeant said.

"Sorry, Sarge." The technician didn't sound particularly apologetic.

Cammie grinned in spite of herself, tracing the modifications to the fuel system. She hadn't seen anything quite like it before, not back home and not with the Vanguard. She leaned closer, then reached into the tangle of wires and piping to check the feed valves and the tanks. There was something odd there. The parts were new, not rebuilt and repurposed, and there was something about the way they connected . . . "Is that the way you'd set this up?" she said to the nearest technician, and he leaned closer to see what she was looking at.

"Oh, yeah, I see. No, I wouldn't do it that way, but everybody's got their own style—"

"Hey! Hey, you, what do you think you're doing with my bike?"

Cammie straightened to see a stocky man in stained leathers hurrying toward them, trailed by a fair-haired woman in a hip-length leather coat. Captain Herrera was a few steps behind her, frowning as he looked over the scene.

"Yeah, you, bunny ears, I'm talking to you." The stocky man came to a stop on the other side of the bike, hands on hips, glaring at her. "Nobody touches my bike."

"Don't want your crappy bike," Cammie snapped, and was instantly sorry. She sounded like a child.

"Hey, now," Migas said, taking one step to the side so that he was between Cammie and the stranger. "What's your problem, man?"

"I want you to leave my bike alone," the stocky man barked.

The sergeant folded her arms across her chest. "We've been working on all your bikes, thought you might like to have them in working order before you leave. But, hey, you want us to take them apart again, we can do that—"

"Nobody asked you to touch our bikes," the man yelled. "Least of all some dumbass kid—"

"Watch your language," the freckled technician, Taggert, said.

"Liam!" That was the woman, sliding to a stop beside the stocky man to tuck one hand around his arm. "Liam, they meant well—"

"It's standard procedure for Vanguard technicians to go over any private machinery that refugees bring into De Soto," Herrera said. "Security. You were told that."

"And we try to put it back into working order, too, so you have something to take with you when you leave," the sergeant muttered.

"Sergeant," Herrera said, and she subsided.

"Sorry, sir."

"My bike was fine," the man snarled.

"Liam," the woman said again. "I'm sorry—Sergeant, is it? We had kind of a rough ride getting here; we're still a little on edge. Captain Herrera just cleared us through Base Security."

"*Provisional* clearance," Herrera said, with a look at the stocky man. "Which can be revoked."

The woman went on as if he hadn't spoken. "My name's Aris Webb. He's Liam Foxe. Like I said, we came over the Eighty-Eighth—thanks to Vanguard and those crazy mechs. And we do appreciate your help with our gear."

"Standard operating procedure," the sergeant said stiffly.

Aris nudged Liam in the ribs and he mumbled something. "I'm sorry," she said, "I didn't hear you, and neither did these helpful folks."

Liam heaved a sigh. "I'm sorry I yelled. It's like Aris said—we're all still on edge."

"It ain't easy, crossing the Eighty-Eighth," Taggert said.

"We heard you lost some folks," the sergeant said. "We were sorry to hear that."

"Thanks." Aris tightened her hold on Liam's arm. "Jake . . . he was Liam's brother, and a good friend."

And that was a good reason to be touchy, Cammie thought.

"I shouldn't've yelled," Liam said. "I didn't think a kid would be working on things like this—but obviously, I was wrong."

"She's not a kid—" Migas began, and Cammie stepped back on his toe. He yelped, less with pain than surprise, and looked down at her. "What?"

"Let it go," she said softly. He grimaced, but subsided.

"They're nice machines, and we didn't need to do much," the sergeant said. "Let me walk you through what we did."

"I'd appreciate that," Liam said.

Cammie took a step backward. "Come on, Migas."

"Yeah, I don't know—"

"I thought you were hungry."

"Yeah, I am." Migas lifted a hand toward the technicians. "Catch you later."

Taggert lifted a hand and the sergeant nodded in acknowl-edgment, then turned her attention to the refugees. Herrera spared her a nod as well, but his attention was on the refugees. Cammie turned her back on them, telling herself everything was fine, and Migas fell into step at her side.

"Boy, what a jerk."

"Sh—" Cammie stopped herself, reached for a play-ground insult. "Dafthead." It wasn't really satisfying and she sighed. "I wasn't going to hurt his precious bike."

"They were doing him a big favor," Migas said. "Like the sergeant said, if you've got your own transport, it's easier to find work once you're resettled."

"You'd think they'd think of that," Cammie said, and sighed. "I know, they've just had some of their friends killed. Of course they're upset."

"Some people manage to be upset without being jerks," Migas said. "Case in point, Chase. Or Miranda. Or Kazu. Well, not that I'm sure I've seen him upset, but I think he has been—"

"Let's get lunch," Cammie said, and waved for the nearest door sensor to let them through.

The full lunch service was over before they got to the mess hall, but there was plenty of soup and hot tea to wash away the lingering chill from the floodwater. There were sandwiches, too, though Valentina disdained the ones that were meant to be reheated in their packages; she chose rolls and butter and some of the rich chocolate brownies. They were nothing like what she remembered from home, and that was the main thing. There was no point in letting herself get nostalgic; she was a long way from home, and that was unlikely to change anytime soon.

She was warm now—ridiculous, really; it wasn't as though it was cold outside, but the pressure of wind and rain and water on her Holon had left its reflection in her body. The tea and the soup had helped, and she was almost content as she nibbled at her second brownie. Kazu grinned at her from across the table.

"You want mine, too?"

"No, thank you, I have plenty." More to the point, the Vanguard had plenty: She was still getting used to a place without chronic shortages. She licked chocolate from her finger and reached for her mug of tea. "Where is Cammie? Did she decide not to eat?"

Yaz looked faintly guilty. "I thought she was behind us."

"She'll come when she's hungry," Kazu said. "Don't worry so much."

"I wonder," Valentina began, and shook her head. There was no point in saying anything, not when no one else seemed to be worried. It was just that she couldn't shake this feeling of unease.

"You wonder what?" Kazu said.

"If she picked up anything on her sensors, or if she spotted something."

"Are you still worrying about air cover?" Yaz asked. "Because if you are, you can stop. The Union doesn't fly in this weather."

And you would know. Valentina swallowed the words—too much, too sharp for this moment, and Kazu said, "She's probably working on the Holons. With Migas."

Chase mixed in as he spoke, looking from one to the other as he sized up the situation. "You talking about Cammie? She stayed to work on the Holons."

"You see," Kazu said, and his eyes abruptly focused on something behind Valentina. She glanced over her shoulder, toward the entrance and expanse of empty chairs and tables, and saw Cammie and Migas walking toward them, each of them carrying a tray that they'd collected from the only open station. She lifted a hand to wave them over, and they took seats at the long table, Migas making an apologetic noise as he brushed through the arm of Chase's avatar.

"Sorry, man."

"No worries." Chase shifted sideways as though he still had a physical presence, and Valentina repressed a shiver. She loved the Ether, loved to spend time in virtuality, but to be trapped there, to have no body at all . . . It was not something she wanted to imagine. She took another sip of tea to hide her feelings, glancing idly at Cammie's plate. The Scottish girl had chosen the three-pack of tacos, with all the trimmings, while it looked as though Migas was eating a chicken salad sandwich. But of course, she reminded herself, he had not been out in the weather.

"I am wondering," she said aloud, "Cammie, whether you have had a chance to look over the data from this morning yet."

"Data?" Cammie gave her a puzzled look, the ears on her headband swiveling to point forward.

"Sensor data from our excursion," Valentina said. "Any sign of the Union."

"If there had been any Union forces in the area, we would have picked them up while we were out," Yaz said impatiently. "I think we can assume we're clear."

"I'd like to be certain," Valentina said.

"Well, I haven't looked at the logs," Cammie said, "but Caliban should have alerted us if there was anything. I'll double-check after I've eaten, though."

Chase fixed his gaze on Valentina, his eyes blue and glowing against his brown skin. "You're still worried."

She nodded. "I am."

"Have you got anything more?"

"Not unless Cammie turns up something."

"What are you talking about?" Cammie asked.

Yaz flung up her hands. "Valentina thinks there should have been Union air cover. I keep telling her Union fliers can't handle it—"

"But there *should* have been," Valentina said. "They never send out Spider Tanks without backup."

"And if there wasn't, what are you suggesting?" Kazu pushed his tray aside.

"I don't know," Valentina said. It was a good question, though, and she made herself consider it. "If they wanted us to take in these refugees? Wanted to plant someone on the base? Maybe they wanted to track us back to De Soto, if they haven't located it exactly yet. I don't know. It just doesn't feel right."

Cammie looked up from her tacos. "I've told Caliban to take another look through the data. And also, if it's about the refugees, they've been cleared, yeah? Captain Herrara said so. He'd brought two of them down to the hangar, and one of them was really p—*annoyed* that the Vanguard techs were repairing their motorcycles. You'd think they'd be a little more grateful."

"Or at least not start off shouting," Migas said. "It was kind of odd."

Cammie frowned. "Also, there was something weird about their setup, how they'd rigged the bike. I can't put my finger on it, but . . ." She stopped, shaking her head.

Chase looked from her to Valentina and back again. "If you think this is important, I'll get you in to talk to Colonel Varden. I'll back you up, too."

Valentina nodded slowly. "Yes. Yes, I think I would like that. I have a bad feeling."

"I'd like to go with you," Cammie said. "Maybe he can tell me what was wrong with those bikes, or that it's nothing."

"Okay," Chase said. "I'll set that up. Don't go away." He mixed out before anyone could answer, and Yaz sighed loudly.

"I still think you're worrying about nothing."

"I hope I am," Valentina answered. "But it's not a chance I want to take."

Chase was as good as his word. Cammie was dabbing up the last crumbs of a ginger-spiced cookie when his avatar reappeared. "The colonel says he can see us now."

Valentina looked impressed. "You actually—" She stopped, shaking her head. "Yes. Let's go."

Cammie pushed back from the table. "I'm coming, too."

"You don't have to," Chase said. "I can share your report."

Cammie flinched. Why were they all treating her this way? Like she was just a kid when she had something concrete to ask about . . . "I want to. Besides, I'm still waiting for Caliban to check in about this morning. He might have something for us." She glanced sideways to view her internal display as she spoke, but there were no icons indicating a message from Caliban, just a scattering of weather warnings and notes from the base systems.

"All right," Chase said.

They followed his avatar through the corridors, past more workshops and secondary control rooms and some blandly labeled areas that Cammie guessed were either intelligence suites or recreation rooms. Finally they spiraled in toward the base's center, past a discreet checkpoint staffed by deceptively casual guards, and the door slid open to reveal Major Rountree. She looked dead tired, Cammie thought, heavy circles under her eyes, but she gave no other sign of weakness. "Lieutenant. Ma'ams. The colonel will see you now."

She ushered them into the office. Nothing much had changed since the first debriefing. The air was still crowded with virtual displays and scratchy images, and the model of the base and the surrounding area still hovered over the only open area of the desk. Varden compressed it with a gesture, and waved it aside.

"Lieutenant," he said. "And Ms. Romanyszyn and Ms. MacCloud. What can I do for you?"

"I am concerned about the absence of Union air cover yesterday," Valentina said bluntly. "It is not like them to leave their tanks unsupported."

"The weather was right at the limit of what our own aircraft could handle," Varden said. "It seems possible that they just couldn't handle it."

"That is what Yaz—Ms. Madrani—said," Valentina agreed. "And I admit, I have not encountered anything like this weather previously, but it doesn't seem like the Union."

Rountree cleared her throat. "This is a big storm. You saw what it was like this morning just locally, and if anything, it's worse east of here. The whole system has slowed down; it's just crawling ashore. Things are going to stay bad for another couple of days."

Cammie glanced at the screen behind Varden's desk, where a composite satellite image showed the enormous spiral of cloud, the tops picked out in red and yellow and green and lit with sparks to mark the thunderstorms. "Could the Union be using that to cover an attack?"

"We don't think so," Varden said. "You were out in it yourself—you saw what it was like. Everyone is either taking shelter now or they're going to be too busy trying to survive to worry about us."

"Or both," Rountree said.

Varden nodded. "Or both. We had to pull in the last of our live patrols at 0300 this morning, and grounded the airborne drones a little after dawn. We've still got a few ground-crawler drones out, but we're not going to be able to keep them going much longer. None of them have picked up anything, and frankly, I'm not expecting them to."

"What happens when you have to pull the crawlers back?" Chase asked.

"We have several lines of perimeter sensors," Rountree explained. "Covering the roads, of course, and the most likely approaches, backed up by an inner line that connects all our watch posts. The weather won't affect them. If the Union tries anything, we'll see them coming."

"I'm not sure that's what Valentina was worried about," Chase said.

"No." Valentina paused. "I am more worried about these refugees. If the Union did anything to make it less hard for them to get to you, then we have to assume that the Union wanted them here. Or wanted some of them here."

"You're suggesting that there is a Union agent in the group," Varden said.

"That would be the logical conclusion," Valentina answered.

"All this from a shortage of air cover?" Rountree asked.

Cammie saw Chase look at her, and lifted her hand as though she was in school. She snatched it back, swearing silently, and said, "Well, there was another thing. I think. The refugees, they came on motorcycles—well, some of them did. I got a look at the bikes after we came in, and there's something off about the mods. They're not Polity, not the way I've seen anyone do it."

"They came from the Union," Rountree said. "They're going to have Union gear."

Cammie was about to explain the mods, but Chase cut in. "I assume they've all checked out?" Chase asked. "Since I saw they'd been released to the base's nonsecure areas?"

"Captain Herrera said they had provisional clearance," Cammie said.

"They do," Varden said. "And they did check out. There were really two groups, but they both have clean scans and impeccable credentials. There was one group, the original group, from the Carolinas. They were led by a known, tested member of the Underground Railroad, a woman named Charlie Little. She said her cover was blown, so she joined the last group she'd made arrangements for, and we didn't see anything to make us doubt her. The rest of her group checks out."

"And the other one?" Chase asked.

"They're an independent group from outside Tallahassee, not traveling on the Railroad but carrying Polity credentials," Rountree said. "They're not individually known to us, but the people vouching for them are known and trusted agents." She looked at Cammie. "Those are the ones with the motor-cycles."

"Does everyone in the group have those credentials?" Chase asked.

"Just the leaders," Varden answered. "A woman named Aris Webb and two brothers named Foxe."

"I met them," Cammie said. "Well, Aris Webb and one of the Foxes."

"Liam," Varden said. "The other one, Jake, he's dead. He's the one who was supposed to have the information you wanted, too."

"Convenient," Valentina observed.

Varden sighed. "I take your point, Ms. Romanyszyn. But everything they've said checks out."

"We could run a few more interviews," Rountree said. "If there's a Union agent, they'll think they've made it in, and they might get careless."

They're actually taking us seriously, Cammie thought, her and Valentina. She just hoped she wasn't making a fuss over nothing.

"Do that, Major," Varden said. "And have security move them off the refugee protocol and onto enhanced observation. There's no point in taking chances."

"Thank you, Colonel," Valentina said.

Chase nodded. "Yes, thank you, sir. I hope we're wrong, but—"

"I'm not willing to take that chance," Varden said. "Look, I can give you and your team access to the debriefing reports. Maybe you'll pick up something we missed."

"Yes!" Cammie said, pumping her fist, and felt herself blush. "I mean, yes. Thank you, umm, sir."

Varden nodded. "I have the first-pass report on the stolen brains thing." He gestured at a screen, and a bright blue icon popped into existence. He flicked it toward Chase, who caught it and tucked it away somewhere in his internal storage. "Not much to report; like I said, the source was lost in the incursion. Let me know if you find anything, though, or if you need anything more."

Chase looked at Valentina. Cammie couldn't see her expression, but Chase gave a fractional nod. "Thank you, sir. We'll definitely keep you updated."

"Thank you, Lieutenant," Varden said, and turned his attention back to his multiple screens.

Cammie followed the others out into the hall, trailing

behind Valentina's effortless strides. At least the colonel had listened; she was used to people ignoring her, patting her on the head and telling her whatever it was that bothered her wasn't actually important. Though it was probably Valentina whom Colonel Varden had listened to, not her. Valentina was a veteran, decorated, deadly; the observation about the lack of air cover was smart. Without context, Cammie's point about the motorcycles felt trivial by comparison.

"Is that good enough?" Chase asked, and Valentina slowed, her grim expression relaxing.

"Yes. I don't know what else he could have done. And I am painfully aware that I don't have much to offer in the way of evidence. Unless Caliban—?"

She looked at Cammie, who checked her internal systems. "Caliban says he's been over the data and he doesn't see anything. He's checking again."

"So no evidence," Valentina said. "But"—she shrugged with elaborate unconcern, and Cammie didn't believe it for a moment—"I have learned better than to ignore these nagging feelings." She met Cammie's eyes. "And what do you expect to find in these reports, except sad stories?"

Cammie made a face. She hadn't thought about that part, reading about people who'd lost everything, risked everything to get out of the Union, and she definitely wasn't looking forward to finding out about Liam Foxe's brother. No wonder he'd been in a temper; it was probably easier to yell at her than to let himself feel that loss. She remembered that from when Mam disappeared, and then after Dad died, all the times it had been easier to scream at Gran or go do something stupid on the Ether . . . She shoved those memories away, made herself focus on Valentina's question. "I don't know, exactly. Things that don't feel right, like the way that bike was rebuilt. And I'm going to keep working on that. If there's something there, I'll know it."

"Let us hope so," Valentina said, and Cammie felt a surge of confidence.

"I don't notice you offering to help," Chase said.

"No. At least not right now." Valentina allowed herself a small smile. "Tonight, there is to be a hurricane party, both here and on the Ether, and I intend to enjoy that new experience. So I am going to go and rest now." She turned away, brushing past Chase's avatar as though he wasn't there.

Cammie watched her go, wondering uneasily if that was a reference to her nightmares, but it was too late to ask. Though maybe . . . Chase had said she could ask, maybe she could ask him if he'd caught anything on the monitors. "Chase?"

"Yeah?"

Cammie took a breath, wondering where exactly she should start. "Yeah, I . . ." She stopped, made a face, and tried again. "You said—"

"Hang on." Chase's eyes focused on something over her left shoulder and she turned to see Aris Webb walking toward them.

"Is she supposed to be here?" Cammie asked, and Chase glanced sideways at his own displays.

"It's a green area."

Aris lifted her hand. "Hey, hi! It's Lieutenant Chase, isn't it? And Cammie."

Cammie glared, wishing she'd picked any other moment to show up, but Aris kept coming, seemingly good-natured but oblivious.

"Listen, I wanted to apologize for Liam. He's— His brother Jake was killed; he's grieving. He doesn't always think about what he's saying."

"Problems?" Chase said, frowning slightly. He looked at Cammie, but Aris answered with a nervous laugh.

"Cammie was helping the Vanguard technicians repair our bikes. Liam didn't realize what was going on, didn't realize who she was. He hates when people mess with his gear."

Chase lifted his eyebrows a fraction, and Cammie shrugged. "It's okay. Like you said, he was upset. I'm sorry about his brother."

"That's kind of you," Aris said, in the voice you'd use to talk to a child. Cammie's initial good impression of Aris instantly soured. "I'll let him know."

Tell him he can go— Cammie knew better than to say that out loud, and managed a nod instead. "Sure."

"I also wanted to thank you," Aris said, fixing her eyes on Chase. "Those mechs—what a sight! We wouldn't have made it out without you guys."

"You're welcome," Chase said. "We're always glad to help out the Vanguard."

"And believe me, we're grateful," Aris said. "Not that the Vanguard isn't great, but they were overmatched. And then when we saw the mechs come in, well, we knew we'd be all right. I know it's hard to repay something like that, but if there's ever anything we can do for you, any of you—"

"It's not necessary," Chase said. "Really. I don't want to sound pompous, but it really is our duty."

Aris laughed.

She has a pretty laugh, Cammie thought. It was all too apparent what she was trying to do, and it took all of Cammie's self-control to keep from rolling her eyes too obviously. Aris was attractive, though, with a nice figure and light hair tipped with metallic red. She'd managed to bring makeup with her, Cammie noticed, and then reminded herself that she might have borrowed it after she got to De Soto. Either way, though, she was a lot more put together than Cammie would have expected from a refugee, and she looked at Chase to see if he'd noticed. If he had, he wasn't showing it, just kept looking at Aris with that polite junior officer look on his face.

"Like I said, we appreciate it," Aris said. "Are you going to be at the hurricane party tonight? I hear the base is working to make it really fun. Especially with those poor folks from New Janice and St. John's."

"I expect we'll look in," Chase said easily, and Aris smiled.

"I hope to see you there." She lifted a hand and turned away, heading down the curve of the corridor. Cammie automatically checked her map, and guessed she was either heading to the smaller mess hall or back to the refugees' barracks. She glanced at Chase and saw him watching her retreating figure, his expression unreadable. He shook himself then and looked back at her.

"Sorry. You were saying?"

"I was?" Cammie opened her eyes wide, trying to pretend she didn't remember.

"You said you wanted to talk."

"Oh. Yeah." Cammie forced a smile. "Do you know, talking to her put it right out of my mind."

Chase gave a rueful grin. "I know what you mean."

"I mean, give her her due; she's not rude, exactly," Cammie said. "But I'm just not in the mood."

"You sure?"

Cammie hesitated. She'd come this far . . .

"Nightmares?" Chase sounded wary, and she frowned at him.

"Have people been complaining?"

He shook his head. "No. Just—Yaz was worried you weren't sleeping. Nightmares was my guess."

"Sometimes," Cammie said. "Nemesis, mostly."

"Yeah." Chase nodded. "Me, too. Or I did, anyway. Before all of this." He gestured to his avatar, and Cammie winced. That one gesture stood for so much, for everything he'd sacrificed. It made her own problems feel ridiculous by comparison. "I don't dream much now. Or not that I can tell."

"That could be nice," Cammie said, in spite of herself.

"So tell me?"

She shrugged. "He just shows up. In the middle of whatever else I'm dreaming about. He pops up out of nothing with all those arms reaching out—" She shook her head. "How'm I supposed to get back to sleep after that? I might as well go out on the Ether. Or get some work done."

"You have to rest sometime," Chase said.

"I'd like to," Cammie answered. "Any ideas how?"

He winced as though that had hit home. "Okay, no, it's not that easy. Time helps. The Vanguard had people on staff who could handle classified material; we might be able to set up something similar through RTASA."

"I don't want to talk to them," Cammie said. "I can do this on my own—you all did. Besides, Dr. Weller *died* to make this happen. I don't want to let him down."

"You're not letting us down."

"I froze."

"And you pushed through it," Chase said. "You did what you had to, and we saved those people Vanguard could help. Can help. They helped me."

"Yeah?" Cammie gave him a sidelong look. It was hard to imagine Chase needing that kind of help—and even harder to imagine someone who'd dealt with problems on the scale of Chase's doing anything but rolling their eyes when she showed up saying she was having bad dreams like some scared kid yelling about monsters under the bed. She'd *survived*, she hadn't even been hurt. "I'm— I don't want to talk to anyone about this. Bad enough I have to dream it. I don't want to spend any more time talking about it."

"It's up to you," Chase said. "Just . . . will you think about it?"

"Yeah. I'll think," Cammie said. She could tell from Chase's look that he didn't believe her, but to her relief he merely nodded.

"Good enough," he said, and mixed out, vanishing into the network.

5

Aғтеr снаѕе'ѕ аvатаr mixed out, she found herself reluctant to go back to their quarters. Valentina had said she was going to get some sleep; probably Cammie's being there wouldn't bother her, but the others might have returned, and she wasn't really in the mood to talk to any of them. She needed to think more about the modified motorcycle, and she absolutely didn't want to answer questions about how she'd frozen, or whether she was sleeping at night. Back to the mess hall, maybe? The serving lines would be shut down, but there were always sandwiches and crisps and bowls of fresh fruit, and tea and coffee that wasn't exactly good for anything other than keeping her energy up. She wasn't hungry, though, and if she was honest with herself, the enormous empty spaces were kind of depressing. There was always the Ether, but her goggles were back in their quarters: She didn't want to go there.

She could also head back to *Renegade* and work on the Holons, but when she pinged the ship, Caliban informed her that

Migas had secured the ship after they finished their maintenance earlier today.

"I can wake him if you would like," Caliban said, "but you've already done everything necessary. And before you ask, my second analysis of this morning's data hasn't turned up anything either."

"Right," Cammie said, and cut the connection.

She called up the map of the base instead, letting the system locate her in the maze of levels that reminded her more than anything of an ant farm they'd had at primary school. She was close to a couple of rec rooms, one of which seemed to have console games, but a quick query showed them mostly in use, and anyway, they weren't as good as the Ether. Then she saw it, a notation OBSERVATION TURRET (NOT SECURE). The system marked it as disused, but there were also no sealed doors between her and it.

Might as well take a look, she thought, and called up a floating bot to guide her through the corridors.

She could believe the area was mostly disused. The floors were clean, the walls unmarked, but the paint wasn't that fresh, and there were enough open doors to show what looked like empty classrooms, with rows of chairs and a lecturer's screen at the front of the room. It made her think of Dr. Weller standing in front of the team, explaining their new lives, and she shook her head. She still didn't know how she felt about him, about the things he hadn't told them and the things he had, or about the inarguable fact that he'd died giving them the chance to get away. Maybe that was all she needed to know, that and the inarguable fact that it was more exciting to be part of gen:LOCK than it was to be stuck in an installation doing white-hat hacks for the Polity to work off her sentence. More fun, too . . . except when it wasn't.

That was also something she didn't want to think about, and she loosed the bug again, following it down hallways that lit up at her approach, and went dark again after she'd passed. De Soto Base had once held a lot more people; she wondered where they'd gone.

The bot led her down what she thought was a dead-end corridor until she saw the heavy hatch pinned open against the wall. There was a spiral stair beyond it, and the bot transformed to a green arrow pointing up. She followed it, and emerged into a small circular room with long narrow windows set into the walls. It was a little bit like being at the top of a lighthouse, except that she was only barely aboveground, and there was no light, just the stairs and the windows and a narrow metal bench running along the wall under them. The thick glass ran with rain on one side, completely impossible to see out, but on the downwind side, she could see across the landing field toward another set of low-slung buildings. Beyond them, a line of trees thrashed in the storm, but the walls were thick enough that she couldn't hear the wind. She moved closer, laying her hand on the glass, and felt it trembling.

That brought back an unexpected memory—Gran's

house in an autumn storm that had come crashing in from the North Sea to pin the trawlers in the harbor and ground every helicopter from Arbroath to Peterhead. Mam had been off on one of the rigs then, one of her decommissioning jobs, and Cammie had come down, crying, to the kitchen because her windows were rattling and the wind and rain were too loud to let her sleep.

"It's just a storm, Bun," Gran had said. She and Dad had been in the kitchen, Dad with a screen in his lap, busy tracking the weather, though he'd been quick to squash the radar images to nothing when she'd appeared.

"It's loud," Cammie had whined, and Dad had given her a wry smile.

"That it is, Cammie. Maybe we should have some tea, eh, Elsie?"

"No tea for the child, not at this hour," Gran had answered. "Besides, I expect she'd like hot chocolate better."

"Yes, please," Cammie had said, and climbed into Dad's lap while Gran found the pan and the milk and the sugar bowl and scooped cocoa from the tin to mix the drink for each of them. Cammie remembered leaning against Dad's chest while Gran stirred the mixture in the battered pot— thinking sleepily about how weird it was that cocoa powder tasted so nasty on its own, but made hot chocolate and biscuits that were better than anything. Then there had been a flash and a bang and all the power had gone out, leaving them in darkness except for the blue flames under the pot.

She had screamed, and Dad's hands had tightened, holding her safe.

"It's all right," he said. "It's just the power's gone."

"But with no power, there's no lights, and no phone, and no Ether—" Cammie had been ready to cry again, cut off from everything, and her grandmother had reached onto the shelf above the stove to pull out a thick, short candle. She lit it at the gas ring, then set it on a plate and put it in the middle of the table, the wavering flame casting strange shadows.

"Hush now," she said. "We're all here, and all safe. It's just the wind's taken down a line somewhere."

"What about Mam?" Cammie asked. "Is she in the dark?"

She felt Dad laugh softly. "Oh, Bun, she's likely better off than we are. Those rigs are built to take the weather. She's probably tucked up in her bunk right now, reading a nice mystery, or out on the Ether talking to her friends."

"But she won't be able to find us on the Ether," Cammie said. "We can't get there."

"And she'll know exactly why," Gran said. "It's just a storm, child." The hot chocolate was done; she poured it carefully into three mugs, then rummaged in the cabinet to bring out the package of her favorite biscuits. Usually she served them out one at a time, and only for special occasions, like a gold star from school or a project that had come out especially nicely. This time, though, she'd emptied them onto a plate and set it on the table, then lit a second candle and came to

113

join them, a bottle in her other hand. She'd added a tot to her own mug, and to Dad's, and they'd sipped hot chocolate and eaten all the biscuits, and at some point Cammie must have fallen asleep, because the next thing she remembered, she was in her own bed and the touch lights were glowing at the base of her tablet, informing her that it was morning and the storm was over and she had texts waiting.

She settled herself on the cold metal seat, choosing a spot where she could watch the waving trees. Chase could mix in if they needed her, the gen:LOCK network would find her anywhere in the base; this was a nicely private place to look over the reports that Colonel Varden had allowed her to access. She pulled up a screen and found the links, laid them open one by one. After a bit, Nugget wormed his way out of her jacket and began wandering around the open space.

"Don't go too far," she said, but didn't look up from the screen. After a bit, Nugget returned and hopped into her lap, radiating a warmth that was welcome, sitting on the cool metal. She lifted him to her shoulder, and kept reading. The colonel was right; there was nothing there that she hadn't heard before, though the details were sad enough to make her flinch. The group from the Carolinas had three people who'd walked all the way from Delaware, taking turns carrying a baby; they'd had to sedate the infant to keep it from crying, and there was a note from the base's chief medical officer that they were going to start weaning the baby off the drugs right away. There was the preacher who'd been part of the Underground Railroad, and the deputy who'd been ordered to arrest him and the family he was hiding, and instead had warned him and joined the escape.

Maybe the deputy was the problem? Cammie thought, but there was nothing in the file to suggest that Na'Talia Jackson was anything more than a woman who'd been asked to do one thing too many. The group's leader was a farmer named Charlotta Little, who'd been trying to arrange the movement of another group of six, and had ended up with the entire group, all fourteen of them, crammed into an eight-wheeled farm hauler and a couple of four-wheelers. It was amazing they'd gotten this far, past the Union check-points and the roving patrols, but you had to say that about everybody who got across the 88th. Major Rountree's notes said that all the verifiable statements had checked out, and that both the preacher and Little were known agents. The only question mark was the deputy, and even Rountree seemed half-hearted about it.

That left the group from Tallahassee, and Cammie paged quickly through their files. That was where she thought the problem would be, though she was willing to admit that might be because she didn't like the ones she'd met. Liam Foxe was a jerk, and Aris Webb . . . Aris had talked to her like a child. That wasn't exactly proof of anything, but it definitely made it harder to treat Aris fairly. There had been ten of them when they started out from, not Tallahassee, apparently, but towns not far from it, with weird American names like Capitola and Miccosukee and Wetumpka and Lloyd. They'd all worked at the same factory, assembling tanks and other machines for the Union, and they all said they hadn't had any choice about the work. It was all there was, and everyone had to work, under Union rules; they weren't given safety gear, and the machines chewed people up on a regular basis. They were all on the second shift together, friends who rode and rebuilt motorcycles in their spare time, with the same foremen demanding more and faster from everyone, and finally, Aris had suggested that they try to get away before things got worse. She and the Foxe brothers had been the heart of the group, everyone agreed, and it had been their plan they followed.

They hadn't had the luck of the Carolina group, though, or maybe it was that they didn't have the experience. Three of them had been caught—or maybe killed, no one seemed entirely sure—when the group tried to blow past a roadblock, and they'd lost three more at the rendezvous, including one of the Foxe brothers. Jake was the one who'd heard a rumor about "stolen brains," according to both his brother and Aris, but he'd refused to give them any details. *He wanted to protect us,* Aris had said, and the interviewer noted that she had been crying when she said it. *He said if we didn't know, the Union wouldn't zombie us. But of course they would have.*

Rountree had asked what she meant by being "zombied," and Aris explained that was what everyone in the county said happened to the people who the Union took. They disappeared, of course, but everyone said they were used to work the Union's biggest machines, wired into the consoles like interchangeable parts, because people were cheaper to program and easier to replace than actual robots . . .

Cammie shivered at the thought, hunching her shoulders away from the metal wall, the roar of the wind loud in her ears. That was a horrible thing to think about, made worse by the fact that she certainly believed the Union would do exactly that.

Dr. Weller hadn't given her all the details of his mystery program when he had come to Polity Cybersecurity to recruit her, but he'd also given her a chance to back out. She stopped, looking past the screens to the line of trees at the edge of the landing area. The rain was blowing past in solid sheets, hard enough to send shallow waves sweeping across the pavement. Well, maybe it wasn't much of a choice, not when he'd told them they were the only people who could do it, and showed them what was at stake, but it was more than the Union zombies had. And they remained themselves: That was important. Cammie-in-a-Holon was still Cammie. Even if she sometimes wanted to reprogram herself to be better at it.

So maybe she really was being unfair to Aris. The woman had been in an awful situation, and she'd taken a chance and almost made it. *Had* made it, even if half her friends hadn't. That definitely wasn't her fault. Cammie flipped back through the files. All her friends said she'd done everything possible to get them out.

And yet. There was still something that didn't sit right. If she'd just had a few more minutes to examine the bike's engine . . . Her fingers itched to pull the pieces apart, strip it down to parts so that she could really see what was going on. The Vanguard techs were right, of course, everybody built things differently, but there was something there that didn't make sense. That didn't fit the story.

She closed her eyes, wishing she had taken pictures. The Vanguard techs might have something, she could look for that later, too, but if she could just remember . . . The problem was in the fuel delivery system, and she made herself work through the pieces one by one, visualizing each one along with its connections. They were all new, that was one thing that was surprising, new and top-line. Presumably, parts like that were still available on the Union side of the 88th, but she would have expected them to be too expensive for a bunch of factory workers. And . . . they were using high-pressure fuel injectors, when most home-built machines still used the lower-pressure versions that were easier to adjust and safer to work on outside a well-stocked garage. It wasn't conclusive, but it was definitely not what she would have expected.

She waved her hand to close the files and banish the window, and tucked Nugget under her arm. Maybe the bikes were still in the hangar. It would be worth trying to get another look at them, and then she'd know if she was really onto something, or if she was just being unfair.

The hangar was mostly empty, though, just a couple of techs working on a flying drone damaged by the weather in one bay, an older woman deep in discussion with a younger tech over what looked like a schematic for body armor, the usual guards keeping an eye on things. The bay where the techs had worked on the refugees' bikes was dark and empty, the bikes themselves nowhere to be seen. She pinged Caliban.

"Did you see what happened to the motorcycles that were over here?"

"I wasn't aware I was supposed to be watching any motorcycles," Caliban answered. "I assume you're referring to the repair bay in front of which you're presently standing? I can review security footage if you'd like."

"Yeah. Please." Cammie paused. "Is Migas there?"

"He's gone off looking for a snack," Caliban answered. "Or so he said. I think he's gone to play *Siege*."

That was a tempting thought, but Cammie pushed it away. "Did you find the footage?"

"One moment." There was a pause, and a bright blue square opened in front of her eyes. "Is this what you were looking for?"

She recognized the techs she had been talking to before, along with Liam Foxe and the willowy shape of Aris Webb. They talked, from the look of it Aris doing her best to smooth things over, and then Liam nodded and walked away. Aris stayed, talking to the technicians, and a little later Liam came back, followed by a shorter person with a bandaged hand. They wheeled the motorcycles away, and Cammie tensed. That was only three machines; the fourth one might still be around. "Cal. What did they do with the fourth bike?"

The image in front of her abruptly sped up, slowed again to show Aris returning, to walk away with the last machine.

"Fff—" She swallowed the word. "Right. Never mind."

"If you wanted to talk to a particular refugee," Caliban said, "I could provide their location."

Not Aris. Cammie paused, startled by the strength of her own reaction. Maybe it would make sense to talk to the leader of the other group. "What about Charlotta Little?"

"Charlie," Caliban said.

"What?"

"She goes by Charlie." Caliban paused. "She is in the mess hall right now. You should be able to catch her there."

"Thanks."

Cammie made her way back to the mess hall, even emptier now in the middle of the afternoon. The tables stretched empty between covered serving stations, and a single attendant was sweeping behind a counter. A trio of damp-looking Vanguard soldiers were sitting at a corner table, and an older woman was sitting by herself toward the back of the room, staring into space, her fingers occasionally moving as she manipulated unseen data.

"Caliban?"

"Yes, that's her," Caliban answered. "Do you want me to make an introduction?"

"Not necessary." Cammie turned her attention to the serving lines. The beverage lane was open, and next to it a station offered wrapped sandwiches and salads and a big tray of biscuits in assorted flavors. She fixed herself a cup of tea, filled a plate with a selection of the biscuits, and started toward the table where the older woman was sitting.

She looked up at Cammie's approach, flexing her hands to close whatever she was looking at, and Cammie hesitated. This really wasn't her business, and what if she was wrong? She'd risk getting an innocent person into serious trouble, and make herself look stupid in the bargain. And she had no idea what to say, anyway. Except that if she was right and Valentina's suspicions about the lack of air support proved true, somebody needed to do something.

"Hi," she said, and gave the woman her biggest smile. "I'm Cammie."

The refugee leader nodded slowly, and brushed her invisible data back into storage. "Charlie Little." She wasn't a lot taller than Cammie herself, though she was broader, with swollen knuckles on the hands that wrapped her coffee cup. She had the weathered skin of someone who'd spent a lot of time outdoors, and her gray hair was cut close to her scalp. "What can I do for you, Cammie?"

"Well." Cammie pulled out a chair and sat down across

from her, setting her tea and biscuits between them and planting her elbows on the table. "I wanted to ask you some questions. Oh, and I brought some biscuits. You can have one if you'd like."

"Those aren't biscuits—you mean cookies?"

Cammie rolled her eyes. "Yeah. Whatever you lot call them here. I need to talk to you."

"I've talked to just about everybody on this base, seems like," Little said. "No offense, but why should I talk to you?"

"I'm with the big mechs that helped rescue you," Cammie answered. "Well, I'm one of them, actually. So there's that."

"You drive one of those monster mecha?" Little looked impressed, and Cammie remembered she'd seen the older woman at the hauler's controls.

"Drive 'em, build 'em, mod 'em." Cammie shrugged, not able to hide her pride. "I kind of *am* one of them. But that's classified."

"Nice." Little's taut expression eased into a crooked smile. "Those are pretty damned impressive machines."

"I like them," Cammie said, and Little's smile widened.

"Okay, I'll bite. Ask your questions."

Cammie leaned forward a little farther. "The report said somebody turned in your group. Was there anything, I don't know, weird about how it happened?"

"Weird?" Little was looking at her like she had two heads, or maybe it was the way her ears were swiveling nervously on her headband.

"You know, weird. Unexpected. Like it shouldn't have happened or something." Cammie grimaced, not sure how to say it without giving away the answer she expected, and Little's expression sharpened.

"You mean, were we set up?" She paused, considering, then shook her head. "Nah. You got to understand, Tyrell County's not that populated, and where we are, everybody knows everybody, so I knew we'd get caught someday. And this time, from what Na'Talia said, Vickie shot off her mouth in Gum Neck after she'd been drinking, and the Union busted her. They'd already ordered Na'Talia to arrest the reverend. So we grabbed our bugout bags and ran."

"This Vickie, she didn't plan it, then?"

"Vickie's my ex," Little said. "But she hates the Union more than she hates me. And she always did talk too much." She sighed. "I hope she's okay."

They both knew how unlikely that was. Cammie pushed the plate toward her. "Have a biscuit."

Little took one, and they sat in silence for a moment. Cammie nibbled on a piece of shortbread studded with candied orange, and put it down.

"What about the people you picked up in Tallahassee? Anything weird about that?" Little hesitated, and Cammie bounced in her seat. "There was, wasn't there?"

"I don't know," Little said. "Look, just because they do things differently from me, that doesn't make them wrong. And it sure as hell doesn't make them Union."

"There's different, and there's . . . not quite right," Cammie said. "Oh, you know what I mean!"

Little nodded reluctantly. "Yeah. But I'm probably wrong."

"Or maybe not." Cammie leaned forward again. "And if we're not—"

"Yeah. Yeah, I know." Little sighed. "It was weird how we ended up meeting them. I mean, it might just have been luck, but . . . it was weird. The Union kept pushing us north, and a couple of times I was sure we were screwed, but they backed off. And then we ran into the kids."

"Like the Union was herding you," Cammie said.

"Maybe," Little said, but Cammie could tell she meant *yes*. "And the kids, they were careful, but not careful enough. Not careful in the right ways. But maybe that's just because they were coming out of the Tallahassee area. I don't know what things are like there."

"So they ran into you," Cammie said. "And you just happened to have the codes to call Vanguard for a pickup."

"That thought had crossed my mind," Little said. She shook her head. "But the boy who was leading them, the older one, he got killed—"

"Meaning the others didn't have to give us any useful information," Cammie said. "Because everybody else said only Jake Foxe knew the details."

Little nodded. "Though I'd have said Liam and Aris were just as much in charge as Jake was. I was surprised she didn't know."

"She said Jake was trying to protect them," Cammie said.

"Could be."

Cammie looked at her plate again, not liking the way any of this was adding up. "Tell me about Aris Webb."

Little pursed her lips. "I'm not sure I ought to. Nothing to do with you, but . . . I flat-out don't like her. And there's no way in hell I can manage to be fair to her."

"So tell me why you don't like her."

"That's where I'm not being fair." Little breathed a laugh. "She's not exactly authentic, you know? Like, you can tell when she's trying to charm you or smooth something over. She's always trying to *manage* people. She means well, I'm pretty sure of that, but—" She shrugged. "I expect you've met people like her."

"Yeah." Maybe that was all it was, Cammie thought. She'd always hated people who put on a face to get what they want; what did Americans call them? *Phony.* But Aris was a survivor, someone likely accustomed to doing those things to survive. And she'd lost half her friends; she had every reason to be raw and awkward. Maybe it really was nothing. "What about the deputy?"

"Na'Talia?" Little scowled. "What about her?"

Cammie hesitated. "She was Union, or at least a Union supporter, yeah?"

"She's a deputy sheriff," Little said flatly. "That doesn't make her Union."

"But the Union controls law enforcement," Cammie

continued. "They do that everywhere they take over."

"She warned the preacher," Little said. "She didn't have to do that. She could have stayed if she'd just kept her mouth shut. She's all right. Look, what are you accusing us of?"

Cammie felt the conversation sour, tried to right it. "I'm not accusing anybody of anything. Something just felt off, that's all. I thought I might look into it."

We shouldn't even be here. Vanguard doesn't need gen:LOCK for these kinds of jobs; they'd have been fine without us. We're only here because there was intel related to us. And that was something she ought to talk to Chase about, not say out loud to one of the people who might actually be part of the problem.

"Well, ain't us," Little said. "Look, I've known Na'Talia since she was in diapers. She's a good kid. If anybody's sketchy, it's that gang from Tallahassee. But I don't think it's any of us. And honestly, I don't think there is anything wrong."

"All right," Cammie said, but the older woman had already pushed herself up from her seat, grabbing her mug.

"And that's all I've got to say." She stalked away without waiting for an answer.

Cammie watched her go, feeling vaguely ashamed of herself. She hadn't meant to insult the deputy, just to get information. This wasn't the way things worked in games. There you could just ask, and keep asking, and the NPCs never got offended or anything. But then, as Gran always said, the Ether wasn't the same as the real world.

And she still thought she was right. There was something off about this mission, something wrong with the way they'd been drawn in, only to find out there was nothing to share after all. It still wasn't much, but if you coupled it with the lack of air cover and the wrong parts in the motorcycles, it was more than nothing. Maybe. She kicked the leg of her chair, trying to make up her mind. Maybe she should look though the debriefing files one more time and see if there was anything she'd missed before she tried to talk to Chase. Or maybe she should just let the whole thing alone for a while—that was what Gran had always suggested when Cammie hit a knot of code that she couldn't unravel. Put it down and do something else, come back to it when you were fresh. Maybe that was the thing to do.

She made her way back to their quarters, slipping in quietly. Sure enough, Valentina was napping in preparation for the party later. The others were all elsewhere, and Cammie climbed silently onto her bunk, settling Nugget onto his charging pad beside her. She found her Ether goggles and let herself drop through the nearest portal.

Once again, the Ether was less crowded than she had expected, though its candy-bright colors were as lively as ever. A stats check showed that still more people were without power, locked out by the storm, and she shifted back to the gaming networks, checking out the area where players met to collect their teams. Most of the groups were tagged as closed, people who'd already assembled the group they wanted to play with; she set her own status to *available* and *seeking party*, with a link to her stats, but the only pingback was a generic *get stuffed, rabbit*. That came from someone who'd barely made it out of the game's first levels, and she rolled her eyes at him before turning her attention elsewhere. Most of the pickup groups were lower level, though, and she wasn't sure she felt like going to all the work of convincing the other players that she was good enough when they weren't going to be able to play at her level.

"Caliban?"

"I'm sorry, I'm currently engaged in repair work."

"Couldn't you spare some of your brain to have fun with?"

"I am working at full capacity at the moment," Caliban answered.

Cammie sighed, but knew better than to try to talk Migas into letting her have even part of Caliban. And of course he was right: The Holons and *Renegade* had to take priority, but it left her with nothing to do. She scanned the room again, crafted a virtual spitball to lob at the player who'd called her "rabbit," then dropped out before it splatted against his avatar.

She wasn't in the mood for music or dancing, or for socializing outside the confines of a game. She called up the list of available interactive volumes, and ran down her options, her frown deepening. Not pirates, not ninjas, not Triremes and Trylons, definitely not Mecha-Land, that was too much like work . . . Maybe she should take the time to look back at her secret garden, see if she couldn't install some of the necessary updates. At least then she'd feel as though she'd gotten something done.

She dropped to the specialty levels, found the pink-and-green-and-cream portal, and let herself through. Her door was waiting; she unlocked it and stepped out into the ragged grass. Everything was pretty much the way she had left it, except the error menu that popped up as soon as she appeared, telling her how many upgrades she needed to make. She swore at it, but waved a hand to open the maintenance window.

The list there seemed even longer, and after a bit she sat down on the slope to work through them. First, the OS updates, all of which had to be installed in sequence; she set them running, and flipped through another series of screens to recover her libraries. The file formats of the oldest images were outdated, and she dug out a conversion tool, began upgrading them one by one. It would be good to have her grass back, her plants and birds and the messages that she'd saved to hang on her tree. The Wonderland roses were missing, though, and she pulled up a secondary screen only to discover that the maker had ceased to maintain the program two years ago. A couple of people had listed workarounds, and she downloaded one, but it failed to launch.

This is going to take time, she told herself. *You left it alone and you've got a lot of work to do to catch up.* Progress bars filled the air around her, crawling slowly from red to green;

one filled and clicked out, but another one took its place. Nothing around her changed. The grass stayed the same, the plain generic, and the message tree remained stubbornly empty.

Something moved then, fading in from behind the message tree, a familiar shape in gray, and she shot to her feet, not entirely sure she wanted to see that right now. Her father's avatar moved toward her, feet not quite touching the grass, his face just slightly out of focus but still recognizable, still with his familiar smile.

"Hello, Bunny." His voice was breathy—she'd made the recording in the last month before he died, when they'd all known there wasn't going to be a happy ending, and he'd told her to build the avatar for him, for after he was gone. And today she couldn't stand it, couldn't bear to think about that, not when everything else was falling apart and she didn't know what to do about the refugees or her nightmares or the fact that she still couldn't shoot or anything . . .

She snatched off her Ether goggles and scrubbed hastily at her cheeks, hoping no one had noticed. The barracks room was still quiet and dimly lit, just Valentina sprawled on her bunk. Cammie sat up, resting her head on her knees, and Nugget came to nudge against her. She swept him into an embrace and flopped back down again. *Fine*, she thought. If the Ether wasn't going to help, there were always her drones to work on.

Valentina rolled out of her bunk at the chime of her internal alarm, pleased to see that the rest of the team had gathered around the table. "Have I missed anything?"

"Nothing important," Yaz said.

"We were looking at the latest weather," Chase said.

"Yes?" Valentina called up her own screen, her eyebrows rising as she took in the numbers. "I thought these storms were supposed to weaken as they came ashore."

"They do," Chase said, with more confidence than she thought was entirely warranted. "It's slowed down, and that means it'll weaken more slowly, too."

Valentina paged through the data, satellite images of a great circle of clouds, radar showing bands of rain and thunderstorms, notices from the base itself. "There are no patrols out now?"

"They can't handle the weather," Yaz said. "But then, neither can the Union."

So we hope. Valentina didn't actually want to provoke an argument, and swallowed the words. "But at least there is a party to celebrate this."

"Online and off," Kazu said, sitting up abruptly from where he had been lounging on his bunk.

"And which will you attend?" Valentina slanted a glance in his direction.

"Offline," he answered promptly. "Actual beer!"

"But it will be in the mess hall, and full of Vanguard people," Valentina said.

"Hey," Chase said. "What's wrong with that?"

"There are many more . . . interesting . . . options on the Ether," Valentina answered, and allowed herself enough of a smile to show that she was joking.

"But no beer," Kazu said, also with a grin. "We should have beer."

"I will admit that virtual beer is a waste of electrons," Valentina said. "But think of the music—the *dancing*."

"The commissary staff's posted a list of what they're serving," Cammie offered. She spread her hands, opening a window to display what looked like a crude map in bright primary colors. Valentina blinked at it, and realized she was looking at a cake. "Hurricane cake!"

It was indeed a cake decorated with an icing map and various landmarks that looked as though they had been made out of chocolate or candy or possibly both.

"Where's the hurricane?" Chase asked.

Cammie closed her hands and opened them again, revealing a tray full of white spiral rosettes. "Ice-cream hurricanes! You add them to the cake, see?"

"We can't miss those," Kazu said. He reached for a screen of his own. "Hot dogs and hamburgers, good, and . . . 'Memphis-style barbecue.' Also french fries and homemade potato chips. And more ice cream." He scrolled further. "Ah! And hurricane punch, age-restricted. Everything we need to have a proper party."

"No band," Valentina pointed out. "No dancing."

"I could bring my guitar," Kazu offered.

"That is not music for dancing," Valentina said.

"Of course it is." Kazu grinned. "I could teach you."

"I value my toes unbroken," Valentina answered. "A proposal, then. We'll attend both parties, one hour each, and see which one is better."

"I'm going to the one on the Ether," Chase said with a crooked smile, and Valentina hoped he didn't see her flinch. What, after all, would be the point of joining the others in the mess hall? At least on the Ether, he would be the same as everyone else. "What about you, Yaz? Cammie?"

"I think I'll try the Ether, too," Yaz said.

Cammie shrugged. "I haven't made up my mind. The Ether, or ice-cream hurricanes. It's not an easy choice."

Valentina looked at Kazu. "Where shall we start?"

"Cammie," Kazu said. "Flip a coin for us. Heads, the mess hall; tails, the Ether."

"Agreed." Valentina watched as Cammie plucked a shape out of thin air and set it spinning.

"Heads."

"The mess hall!" Kazu crowed, and Valentina hauled herself to her feet.

"Very well. We will see the rest of you later. Perhaps."

She followed Kazu out into the corridor, watched him snatch a guide-bot out of the air, and fell into step at his shoulder. He gave her a sideways glance. "I'm worried about Cammie," he said.

Valentina hesitated, then shrugged one shoulder, unable to pretend she didn't know what he meant. "I do not think she has been sleeping well. Again."

"This morning . . ." Kazu shook his head. "She hasn't made that kind of mistake in a long time."

"No. But she was fine in combat."

"And that's progress," Kazu agreed. "But we should do something."

"Such as?" Valentina cocked her head at him.

"If I knew that, I wouldn't be asking you."

Valentina looked away. "I don't know what to say to her. Besides, isn't that Chase's job?"

"We're a team."

That was unanswerable. Valentina said, "I have spoken to her before—so have you. It didn't get so very far."

"She's not a kid," Kazu said. "We shouldn't have talked to her like one."

"Technically—"

"None of us are kids. Not anymore."

"All right," Valentina said. "I will think about it."

Kazu nodded. "And so will I."

"Yes. But in the meantime . . ." Valentina tucked her hand into the crook of Kazu's arm, enjoying both the surprised jump and the equally quick relaxation. "There is a party waiting."

6

CAMMIE LOOKED AROUND the barracks room, empty except for Yaz, Ether goggles in place and her head down on her folded arms. Chase had mixed out, heading for the Ether; Cammie swung her Ether goggles in her hand, trying to decide on her next move. Follow Valentina and Kazu? The cake and ice cream were tempting, but she thought there would be more to learn on the Ether. And she could always come back to the mess hall party later. She put on her goggles and slipped out onto the Ether.

Chase and Yaz were well ahead, but a personalized invitation flowered in front of her, inviting her to the base's party. A second invitation opened, inviting her to a more general hurricane party. It looked as though the spaces were interwoven so that people at the base could take part in some of the carnival-style games attached to the larger party, and she happily hurried toward the portal. She recognized some of the names on the general flyer, and anything they set up was going to be impressive.

She passed through the portal, feeling the quick tug as the

system verified her invitations and matched them to the ID she was using. A curtain of mist marked the divide between the two parties, transparent enough from this side that she could see the towers and neon-pink frameworks of the Gaia Sisters' latest in-and-out simulation, and she crossed the barrier without hesitation.

As she'd hoped, the in-and-out was a flying sim—no one did better flyers than the Sisters. This one was based on the hurricane itself, a massive tower of clouds contained within the pink frame, rotating slowly. She could see a few players caught in the outer edges, working wings and glider frames against the illusory winds, before they were sucked into the center. That looked like fun, and not at all like work, and she searched for the start point.

"Cammie!"

She turned to see a familiar avatar, a green-skinned woman with Earth's continents spread across her cheeks. She was wearing a loose dress that swirled in her own private wind, and at the moment she was carrying a staff topped with the Sisters' glowing globe. "Littlest!"

"Good to see you," the Littlest Gaia Sister said. "You haven't been around in a while."

"Working," Cammie said vaguely.

Littlest lowered her voice. "I heard you'd been busted. Are you okay?"

Cammie shrugged. "Yeah. I was sentenced to reparations, Polity Cybersecurity."

"Bit of a change from the old days," Littlest said.

"It's all right." The Gaia Sisters were mostly legit, though like anyone who worked in Ethertainment, they kept a close eye on the black hats. Nobody wanted to see a game or a sim or a shared space turned into malware bait, and Cammie was pretty sure Gaia was paying protection money to keep their products clean. And if Cammie was still with Polity Cybersecurity and not gen:LOCK, she might be able to do something about that, but not where she was. "This is new."

"Our biggest yet," Littlest said. "Ride the hurricane! We're using real-time data for the wind, direction, and speed, and you can fly a plane or take the fantasy mode and go in direct. I like dragon mode, myself." She lowered her voice again. "For you, on the house. First ride, anyway."

"Thanks." Cammie accepted the menu, chose a pale green dragon with pink-and-cream frills and whiskers. Littlest looked sideways, checking the sim's status, then nodded.

"All set. Have fun!"

"Thanks, Littlest," Cammie said, and stepped through the ring of lightning that appeared in the air in front of her.

She was instantly a dragon, soaring on pale green wings just outside the roiling tower of clouds that was the simulated hurricane. She circled, checking her controls, getting a feel for the play of air on wings, then switched to game vision and looked for an entrance point. Patches of violet light flickered on the clouds; she chose the nearest, folded her wings, and dove for it.

The wind caught her as soon as she hit the cloud, trying to throw her sideways and out, but she'd been expecting that. She kept her wings closed, stomach lurching as she dropped into simulated rain and lightning, feeling for the moment the wind eased. It came, and she extended her wings, turning to let the strongest current carry her in toward the center. The sim flung her up, beat her down; a blast caught her wing and sent her tumbling, but she righted herself, grinning fiercely, and dove back in. This was what she'd needed, the chance to play, no consequences, no thinking required, just follow the violet light and ride the wind—

She popped out of the last layer of cloud into sunshine and smooth air, extended her wings to their fullest to glide, and caught her breath. She could see half a dozen other players in the eye with her—more dragons, a couple of eagles, a hang glider, and, inexplicably, someone riding a surfboard—and one by one they rose up to the top of the clouds and vanished. She let herself circle the eyes a couple of times, enjoying the victory, then followed them up into the sun.

She popped out again onto the concourse not far from the entrance, and a moment later, Littlest mixed in beside her. "Well? Did you like it?"

"It was excellent," Cammie answered. "Did Arabel make it?"

Littlest nodded. "Pretty much all her work, with a little help from Bryn. All based on real-world data, and still perfectly safe for players."

"It's fun."

"Want to go again?"

Cammie checked her disposable account and the ride's price, and hid an inward wince. "Maybe later."

"Cybersecurity keeping you on a short leash?" Littlest asked, and Cammie shrugged. It was as good an explanation as any, and safer here in the open Ether.

"Kind of."

"Too bad." Littlest's eyes slid past her, fastening on someone behind Cammie. "Welcome! Care to ride the hurricane? Fly a plane or try fantasy mode—it's all based on real-time data."

"It's great," Cammie said loyally, and turned to see Aris and a trio of Vanguard soldiers. Two were technicians she remembered from the morning, and the third, who had his hand cautiously on Aris's back, wore a pilot's insignia.

"Have you been through?" the freckled technician, Taggert, asked.

Cammie nodded. "Yeah. Went through as a dragon; it was super fun."

"Too much like work," the pilot said with a wry smile. "But if you all want to go . . ."

"Maybe later," Aris said, and turned away, taking the others with her.

"We'll be here all party long," Littlest said cheerfully, but rolled her eyes in Aris's direction. That was interesting, that Aris bothered Littlest just as much as she bothered Cammie and Charlie, and Cammie tilted her ears to hear what the Vanguard group was saying.

"None of my business," Aris said, "but why does the Vanguard have a kid like that working for them?"

"She ain't exactly a kid," Taggert protested.

"Oh, come on," Aris said. "She's running around the Ether dolled up as a bunny rabbit. That's not exactly an *adult* thing to do."

"It saves me a lot of hassle," Cammie shouted. She covered the gap between them in one deliberately rabbitlike leap, and faced them, hands on hips. "Usually, anyway."

"It's rude to eavesdrop," Aris said.

"Maybe you shouldn't talk so loud." Cammie glared at her.

"I wasn't talking to you," Aris said. "And, I mean, a bunny? Who over the age of twelve uses a bunny rabbit for an avatar?"

"Some people make that assumption, yeah," Cammie said. "But mostly they're people I don't want to deal with. Guys I don't want hitting on me."

Littlest had come up beside her, eyeing the Vanguard group with displeasure. "I might point out that if you mention rabbits in certain shadows, you get a very nervous response. You don't want to mess with her."

"She ain't a kid," Taggert said again. "Not with—" He stopped, remembering security, and substituted "Not with what she does. And you owe her for that, Aris, you know you do."

Aris looked like she wanted to deny it, but they were starting to attract attention, not just from passersby but from Ether Security. "Yeah. You're right, I do. I'm sorry. I didn't mean to insult you."

Cammie gave a stiff nod. She wanted to keep yelling, tell Webb exactly how stupid she was being, how the bunny avatar was protection and camouflage and none of her business anyway, but she knew that would make her the one who was in the wrong. "I didn't mean to listen in," she said.

Aris showed perfect teeth in a beaming smile that made Cammie clench her fists. "There. We're all good, then?"

"Yeah." Cammie watched them walk away, and Littlest whistled softly.

"What an arse."

"That's an insult to arses," Cammie responded automatically, and Littlest grinned.

"You want me to give them an extra-rough ride if they come back?"

"I wish." Cammie shook her head. "No, let them alone; she's been through a lot lately."

"If you're sure," Littlest said, and Cammie sighed.

"I'm sure."

"Want to go through again?" Littlest asked. "On the house."

"No, thanks," Cammie said. "I've got another party to go to."

"All right," Littlest said, and Cammie let herself drop off the Ether.

She pulled off her Ether goggles, blinking in the too-bright lights of the barracks room. Yaz was still out, her head down on her folded arms, eyes hidden behind goggles. Cammie conjured up a bot to lead her back to the mess hall. Whatever that was like, it had to be better than the lame gathering on the Ether—though that had been fine until Aris showed up. And maybe she just didn't like Aris—maybe, like Charlie Little had said, maybe the woman just had a talent for rubbing people the wrong way. She hadn't said anything lots of other people weren't thinking.

Cammie knew she was young, younger than anyone else in gen:LOCK; Dr. Weller hadn't wanted to take her for exactly that reason, and wouldn't have taken her if there had been more than six candidates with gen:LOCK compatibility. He'd even half apologized, his sentences winding back in on themselves the way they always did, saying he wouldn't have put her at risk if he had another choice. *It doesn't matter*, she'd answered. *There's a war on, isn't there? Wars are for the young.* He had nodded. *Yes, but that doesn't mean we old men like sending you out into it.* It seemed strange that he should be dead while she was still alive. She doubted that was what he'd expected. Logically, it should have been one of her team who died . . . all of them, even, whether it was facing Nemesis or behemoths or just an overwhelming Union force. And instead, Weller had lured the Union into his lab and sacrificed himself to buy time for them to escape. She only hoped she'd be smart enough and brave enough to make the same choice if she had to. Though, surely, they wouldn't face anything like that again any time soon.

She shook those thoughts away as she reached the mess hall. The doors were open, and light and sound spilled out into the corridor, voices and laughter and the leaping beat of what sounded like an actual band. Sure enough, when she stepped inside, she could see an improvised platform at one end of the hall, where the tables had been stacked to the side, and a group of musicians who looked like Vanguard soldiers were playing a ragged cover of "Talk to Me." She was a little surprised that Kazu hadn't joined them, but then, it wasn't really his kind of music.

The base staff had strung multicolored steamers across the ceiling and added balloons and lanterns, all in lime green and hot pink so that it almost looked like the Ether. She could smell the food, and sure enough, there was an open grill table as well as a cylindrical cooker, and there were lines twenty people deep at both of them. The promised cake stood in pride of place, already with a few bits of ocean missing, and the cooler next to it had to hold the ice-cream hurricanes. There was also an ice-cream machine, complete with a choice of sauces and toppings, and as she watched, one of the refugee children put a bowl under the spigot, staring with widening eyes as he pulled the lever and no one told him to stop.

"That one is going to be sorry later," Valentina said, coming up beside her.

"I don't know, maybe not," Cammie said. "Besides, it might be worth it. Imagine, all the ice cream you could eat, and nobody to tell you no."

There was an odd look on Valentina's face, just for an instant, as though that was something she still couldn't quite imagine, and then the moment passed. "Let us hope he doesn't spill it."

"Cammie!" Kazu threaded his way out of the crowd, two beers held high to avoid spilling them. "Wasn't the Ether party any good?" He handed one beer to Valentina, and cracked the seal on the other.

"It was good," Cammie said. "Look, Kazu, what you're drinking—"

"It's not legal in this country," Kazu said complacently.

"It would be perfectly legal in Scotland," Cammie said. "Look, there's even food."

"We are not in Scotland," Valentina and Kazu said, in an almost perfect chorus, and Valentina went on, "Have some of that ice cream you were admiring."

Cammie could see that there was no chance of changing their minds. "I want one of the hurricanes," she said. "After I've eaten something."

"I've eaten," Valentina said.

"I could always eat again," Kazu said. "Come on, Valentina, keep us company."

Valentina sighed. "Oh, very well. But then we'll try the Ether party, yes?"

"Yes," Kazu agreed. "But first, more barbecue!"

They filled plates at the various stations—even Valentina took some small helpings—and retreated toward an unoccupied table. The band chose that moment to take a break, and someone put on a recording, fast and synth-filled, and Valentina gave Kazu a teasing glance.

"Perhaps you should fetch your guitar."

"If I had it with me, I'd definitely play," Kazu said. He mimed shredding a chord. "I'd liven things up."

"Or drive everyone away." Valentina was smiling, though, and Cammie relaxed. This was starting to feel more like a party.

"Cammie!"

She didn't recognize the voice, and turned to see the refugee leader, Charlie Little, weaving her way toward them, a younger, dark-skinned woman following her. "Hi, Charlie." She made the introductions quickly, and Little nodded.

"We're pleased to meet you. This is Na'Talia Jackson, she's part of our group. We wanted to thank you for getting us out of trouble yesterday."

"Was it only yesterday?" Valentina murmured.

"You're very welcome," Kazu said.

Jackson looked wary, and Cammie realized that she wasn't getting the eyeline translations. Little said, "He says you're welcome."

"I lost my glasses," Jackson said. She had a soft voice, and the same broad accent that Little had. "And I don't have implants. I was going to get them next year . . . but I guess that doesn't matter now."

"We'll get you glasses," Little said. "Don't worry."

"I can't help it," Jackson said. "They aren't cheap."

Little put a consoling hand on her shoulder.

"Where will you go from here?" Valentina asked.

"West," Little said, with a wry smile.

"I've got cousins in Arizona," Jackson said. "They might take me in. Anyway, like Charlie said, we're grateful. I wasn't sure we were going to get out of that."

"Glad to have helped," Kazu said, and Valentina translated this time.

The refugees nodded, and moved away. Valentina looked sideways at Cammie. "You had met them before?"

"I'd met Charlie," Cammie answered. "I wanted to see if she thought there was anything funny about all of this."

Valentina lifted an eyebrow. "Was that wise? Now they know you're suspicious."

Cammie froze. Was that why they'd come over here to thank them all of a sudden? Charlie had walked off in a bit of a huff earlier. "I didn't think—"

"I would not have talked to them," Valentina said.

"And you wouldn't have learned anything," Cammie retorted. "We couldn't just sit on our thumbs and do nothing."

"Point, I suppose." Valentina sighed. "And did you learn anything?"

Cammie shrugged. "She said she didn't quite trust the

other group, but admitted she didn't have any real reason for it. The other woman, Na'Talia, she used to be a deputy sheriff, but she warned them that the Union was coming."

"That is very interesting," Valentina said. "The Union has been known to set up such officers in deep cover."

"Are we going to do this again?" Kazu demanded. "The colonel's been over all of that, and he didn't find anything. We should enjoy the break while we can."

"I still say something is not right," Valentina murmured.

"Valentina's right," Cammie said. "The people from Tallahassee, they used high-pressure fuel injectors on their bikes, and they're not just expensive, they're impossible to work on without expensive tools. I don't know how they could afford them if they were just factory hands like they say they are."

"So until you figure it out," Kazu said, "you might as well enjoy the party."

There was some logic to that, Cammie had to admit, and she also had to admit that for once she liked the real party better than the one on the Ether. But of course, a lot of that had to do with Aris. Wherever she went, she brought trouble with her.

Kazu took his time finishing his beer, mostly to tease Valentina, who was obviously ready to move the party to the Ether. "Perhaps I should have another," he said, just to make Valentina roll her eyes, and Cammie banged her fist on the table.

"That's just not fair. You don't get two when I don't get any."

"Hey, I don't make the laws," Kazu said.

"No, but you don't have to enjoy them so much," Cammie answered.

"We had a deal," Valentina said. "Time to hit the Ether."

"Right, right," Kazu grumbled, but followed the other two back to the barracks. He stretched out comfortably on his bunk, settling in his Ether goggles, hearing the faint familiar rustling that was Cammie and Valentina donning theirs. He felt a little guilty about Cammie, or at least about the beer: If Cammie was old enough to drink in Scotland, it seemed a little unfair to treat her like a child in what was left of the United States. Or maybe what was unfair was to treat her like a kid when she wasn't acting like one, when she was putting her life on the line with the rest of gen:LOCK.

That was something he didn't like to think about, not when it was so easy to fall into the habit of treating her like a little sister, like someone he didn't want getting hurt. He liked the way she looked so happy when he fried her an extra egg for breakfast, liked the way she rolled her eyes when he teased her. He liked the way she worked at the things that were hard for her, whether it was controlling the urge to curse, or programming the drones to target her shots for her, or picking herself up and bracing the bridge when she'd frozen for a second. Or fighting the nightmares that still sometimes woke her. He probably ought to say something about them, he knew, but words—feelings—weren't really his strength. *I'll mention it to Chase*, he thought, not for the first time, and let himself drop onto the Ether.

Cammie and Val were there ahead of him, Cammie in her usual rabbit avatar, Val as elegant as ever in his dark blue suit patterned with stars and galaxies, one eye and part of his cheek shadowed by a sweep of red. As always, it gave Kazu a little pang to see Val instead of Valentina, and to know that one day, maybe even one day soon, he might take on that shape in the real world as well. Then again, Kazu remembered Mindshare, Val appearing out of nowhere to bow and lead him into a beautiful, deadly dance. Kazu had trained for most of a lifetime to fight with something approaching that feral grace, and he was still faintly surprised at how willing he was to put himself into Val's elegant and capable hands. But then, Val couldn't do what he did without Kazu's cooperation, without Kazu's strength and training to give their dance power. They were good together, and that was all they needed to know.

"Where have you been?" Cammie demanded, hopping impatiently. "We've been waiting forever."

"An entire eighteen seconds," Val said, with his crooked smile, and Kazu shrugged.

"I'm here now. Where's this party?"

Five invitation icons materialized and bounced off him before he managed to catch the last one. "Hey."

The icon unrolled with the sound of tinny trumpets and a

shower of glitter, announcing the De Soto Base hurricane party. *With links to civilian party space*, it added, in English letters that his system translated to kanji. "Did you say you'd already been on, Cammie?"

"Yeah." She bounced again. "There's a hurricane ride, done by Gaia Sisters. It was really good." Both her ears and her voice flattened a little, and Val frowned.

"It doesn't sound like you enjoyed it."

"I did!" Cammie's ears flattened again. "It's just . . . I ran into one of the refugees, Aris Webb. I don't like her very much, that's all."

"What's she done?" Kazu demanded.

In the same moment, Val asked, "Which one is she?"

Cammie crooked her fingers, pulling a small display screen out of the Ether. In it, a picture formed, a tired-looking young woman with her hair scraped back in a tight ponytail. Kazu shook his head. "I don't know her."

"She was one of the ones on the motorcycles," Cammie said. "Her boyfriend got killed, so I'm really not being fair."

"That doesn't make her trustworthy," Val said.

Kazu looked from one to the other. "But what did she do?"

"She didn't *do* anything," Cammie said. "Except treat me like a kid, and insult me about my avatar. But I keep telling you, there's something not right here, and she's in the middle of it."

"That's foolish of her," Val said. "To treat you like a child, I mean."

"But if she hasn't done anything," Kazu said, "how can you say she's in the middle of things?"

"I told you, their story and the way they rigged their bikes—it doesn't add up," Cammie said. "And it's like Val said, there should have been air cover, a whole bunch of things. It just doesn't feel right."

"Colonel Varden didn't find anything wrong," Kazu said. "I don't see it."

"That doesn't mean there's not something there." Cammie looked as though she was about to thump her foot in frustration.

"You were going to look at the debriefing files," Val said. "Was there anything?"

"Nothing definite." Cammie shook her head. "Just what I said before, Na'Talia was a sheriff's deputy. And Charlie Little said she didn't trust the group from Tallahassee."

"I think there is reason for concern," Val said. "But we need more to go on."

"You should take this to Chase," Kazu said. "There's nothing we can do about it."

"I've already talked to Chase, and the longer we wait, the more chance that they'll do . . . something." Cammie waved her hands. "And, no, I don't know what, but they're not going to all this trouble just to sit here."

"There's a hurricane outside," Kazu said. "We're cut off."

"Except they're already here," Cammie noted.

"We think. Maybe." Val shook his head. "Cammie, we

have nothing more than we had before. It's not enough."

"This is something for Chase," Kazu said again, more firmly. "He's the one to handle this."

"If I had something to take to him, I'd do just that," Cammie snapped. "Only I don't. And none of you eejits are doing anything to help me. So fine! I'll take care of it myself."

She turned on her heel and leaped away, her avatar mixing out in mid-jump.

"Cammie," Kazu began, and stopped, shaking his head. "What are we supposed to do?"

"If I knew that—" Val began, and shook his head in turn. "I also have an uneasy feeling about all of this. But I agree with you, there's nothing we can do without actual evidence."

"And we're not the people to get that," Kazu said. "That's Major Rountree's business. Or Captain Herrera. Base Security. They must have plenty of that."

"One would assume," Val said.

"So we let them do their job," Kazu said. "Now. You said you were going to show me a better party than the one we came from."

Val smiled slowly. "I think I can do that."

Cammie mixed in at the interface of the base party and the public party, confident that she was not being followed, and already a little ashamed of her spurt of temper. She knew she needed more evidence; that was what she was trying to find. But no one was willing to help her investigate. Even Val, who had taken his concerns about the lack of air cover to Chase and Varden, was now saying it wasn't their job.

She let herself ease through the interface, careful not to trigger even the benign counters that kept track of visitors, and found herself back on the midway of the public party. The Gaia Sisters' storm sim loomed in the distance, but by now it had attracted a sizable crowd and there was a wait to enter. And she still didn't have any extra money in her bank account. No, what she should do was figure out some way to find out more about the refugees, though what she could find that Major Rountree hadn't uncovered . . .

She stopped abruptly. Rountree would have checked the Vanguard records, the Polity servers, and whatever they'd been able to pry out of the Union systems, but Cammie knew as well as anyone that Polity Cybersecurity didn't exactly have unlimited access to the opposing side. On the other hand, she still had connections in the shadow markets, people who dealt with both factions. Somebody there might be able to get information for her . . . for a price, of course, but she knew Polity Cybersecurity had an account for that. gen:LOCK would, too. And if not, there were still people out there who owed her favors. It might be time to call them in.

There were also ways into the shadow nets if you knew what to look for. She started down the midway, pretending to study the floating menus outside each of the Ethertainment sections, but in reality looking for a faint flash of blue from any apparently decorative icon. This section was swept clean, probably because it was the access point for De Soto Base, but as she passed the in-and-out, the air thickened slightly—not real thickness, of course, but her sense of the code beneath the imagery sharpened. Adcons swarmed here, swooping from avatar to avatar, and she pulled out the sub-routine she'd written as "bug spray." The next swarm slowed sharply and divided, two halves sweeping past without trying to flash their wares, to rejoin once they'd passed her, and swarm someone else's avatar.

There were more hidden icons tucked into the scenery, though none of them had the particular shade of blue she was looking for. She recognized most of them: affinity group sign-posts for private spaces; clue codes for virtual live-action games, most of them faded; assorted traffic trackers, legitimate and less so; the trigger for a prince-in-need scambot lurking among some otherwise harmless advertisement. She paused long enough to reset the trigger so that it would fire at the next white hat who passed, and moved on. Anyone clumsy enough to leave a trigger out in the open deserved to have it jinxed.

She moved on, following the curve of a side path lit with flashing green and gold signs that promised maker sales, and slowed to scan the displays. You never knew what you might find in a spot like this, even if it was always mostly reworking of familiar code. And then she caught it, a flash of bright blue from across the path, gone almost as soon as it registered. She turned casually, pretending to look at specs for 3-D-printed toys, and found it again, a vivid blue spark in the center of a decorative daisy.

She recognized the maker and the safe sign, found the key in her own tool kit, and flicked a finger to activate it. The air around her dimmed, hiding her avatar from view, and a narrow line of purple shadow unrolled in the air in front of her. It widened until it was just large enough for her avatar to fit, a dark crack in the Ether's brightness.

Polity Cybersecurity never allowed its people to enter the shadow nets without backup and watchdogs to make sure they didn't revert to old habits. If she'd done this while she was still with them, they would have revoked the suspension of her sentence and she'd have been back in jail as soon as they could put her on a transport. She'd spent four days in the cells before her trial, before Gran had made bail, and she never wanted to go back there again. But she wasn't with Pol Cy anymore. She was part of gen:LOCK, one of the only people who was gen:LOCK compatible, and she was doing this to help the Polity. She took a deep breath and stepped through.

She landed in the familiar twilight shadows of the Nexus, currently a vaguely French-looking plaza with an enormous circular fountain at its center. Virtual water played from the mouth of a giant fish standing upright on its tail; its scales glowed and flickered, covered with multicolored icons, each one a message for someone in the shadows. She pinged it out of habit, but there was nothing for any of her old personas.

She turned clockwise around the fountain, ignoring the other avatars just as they ignored her, studying the facades of the buildings that enclosed the plaza. They were old-fashioned, made to mimic stone and shadow, with shuttered windows and closed doors, but each door carried a small symbol like a knocker precisely in its center. All the old standards were still there, Criss-Cross, the clenched fist, the lightning bolt, the plain initials MKR where you could sell anything, and buy nearly as much—and then she saw it, the big-eyed alien's head that marked her destination. She pinged it, and a hole opened in the pavement at her feet. She stepped forward and let herself fall.

She landed in near darkness, only the bricks beneath her feet glowing gold. This was the so-called nonhuman quarter, where the pro hackers like her did their business. She polled the empty air, looking to see who was accepting contact, and a handful of symbols popped up. Fate wouldn't have what she was looking for, Dragon-mother didn't deal with the Union, Sofa-hat was as weird as his name, Cataboy always tried to cheat, but XPNSV . . . XPNSV was reliable, and had always moved easily between Union and Polity. They'd linked her with the job that had gotten her arrested, that was a point against them, but on the other hand, they were likely to have the information she wanted. If they were willing to help her. She shaped the query and compressed it, adding the old private checksums that provided her identity, and launched it into the dark.

For a long moment, there was no response, nothing bouncing back, not even a rejection, and she considered another poll. But, no, that would just make her look too eager, and she made herself wait, counting seconds, until at last a spark barely brighter than the air around her circled her and stopped.

"Really?" a voice whispered, genderless and direction-less. "Are you kidding?"

"I want to talk," she said. "I'm looking for information."

"On whose behalf?"

"My own."

There was another pause, long enough that she wasn't sure she was going to regain contact, and then she felt the breath of a sigh.

"Where?"

"Any disposable," Cammie said. She didn't have any throw-away spaces prepared, not anymore, but she was willing to bet XPNSV did.

She felt them sigh again. "All right."

The Ether shifted around her, the shadows fading, shapes blossoming and coalescing until she was standing in what looked like an ordinary white-painted room with a white sofa and a white chair and a white table. A window with white curtains looked out onto a pale white sky. This was XPNSV's usual disposable display, and she relaxed, turning to see a swirl of glittering light materialize out of nothing.

"I heard you were working for the Polity these days,"

XPNSV said. For an instant, the swirl of light mimicked a human shape and seated itself in the chair, crossing long legs, before dissolving again into a rain of diamonds.

"You know I am," Cammie answered. She settled herself on the sofa opposite them, sitting bow-legged on the illusion of very comfortable cushions. "And you know I didn't shop you to Pol Cy when I got caught, so there's that, too."

"True enough," XPNSV said. "Haven't seen you around lately, though. Even among the white hats."

"I've been on a project," Cammie said. "Nothing to do with you."

"So you say."

This was the thing she'd always hated about the black-hat side, the constant suspicion, everyone circling around everything so that you could never tell who was serious and who was joking and who was pretending to joke but was actually out to get you. She'd built her reputation on contract work and had always reserved the right to bail if someone told her too many lies. "I do say so," she said. "Look, you know perfectly well what happened. I got hired to hack Pacific Technologies—which I did not know was a subsidiary of RTASA, by the way—and it turned out to be a trap. I could have told them I got the job from you, but I didn't. So it seems to me you could at least talk straight with me."

"Darling, I don't do anything straight." XPNSV coalesced again, this time to wave a languid hand in her direction, and Cammie rolled her eyes.

"You don't upset me."

"No." XPNSV became a hovering cloud of diamond glitter. "All right. What is it you want?"

"I need information from the Union side of things," she answered. "If you still have connections there."

"Some." XPNSV sounded wary.

"I have three names. I want to find out if any of them have Union connections."

"I can probably come up with something," XPNSV said. "How fast do you need it?"

"Twenty-four hours, if you can," Cammie answered. That would give her time to take anything they found to Colonel Varden before the refugees left the base. "The sooner the better, but I'd rather you were accurate than fast."

"I'm hurt."

"You're pushing it."

"But it's so much fun." XPNSV's tone changed, was abruptly serious. "It'll cost you."

"How much?"

XPNSV paused, the swirl of diamonds slowing almost to a stop. "Who are the people?"

"Two women and a man," Cammie said. "The first woman is called Aris Webb. She's from near Tallahassee, Florida. The other is named Na'Talia Jackson, and she's from Gum Neck, North Carolina."

"Seriously?"

"Yes, seriously. The man is Liam Foxe, also from Tallahassee.

They're refugees, or they claim they are, but they might have Union ties."

"You mean they might be Union agents," XPNSV said.

"It's possible," Cammie said. "Or they really might not be. If I had any better idea, I wouldn't be asking you to poke around."

XPNSV formed enough of a shape to nod in her direction. "How deep are you asking me to go?"

Cammie considered. "Nothing too deep. It's more important not to get caught than to get into their vault space."

"That's a good thing," XPNSV said, "because I'm not hacking the Union vaults. Bad things happen to people who play that game."

"Yeah." Cammie suppressed a shiver. They all knew the stories, hackers found dead in their goggles, their brains fried by something they found in Union space. Half the time, people said it was nothing, urban legend, but hackers disappeared, icons and avatars that had been on the Ether for years simply vanishing, not arrested, not retired, just . . . gone. Even Polity Cybersecurity couldn't entirely disprove the possibility that the Union had found some way to attack through the Ether, though the current theory was that the Union was using the Ether to identify hackers and targeting them through more conventional means. If the Union had a way to attack through the Ether, they clearly weren't weaponizing it en masse . . . not yet, at least. "Don't go there."

"Right."

"So. What's it going to cost me?"

XPNSV paused again. "I've got some contacts who can help," they said. "Shall we call it a bit of in good standing?"

"I'm not with Pol Cy anymore," Cammie said reluctantly. "I'm on a separate research project. But I could put in a good word if that would be enough."

"That'll do," XPNSV said. "What have you got for me to work with?"

Cammie formed a packet with the basic identification data, and handed it across.

"Come back tomorrow," XPNSV said, "and I'll have some answers for you."

"When?"

"Let's say 1500 to 1600, Ether time," they answered. "If you're not there, I won't wait." The room dissolved around her before she could respond.

7

SHE FOUND HERSELF back in the nonhuman quarter's vestibule, the bricks now glowing more green than gold. That meant there were other people in the area, though when she pinged discreetly, she received only anonymized shadows. That was pretty normal, and she looked around for the slightly brighter bricks that pointed the way out of the quarter. They seemed more dimmed than she was accustomed to, harder to spot, and didn't follow the usual pattern. She frowned and risked a quick ping, but once again, there were only anonymized shadows moving away from her. Sometimes the host systems had to set up roundabout roads if Polity Cybersecurity was watching the usual routes, and that was probably all it was, but she readied her defensive tool kit just in case.

The bricks led her on a curving road, first right, then left, then wound into a spiral with a dull red spark at the center. That was definitely not the usual way out, and she pinged it, releasing a second probe bot under the cover of the ping. The ping came back normal, a link to the Nexus, but the bot reported an intermediate space spoofing the connection. That was definitely trouble, and she backed away, looking for the regular exit.

The vestibule darkened further, the color fading from the bricks. She pinged again, scowling. Nothing answered, but deeper vision showed a shadow flowing out of the spiral's red-flecked center. She turned on her heel, grabbing a familiar key, and loosed it to open a door between the looming shadows. Light spilled out as she leaped through, and she spun around to break the connection as soon as she was through. The door vanished, leaving her in a meadow spotted with poppies and daisies as big as her head, each with a wizened face at its center. On the horizon, she could see spikes of green crystal, but turned the other way, looking for an exit. This was a trading space, full of illegal goods, and it was dangerous to linger if she had nothing to buy or sell.

She threaded her way between the daisies, ignoring their programmed chatter, and froze as an enormous bee dove at her out of the sunlit sky.

"Business?" it demanded.

She could feel the static sting behind the image, intrusion countermeasures sharp enough to knock her off the Ether and give her a headache that would last for days, and she reached for the pass she had hoarded from her black-hat days. "Just passing through."

"Expired."

"I retired," Cammie said. "Just let me out, will you?"

The bee paused, and she braced herself for a shock. Then the ground gave way under her feet, and she was back in the Quarter, shadows swirling away from her automatic ping. The path was visible, though, gold and glowing, and she ran toward it. Already its light was beginning to fade, dark shapes gathering, but she could see the way, could still pick out the right bricks among the dying colors.

And then she was through, back into the Nexus. The shadow was right behind her, though, and she activated her own anonymizer and leaped for the first door she could open. That was MKR, and she dropped into a space hung with screen after screen of schematics, white and gold lines on sheets of blue. She caught a glimpse of a wheeled robot carrying a tray, a wheel within a wheel that might have been a monocycle or a space station, and then a set of VR gloves that she was sure she'd seen at RTASA. She filed that for later, not slowing at all, and darted past several avatars and out again into a corridor that seemed to be a river of stars.

That at least was familiar, even if it never used to connect to MKR, and she picked up her pace, heading for the point in the middle distance where several strands split off into separate streams. The second from the left should lead back to the normal Ether, and it wasn't like whoever was messing with her would follow her there.

The stars vanished from beneath her feet, and she fell tumbling into darkness. She twisted to land upright, balancing in the middle of nothingness as though she were in Mindshare, and the shadows resolved abruptly to reveal that she was back in the Quarter's vestibule. This was definitely personal, not a random attack. She put out a general call, looking for friends, pinged XPNSV as well, but the Ether felt sticky, as though her messages were being blocked.

This is not good. In fact, it was getting to the point where she wouldn't be breaking any unwritten rules if she damaged the local fabric, and she reached for her tool kit, pulling out the routines that would let her bridge from one known volume to another. Whoever this was probably wouldn't follow her back onto the Ether's main levels, but breaking through the layers would set off every alarm in the place, and she really didn't want to have to explain this to Pol Cy or to Chase. But if she was quick enough—she had the tools out already, plugging in node addresses and server strings—she could jump to a disused data volume, and there she was, in a cavern between two towering walls of filing cabinets, dust motes drifting in a broad beam of sunlight, and from there to a string of chat rooms, and from there to the little-used volume where her secret garden lived.

She closed the last bridge behind her, breathing hard even though she hadn't actually been running, and quickly scanned the volume. There were a few people in the domain, most of them in their private spaces, but nobody with privileges that she could alert. Still, from here she should be able to jump back to the main levels, and try to figure out what was going on. It was probably black-hat business, enemies left over from before she was arrested, but if it was Union, then she was in serious trouble.

The air in front of her rippled and split, smoke billowing out of it. It wasn't nanite smoke, she knew it couldn't be, but she cringed anyway, and behind it came a four-armed shape with clawed hands, reaching to her out of her nightmare.

"You're not real, *you're not real*," she repeated over and over, but when she looked up again, the claws were still reaching. She screamed, and in the same moment deployed her best firewalls, sealing herself into a bubble that would take serious code knives to break. She grabbed for the gen:LOCK network, the connection maddeningly slow, finally felt it click in.

Help! Kazu, Val, anybody, help! Under attack! Chase, Yaz, help! She added her location and set the call to repeat, then began backing away from the looming shape, the firewall moving with her. It wasn't Nemesis, *couldn't* be Nemesis, there were lots of differences now that she looked closer, but even as it reached for her, she felt invisible daemons chewing at her barriers.

They were the real danger, not the fake Nemesis. If she didn't stop them, they'd unravel her firewalls and dive into her private data—*into gen:LOCK's data.* She mustered countermeasures, chaff to distract, ICE—her best intrusion countermeasures—and chawbots to home in on foreign code and rip it apart.

Kazu mixed in next to her, looking bigger and meaner than ever, followed a moment later by Val. *What the hell is that?*

The fake Nemesis recoiled, shadows rippling and roiling, then split into half a dozen black shapes.

What are these? Kazu exclaimed, and Cammie watched in horror as code in the shape of thousands of spiders began swarming over their avatars like a wave, trying to tear them apart for a way into their source code.

Mix out! Val said, brushing off the spiders. *Cammie, mix out!*

"Can't." Cammie loosed her best hunter, letting it pour over the spider army, washing most of it away. The rest she could squash one by one if she had to, wielding a code hammer in one hand and scattering chaff with the other.

Then Chase was there, and Yaz, ready to join the fight, and Cammie used the moment of distraction to reset her barriers. The spiders tensed, leaped back, and disappeared.

Everybody, mix out, Chase said, and Cammie obeyed.

She sat up on her bunk, reaching for screens to examine her security.

"What was that about?" Yaz asked, pushing back her goggles.

"It seems as though someone does not like our Cammie," Valentina said, smoothing her hair where the goggles had disarranged it. "Though I, too, am curious as to why."

"Give me a minute," Cammie said, her fingers flying as she flicked from screen to screen, resetting access codes and passwords and locking down everything triple-tight. She'd always been careful, hadn't let herself get slack after leaving Pol Cy, but this attack, whatever it was, called for extra measures. It had been close, there, burrowing into the code of her avatar, prying at points that linked her to gen:LOCK, to the Polity's servers; she couldn't afford to leave anything undefended.

"Cammie?" Chase said, mixing in to stand beside her bunk, but she ignored him as well, watching her full suite of intrusion detection routines run through their paces. They flicked green one by one, and she took a deep breath. "Sorry about that. I had to be sure nothing got through."

"What was that?" Kazu asked.

"I'm not really sure—"

Chase folded his arms. "Cammie. What is going on?"

There was no arguing with that voice. Cammie heaved a sigh, her ears flattening. "Well. You see. I was following up on something I saw in the debriefing reports, and I seem to have attracted some attention. I don't know who that was, it could have been a bunch of different people, but we should be all right now. Nothing got through."

"*Nothing got through?*" Chase repeated, his voice like ice.

"Must have been Union, surely," Valentina said.

"Not necessarily." Cammie felt her ears flatten again.

"Where were you?" Chase asked.

"Um. In some, I don't know, private spaces?" Cammie cocked her head at him.

"Black-hat spaces?" Chase asked. "Shadow net?"

"More shadow net than black hat," Cammie said. "They're not the same."

"Don't try to distract me," Chase said. "Why were you on the shadow net?"

"I wanted to ask someone to look something up for me," Cammie said. "An old friend. I wanted him to check on a couple of the refugees. To see if they had Union connections."

"That could certainly have attracted Union attention," Valentina said.

"Or annoyed the cyber-yakuza," Kazu said. "They don't like people playing politics in their spaces."

Chase looked at Cammie. "What do you think it was?"

Cammie paused, not sure if she wanted to admit to the nightmare Nemesis. "I don't know. I didn't catch any samples, I was too busy smashing them. I don't think my contact would have shopped me, but I suppose it's always possible. I didn't pick up any sign of the Union. And I don't know how they would have found me, to be honest."

"We're always being warned that the Ether is not secure," Yaz said, though she sounded skeptical.

Kazu scratched his head. "I . . . I'm not entirely sure, but when we first mixed in, the thing that was attacking you looked like Nemesis. Did you see that, too, Cammie?"

Cammie hesitated again, tempted to lie, but caught Valentina giving her a thoughtful look. "I might have," she said.

"I mean, it had four arms, which always makes me think about that thing. But it couldn't possibly have been."

"Couldn't it?" Yaz looked worried. "If there were copies—"

"If there were copies, we would have run into them before now," Chase said. "Vanguard agreed with us on that one."

"And only the top end of the Union's hackers would have known about Nemesis anyway," Cammie said. "I mean, it's more likely that it was just trying to be a scary shape, something that would distract me from the real attack."

"So which do you think it was?" Yaz asked. "Union or black hats?"

Cammie considered. If it was Union, using Nemesis's shape would have made sense, except that the kind of mid-level agents who ran attacks like this wouldn't be allowed to know about something as important as Nemesis. Though of course they could just have been given the shape to use as a decoy; they wouldn't need to know what it was to deploy it effectively, and that would explain why the shadow didn't quite look like Nemesis. And she had made enough of a name for herself as a hacker, and then again with Pol Cy, that some aspiring black hats would want to take her down for the boost to their reputation. "Maybe some of both? I don't want to get above myself, but maybe someone on the Union side of the shadows put a bounty on me, and it triggered the first time I did any hacking. I haven't exactly been spending a lot of time on the Ether lately, you know. Except gaming, and that doesn't draw notice."

"That makes some sense," Kazu said.

Chase nodded. "Cammie, I need to speak with you alone."

Cammie reluctantly followed him into the hallway, aware that he was keeping an eye on the security cameras just as much as she was. He picked a spot where none of the monitors had a perfect view, and fixed her with a cold stare. "What the hell made you think this was a good idea?"

Cammie blinked. She'd never heard Chase use this fierce, damped-down voice before, never heard him swear, or even come close to losing his temper. Her ears flattened against her hair. "Um. I told you, I wanted to find out if Union sources had anything about the refugees."

"And you don't think Captain Herrera and Major Rountree already did that?"

"I've got better connections than they do," Cammie said.

"You *had* better connections," Chase said. "Maybe they were better, but that was a while ago. Cammie, I've seen your records. You made a deal with Polity Cybersecurity. You agreed to full-time oversight, you agreed to stay out of black-hat spaces unless it was on a specific mission and only with their watchdogs keeping an eye on you, and you agreed that you'd give up your contacts. You also agreed that they could send you back to jail if you broke any one of those promises. Right?"

He waited, and Cammie scuffed a foot. "Yeah."

"When you tested out as gen:LOCK compatible, Pol Cy didn't want to let you go. They said you were dangerous, that you didn't take any of this seriously—didn't under-stand what you were playing with and what the stakes were," Chase said. "The ESU agreed. Dr. Weller went to bat for you because he thought they were wrong. He put his neck on the line, promised that he'd make sure you wouldn't indulge in any private hacking while you were part of gen:LOCK, swore that you understood the damage you could do even by accident, and that you'd never put gen:LOCK—the Polity!—at risk. And now he's dead, and you do this."

"I was trying to help," Cammie said again. "I thought—"

"You didn't *think*," Chase said. "If you'd thought, you'd have seen the risk. If the Union gets into your files, they get gen:LOCK. If they get gen:LOCK—they could take down the Polity." He held up two fingers, pinched them together. "Right now, we're the only edge the Polity has, and you came *this* close to handing it to the Union."

"I didn't think anyone would spot me," Cammie mum-bled. Chase was partly right; that was the problem. She had taken a risk, had put gen:LOCK in danger—but she'd saved herself, saved gen:LOCK. "I won't make the mistake again."

"Damn right you won't," Chase said. "I want your word."

Cammie gave a jerky nod. "I promise. But what if I see something else like this, something that needs to be investi-gated?"

"You bring it to me first," Chase said. "We talk about it.

You do not go haring off into black-hat space on your own. Agreed?"

"Agreed," Cammie said. "I promise."

"Thanks," Chase said. "Now, though . . . now we've got to let Colonel Varden know what happened."

Varden was off duty, but Major Rountree was available, seemingly as alert and tireless as she had been before the storm began. She listened intently, stopping them only long enough to loop in Captain Herrera, who mixed in looking faintly disheveled, and when they had finished, she leaned against the edge of the desk, frowning deeply.

"There's nothing we can do about the Ether in general," she said at last, and Herrera nodded.

"Not generally. We do our level best to control the access points, but a good hacker's kit can nullify what we've done."

Cammie dragged her toe across the carpet. "Sorry."

"If you'd let me take a look at your kit—" Herrera began.

"Focus," Rountree said, and he subsided. "Look, the Ether is always a problem when we're trying to maintain secure space. It's not secure, and we can't make it secure, not without losing what makes the Ether appealing—and useful—to our people."

"The Vanguard can't exactly keep everyone off the Ether," Chase said.

"Not if we want to keep our people happy," Rountree agreed. "But we can definitely tighten things up, right, Joe?"

Herrera nodded. "Already on it, Major."

"We'll pull the plug on the party a little early, too," Rountree went on. "It looks like we'll be able to send out drones sometime around midnight, and that's a good reason to close down the parties."

"Thank you, Major," Chase said.

"But that's locking the barn door after the horse was stolen," Rountree said. "How am I supposed to protect my people when your people are accessing black-hat spaces? And I certainly can't protect her. You're on your own when you play those games."

Cammie started to protest, but Chase caught her eye, and she subsided, frowning. It wasn't her fault that someone had put a bounty on her, and that seemed like the most probable answer. Though if it was the Union . . . But she'd just been trying to help the Vanguard.

"Understood, ma'am," Chase said.

"What I don't need is your people breaching our security," Rountree went on. "And that's exactly what's happened here."

"Nothing got through," Cammie said.

"That we know of," Rountree said sharply. "Herrera's team is still checking out our systems, and that's a lot of extra work we didn't need."

"I'm confident Cammie was able to shut out the intruder," Chase said.

"We can't assume that," Rountree retorted. "If she wasn't a kid, I'd put her in the cells until you people leave—and don't think I won't be reporting this to ESU and Vanguard command. She could have brought down the entire base."

"Understood," Chase said.

"It had damn well better be." Rountree looked at Cammie. "As for you, young lady. You are banned from the Ether, and from the base network unless it's necessary for your job. If you try anything else like this, I *will* put you in the cells. Is that clear?"

Cammie swallowed hard. Part of her wanted to cry, because Rountree was right, there had been a danger to the base, and that *was* her fault. Part of her wanted to yell back, because she'd been trying to get information that they needed and that they couldn't get any other way.

"Cammie?" Chase asked.

"Yes," she managed. "Yes, that's clear."

"Good." Rountree nodded. "Lieutenant, I'm relying on you to enforce that."

"Yes, ma'am."

"Good," Rountree said again. "Dismissed."

They filed back out into the corridor. Cammie stumbled, her teeth clamped tight, her eyes prickling. She wasn't going to cry, and she wasn't going to shout, she was going to act like an adult because she *was* an adult, whatever Major Rountree said—

Herrera mixed in beside them, clearing his throat apologetically. "Ms. MacCloud. I really would love to get a look at your kit; that would be very helpful—"

Whatever. She swallowed the word, knowing it would only make her look worse, and struggled for the right response. She could see Chase watching her warily, and she managed a nod. "Yeah. Okay."

"I appreciate that, Ms. MacCloud—"

"Cammie. It's Cammie."

"Cammie." He was younger than she'd thought at first, with dark eyes and untidy hair. "I'm Joe, then."

"Joe." Cammie didn't really want to share her toys; she needed to be sure she kept an edge, but she also needed to convince them that she was cooperating. She could at least show him the tools that Pol Cy knew about. "I suppose you'd better." She drew up a screen and pulled up the menu of her standard tool kit. She ran her finger down the list, selecting all of them, then copied and compressed them into a tidy packet. "Here you go."

"Thanks, Ms. . . . Cammie, I mean." Herrera's avatar blurred as he checked the packet, and his eyebrows rose. "Oh, these are—they're very nice indeed. Thank you!"

"Yeah. Just don't hold that against me."

Herrera shook his head. "Just—do me a favor, all right? Stay off the Ether."

I said I would. Cammie nodded, and he mixed out. She looked at Chase, but he had the abstracted expression that meant he was listening to some private transmission. He blinked once, and looked back at her.

"The major wants to talk to me. Can I trust you, Cammie?"

"I promised, didn't I?" she said, hurt, and he mixed out. She stared at the place where his avatar had been, her eyes stinging. It wasn't *fair*. She had been doing her best to help, and she was still certain this was the best way to get more information on the refugees. But if Chase was right, and it was the Union—how had they found her? XPNSV hated the Union; they wouldn't have betrayed her. There were other black hats who worked impartially for both sides, and just because she hadn't pinged them, it didn't mean they weren't there. Or the Union could have figured out that gen:LOCK had a hacker on the team, and set passive watchers. That was probably the most likely option, if this wasn't a personal vendetta, which she still couldn't entirely rule out—but she couldn't solve the problem without going on the Ether, and she'd promised not to do that. *Serves them right*, she thought. *Let them spend hours and people figuring out what I could have told them in two hours' searching. If that's what they want, they can have it. I'm going to get some tea.*

She started down the corridor, and as she made the turn toward the mess hall, she very nearly ran into Valentina, who caught her by the shoulders. "Here, careful."

Cammie sniffed hard. "Did you want me?"

"I was going to see if there were any ice-cream hurricanes left," Valentina said. "Would you care to join me?"

Cammie gave her a suspicious look. It wasn't like Valentina to ask for her company. On the other hand, she was banned from the Ether, and she had no desire to try to go to sleep, not after she'd seen Nemesis's ghost on the Ether. The real-world hurricane party would let her put that off a little longer. "Did Chase ask you to look after me?"

Valentina shook her head. "Why would he do that?"

"Never mind." Cammie sighed. "Yeah, I'll come with you."

The mess hall was quieter now. The refugee children had been taken off to bed some time ago, and many of the refugees had gone with them, leaving it mostly a Vanguard crowd. The grill had shut down, and nearly all the cake was gone, just a blue corner and an edge streaked with green-and-brown icing remaining. But the freezer tray with the swirls of ice cream was still half-full, and there was a tray of assorted toppings to add. Cammie piled hers with chocolate and caramel and bright silver-and-gold candies, and looked curiously at Valentina's tray. "Just ice cream?"

"I like just ice cream," Valentina said placidly. In fact, she had two of the hurricanes, and Cammie pointed toward an empty table.

"Shall we?"

"Certainly."

Cammie settled in and allowed herself one bite of the ice cream before pointing her spoon at Valentina. "All right, then. What did you want?"

Valentina gave a slow smile. "You would not believe I merely wanted some ice cream and company?"

"No," Cammie said, and Valentina's smile widened.

"I should know better than to underestimate you. Yes, I

was curious. Tell me about these refugees, the ones that you suspect?"

"Now you're interested again?"

"Now you have been attacked on the Ether," Valentina said. "That is—if it is not corroboration, it is certainly an interesting coincidence."

"The thing is, it might be old business," Cammie said. "There were people who didn't like me, back when I was freelancing—"

"When you were black-hat hacking," Valentina corrected. "Before Polity Cybersecurity made you an offer you could not refuse."

"Before I—" Cammie stopped. "Well, yeah. It was join or go to jail, and believe me, I didn't want to be locked up."

"I entirely sympathize," Valentina answered, and there was a note in her voice that made Cammie wonder just how she had been recruited for gen:LOCK. "So. Tell me about these people."

"There are three of them," Cammie said. "Two from the Tallahassee group, Aris Webb and Liam Foxe. They and Foxe's brother Jake, he'd been one of the ones who was killed, they're the only ones who admitted knowing anything about the 'stolen brains' story. And Na'Talia Jackson, the one you met. She used to be a sheriff's deputy, which means she was working with the Union."

"If I were with the Railroad, I would wish to have contacts in law enforcement," Valentina said.

Cammie nodded. "I know. And their leader, she was the other one you met, she says she trusts her. And I feel like she's telling the truth—Charlie is, I mean. Only maybe I'm not being fair, because I really don't like Aris."

"What is wrong with her?"

"She treats me like a kid, remember?" Cammie said with loathing. "She has no business doing that."

"It would seem unwise," Valentina agreed.

"But she just lost her boyfriend, so she's not exactly at her best." Cammie shook her head. "I don't know . . . I just really don't like her."

"You mentioned she said something about your avatar?"

"She said that only a kid would hang out on the Ether in a bunny avatar."

Valentina's expression didn't change. "There are many people who use an animal avatar. Or one that's nothing like their off-line self."

"Exactly! And it's none of her business, anyway." Cammie paused. "Though, I don't know, maybe I should rethink it. Redesign it a little, or something."

"I would not, unless you wanted to." Valentina gave her another sideways smile. "I expect it has its advantages, yes?"

Cammie nodded. "Nobody hits on you, nobody hassles you . . . You know what it's like being female on the Ether." She stopped. "Or maybe you don't. I've only seen you on as Val. I'm sorry if I got that wrong."

"I have been Valentina on the Ether," Valentina said.

"Usually when I was Val in the real world, but not always. And, yes, I know what you mean. That was why Ether Valentina was built to draw attention. If anyone harasses me, I am happy to slap them down."

Cammie didn't doubt that. Anyone stupid enough to hassle Valentina, online or off, was asking for trouble. "When I started going on the Ether, outside my family's space, I was, oh, maybe ten? By the time I was twelve, I was entering competition makerspaces, and I picked the rabbit because I liked it, and because it was the avatar that nobody treated differently. Everything else, they treated me like either I didn't belong or I was something weird and special, but the rabbit, they treated like an ordinary person. And then, after my dad died, and it was just Gran and me, I needed to bring in some extra money, and the rabbit was inconspicuous. Nobody took me seriously until it was too late. And by the time I thought of changing it, I was established. It was my trademark."

"It was a clever choice," Valentina said.

"It would have been smarter if I'd thought more about it," Cammie muttered. "Planned it. And I don't know why I just told you that; I haven't told anybody else—"

Valentina held up a hand. "If you want me to forget I heard this, I will do so."

Cammie shrugged one shoulder. "I don't know. I suppose it's not a secret."

"I will not run telling everyone," Valentina said. "And I still think you are right. There is something going on here that we haven't seen."

That was reassuring, but Cammie heaved a sigh. "I'd rather be wrong."

"A moment, Lieutenant, if you would?"

Rountree's voice sounded in Chase's ear, and he suppressed a sigh. He recognized that tone, the one that all senior officers used when they weren't going to accept an argument, and he mixed back in to her office, schooling his expression to polite neutrality. "Major?"

She wasn't fooled. "Ms. MacCloud. What was she really doing in the shadows?"

"Exactly what she said," Chase answered. "She's been concerned about the refugees; we've spoken to Colonel Varden about it, ma'am."

"I know." She studied him, mouth closed tight, before she finally spoke again. "And this wasn't related to gen:LOCK? Or RTASA?"

"No, ma'am." He didn't think to wonder until the words were out of his mouth. Was it possible Cammie had some other agenda, some favor she was doing for RTASA or one of the Vanguard techs? No, she would have said so after the fight—that would have been a reason for someone to attack her, and he believed she had been both surprised and shocked.

"So was she freelancing?" Rountree demanded. "I finally pried her record loose. She has quite a reputation."

"The only thing she was doing was trying to find out about some of the refugees," Chase said. "I know she came to us from Polity Cybersecurity—"

"Which she was only assigned to in lieu of significant jail time," Rountree said. "I think you can see why I might be concerned, Lieutenant."

"I understand." Chase groped for the right words. "Major, Pol Cy and the ESU checked her out, as did Vanguard. I trusted them then, and I trust them now. More than that, though—I trust Cammie. She's a solid part of the team, and I know she's completely loyal to the Polity. She'd never knowingly do anything to help the Union."

To his surprise, she sighed. "I could wish you weren't so certain, Lieutenant. Because if she's not off on her own . . ." She shook her head. "We've checked the refugees, first our regular check, which is pretty damn thorough, and then a second time because you were nervous. They came up clean. If there is someone on the inside, it's one of ours, and I— Well, I would have sworn they were clean, every one of them."

"It's more likely to be one of the refugees," Chase said. "Everything started with them. We wouldn't be here if we hadn't heard they had intel."

"So you think this is about you?" Rountree asked. "About gen:LOCK?"

"We're what's different," Chase answered.

Rountree gave a small smile. "Fair enough. And it's true if they had an agent here, they could have hurt us a lot worse before the storm hit."

"How's that going?" Chase asked, and she shrugged.

"Following the meteorologists' predictions pretty closely, though it's slowed down more than they said it would. We've had a good foot of rain here already. We'll weather it, though."

Chase nodded. He'd wondered about an underground base in the middle of all the flooding, but clearly De Soto had that well in hand. *Or if they didn't,* a voice whispered at the back of his mind, *they haven't had to tell you yet.* That was something he was not going to think about. He had to trust the Vanguard, had to trust Varden and Rountree. *Like that worked out so well before,* the voice whispered, and he shoved it firmly aside. "Good to hear."

"Joe—Herrera—he's good," Rountree offered. "His firewalls are solid."

"Yes, ma'am." Chase nodded again, wondering if he should push any further.

"And I'll notify Colonel Varden, of course," Rountree added.

"Thank you, ma'am," Chase said, and mixed out. In the quiet recesses of the gen:LOCK network, he slowly made himself relax. Rountree was just doing her job, keeping the base secure. And he'd seen enough questionable stuff to know that the authorities might just lie to him if they thought it was justified. He couldn't blame her for making the same assumptions. With gen:LOCK, Dr. Weller hadn't told anybody everything until he'd had to. Until it had been too late.

That wasn't something he wanted to think about right now—wasn't something he ever wanted to think about, if he could manage it. He checked the network, reassuring himself that everything was normal, that everyone was where they ought to be. Cammie and Valentina were just leaving the mess hall, and he hesitated. He'd come down pretty hard on Cammie, even though every harsh word was more than justified. Maybe it was time to talk. He waited until they left the mess hall, and mixed in beside them.

"Everything all right?"

Valentina gave him a knowing smile. "I will leave you, then." She turned away, and Cammie scowled.

"Not fair." She looked back at Chase, still scowling. "Yeah?"

"I wanted to be sure you were all right," Chase said.

"I'm fine." She didn't sound fine, and Chase waited. They both knew he couldn't stop her if she wanted to walk away, and he thought that knowledge was what made her sigh and shrug. "What more do you want me to say? I get it. I've promised. It's settled."

"It looks as though you were right, the Union wasn't able to get a foothold in our systems," Chase began.

"I told you they hadn't."

"You know we needed to be sure."

For a moment, he thought she'd argue, but she sighed. "Yeah." She gave him a sideways look. "I really was trying to help."

"I know."

"What if I'm right?" Cammie asked. "What if one of the refugees is a Union agent?"

"We'll have to trust Base Security to stop them," Chase said. "Can you do that?"

She hesitated, just long enough that he was beginning to wonder what he'd have to do if she said no, and then she sighed again. "Yeah. I promise."

"Thanks," Chase said, and mixed out again.

It was dark in the barracks except for the faint light from Cammie's screen. She had kept it shielded for the first hour or so, waiting for the others to fall asleep. The last thing she had wanted was anyone checking to be sure she wasn't on the Ether, or another lecture about staying up all night gaming—but now that the room had gone quiet except for the familiar sounds of breathing, she shifted to a more comfortable position.

Why couldn't Chase have just left her alone? She'd promised to stay off the Ether, she'd even admitted that she'd screwed up. What more did he need to hear? Maybe she should have stayed out of the shadows. She doubted whoever had made the four-armed thing would have found her if she'd stuck to the safe parts of the Ether. Or at least the public parts. But she still thought they needed to know more about the refugees, and XPNSV was still her best bet for that. Assuming it wasn't XPNSV who'd shopped her to her attacker, though that had never been their style. They had a reputation for staying bought, and for making any conflicts known to their clients. They would have told her if they were working for someone who was after her.

So who was it, then? She ran down the list she had never dared commit to a file, names of people she'd known in the shadows who had a grudge against her. With Fate and Archidoxy, it had been purely professional; she would have risked talking to Fate if XPNSV hadn't been available. Stormboss was a Union sympathizer and made no bones about it, but she hadn't seen any trace of him after she'd joined Pol Cy. There was a chance he'd actually joined the Union, or maybe something had happened to him in the real world. LostGirl had always been a pain, but Cammie didn't think she'd work with the Union; PaMELa and JaneSmith and Corey had all been professional rivals, but she'd been out of the business long enough that she doubted they'd still care. Unless it was someone who resented her joining Pol Cy? That was a much broader category; any of the black hats might want to cause trouble, might even want to damage her, but the attack had been too elaborate. She couldn't imagine going to that much trouble over events—jobs stolen, insults, a little bit of cyber vandalism—that were not almost a year in the past.

And anyway, it wasn't likely it was any of them. None of them would have tried to dissect her avatar to get at her logins and passwords. They'd all have had better ways to go after the same information: If they'd meant to hack her files, they'd have followed her discreetly and leveraged known nodes and styles and her favorite ICE and firewalls to try to get in. This kind of brute force meant that her attacker was a stranger; it was also the sort of thing the Union specialized in. She pulled up a second screen, checking her security settings for the hundredth time tonight, and confirmed that everything was green. No, this was Union style, and that meant that the four-armed shape wasn't just a lucky guess. Her attacker had known that Nemesis was the one thing that might make her freeze long enough to let the demons get close.

But of course that didn't mean that whoever had attacked her had known what the shape was. More likely, they'd been handed it and the tool kit, the premade rippers and code slashers, and told to keep an eye out if she went through the Nexus. She'd taken jobs like that herself, back in the day, though she'd never been asked to do more than steal code. Very possibly that was all the attacker had thought they were doing, too.

And that brought her right back around the circle. If she could go out onto the Ether, she could probably track down whoever had attacked her—no one was going to be happy that they'd made that much trouble in the shadow spaces, enough trouble to get things noticed—but even if she did find them, they weren't likely to know anything useful. And she'd promised to stay off the Ether.

She yawned and flicked away the monitor, then closed down her tablet. Maybe it had been a busy enough day that she could actually sleep. She pulled the blanket over herself, Nugget snuggling close on his charging pad, one foot resting against her hair, and settled herself to sleep.

She dreamed, of course, first of the storm and then the flooding stream, and the refugee vehicles struggling to cross. She dragged herself half-awake then, remembering the weight of the bridge and the shock of the water breaking against her and Kazu as the last of the haulers scurried across just before the bridge tore free. That was actually a win, a real success; she rolled over, folding her pillow to a more comfortable shape, and pulled the blanket up over her head. Nugget stretched like a cat, servos whirring softly, and she let herself drift off again.

This time, she dreamed she was back in her secret garden, the message tree restored to its golden glory, the new grass icon she'd retrieved for the space now flowing underfoot. The sky was clear, bright and blue with only a few fair-weather clouds floating toward the distant horizon, and the tower where she would see her mother's avatar had been completely repaired. She started toward it, only to see the ground change under her feet. Everywhere she stepped, she left dark footprints, as though she'd walked through some kind of poison and was destroying the delicate greenery.

She stopped, checking her avatar, checking the code, and found nothing wrong. She leaned down, determined to get a sample this time, and saw that the edges of the footprints were no longer black, but deep purple, seething outlines that began to crawl toward each other as she watched. She reached for generic ICE, but it shattered against the color that crept like a line of dark fire across the unreal grass. Where two lines met, a wisp of smoke began to rise. She rummaged in her tool kit, but it was suddenly empty, her best tools missing, the safeties gone, so she could only watch in horror as the purple fires met and joined and gave up ever-stronger plumes of nanite smoke that stretched toward the vaulted sky of her garden.

She knew what was in that smoke, what had to be behind it, and turned to run, but her feet were caught fast in the blackening grass, her toes dissolving into a purple-tinged fog. She fought to take a step, and then another, but her feet were gone, and she teetered on the stubs of her ankles. If she could just reach her gate—but the fog was creeping up her legs, winding around her calves, and the fur of her avatar was fizzing away into static as the smoke rose up around her, cutting out the sun.

Nemesis lurched out of the cloud, larger even than she remembered, its body all jagged angles and glowing eyes and glittering claws at the ends of its fingers. It reached for her with all four arms, and the nanite smoke swirled out ahead of it, circling her like a nest of snakes. The strands pinned her arms to her sides; she fought them, kicking with what was left of her legs, her fingers dissolving as she clawed at the strands. Nemesis loomed closer still, reaching for her chest, where the mainframe was tucked into her body. Its claws closed over it, and another hand closed over her head, twisting and tearing as she screamed—

She awoke shaking in the dark, once again unsure if she'd actually made a noise. Everything around her seemed quiet enough. She could hear Kazu snoring softly; surely, if she'd woken him, he wouldn't be faking that. Her heart was still racing, she could feel it hammering under her ribs, and Nugget had slipped off the charging pad and was padding at her head with all four feet.

The sensation of his feet was probably what made her dream about Nemesis ripping her head off, she thought, and scooped him into her arms. "I wish you hadn't done that," she whispered, holding him close, and felt him warm slightly, a comforting presence. By the fair light of the charging pad, she could see the shadows of the other bunks. Probably she hadn't screamed out loud, though her throat felt as tight as if she'd been yelling.

The garden was fine. Probably fine. She'd been thinking about it a lot lately, so of course that was where her subconscious had chosen to show her Nemesis. That was how nightmares worked; she'd done enough reading about them to know that. She understood how and why they happened, how she was stuck replaying the stupid trauma until some-day, somehow, it would stop . . .

She sat up, resting her head on her knees. In the mean-time, she needed . . . well, she didn't *need* to sleep, that was for sure. Nightmares like that were worse than being tired, left her on edge and prone to making mistakes. Normally, she'd go out on the Ether, find something to distract herself with and sleep later, but she'd promised to stay off the Ether. She wasn't even supposed to use the base network unless it was for work, and it would be awkward to explain why she was "working" in the middle of the night when everyone else was sound asleep . . . She wished she could take a quick look at the garden, run a few more patches. That would prove she had nothing to worry about. Unless the attack has somehow found her access codes.

That wasn't very likely. She'd destroyed the bots before they'd worked their way through more than the first and lightest layer of her security. There was no way she would mix in to find Nemesis or its Ether ghost waiting for her. It was just a nightmare, and the thing she had seen on the Ether was a bot sourced to some Union-sympathizing black hat. Nothing bad was happening to the garden.

She hugged her knees to her chest. Nugget squeaked, his corners sharp against her, and she set him down on the foam mattress, rubbed his left ear to encourage him to give off a little more light. She couldn't check it, of course. She wouldn't break her promise, not for something as trivial as this. Even thinking about it was ridiculous.

And of course, there was no actual need to check the garden; it had waited for years without her attention, and it could wait a little longer. In fact, she could let it go altogether if she wanted to. There was no rule that said she had to keep maintaining it, not when she was pretty nearly an adult. Maybe it was time to shut it down, stop paying the maintenance fees.

Except if she did, it would be gone, and she'd never be able to get it back.

She rested her forehead on her knees, remembering sitting with her father, him in his mobile chair, her perched on a padded bench beside him as he showed her the space he'd bought. It hadn't even been her birthday, or Christmas; he'd grabbed the space as soon as it became available, done minimal setup, and turned it over to her. *You've got a knack for this coding, Bun,* he'd said. *Let's see what you can do.* The first big thing she'd done was to build the message tree, and give Gran the access code. Gran wasn't particularly fond of the Ether—she used it nimbly enough—but, she said, *I like to make real things.* Still, she'd seemed to enjoy the message tree. Cammie shivered. If she abandoned the garden, she'd lose something that made all those memories real.

And yet. She closed her eyes, remembering the place as it had been the last time she'd looked at it, all her best mods stripped away. The list of updates had been enormous; it was going to take forever to set up a queue that would let the critical changes run first, not to mention trying to find replacements for some of the older programs. She'd probably have to build most of those from scratch, and when she'd have the time . . . And even when it was finished, it would still be tawdry, childish, out-of-date. If she were building it now, she'd do everything differently . . . and she'd lose what she had. *Fix it first*, she told herself. *Then you can decide what to do.* She lay back on her bunk, tears prickling unhappily in the corners of her eyes. She wouldn't cry, not when someone might hear. She clutched Nugget to her chest instead, heedless of sharp corners, and buried her face in the pillows.

SHE WOKE TO a buzzing sound, and sat up before she realized that it was coming from her discarded Ether goggles. She put them on and the buzzing resolved into words.

Cammie! Are you there? Migas needs us.

That was Chase's voice, and she shook herself hard, reached for a screen to provide light and some idea of context.

Chase?

Someone's trying to hack Renegade, Chase answered.

For f— Cammie mentally swallowed the word. *Right.* Her hands were already busy, sweeping away one screen, replacing it with another that gave access to gen:LOCK's systems, but she felt Chase shake his head.

No time. We need to do this in Mindshare.

For a heartbeat she hesitated. Suppose this was another trick, another attempt to draw her into the Ether, where she could be attacked? But if it was, it meant the Union had hacked gen:LOCK, and that was worse trouble than hacking *Renegade*.

Coming, she said, and let herself fall into Mindshare.

Instead of the usual empty plane, she fell into a jungle, a pit of vines that writhed like vipers and snapped fanged mouths like black flowers at her as she fell. She struck out at them, calling a subroutine that manifested as a flaming ax and made the flowers shrink back, hissing. *Chase!*

Over here!

She could see him now, caught in a knot of thicker vines, and beyond him, she could see Caliban, almost submerged in a sea of green and black. If Cal went down, *Renegade*'s systems would be open. There was no time for anything but the full link, and she reached for Chase, handing him the subroutine and everything she knew about using it. The ax blossomed in his hand, the flames even taller than when she was using it, and he spun in a circle, striking at the weak points she could feel. She copied him, used his strength to overleap a thick coil and strike down on it as she passed, chopping it neatly in two.

And then she was at Chase's side, switching to another ICE routine that manifested as a flamethrower, withering the nearest vines to ash.

Up, Chase said, and she stepped into his outstretched hand, let him launch her up and over the struggling Caliban, fire lashing out to clear a circle around them. The vines recoiled, and she filled the space she'd gained with more fire, then turned her attention to Caliban. Chase had already reached his side, was slashing at the vines, carving them away with great sweeps of his ax. Cammie switched subroutines again and piled in from the other side.

Together they hacked away the vines, stamping on them and kicking them into the flames, and suddenly Caliban was free, the last of the clinging green lines dissolving into a shower of sparks. They stood in the center of a ring of fire, Mindshare empty around them. Cammie tested the network, and found it clear.

Well, Caliban said, *that was certainly exciting.*

Yeah. Chase was already pulling back from their link, but Cammie caught a flicker of unease, maybe even disapproval, before the connection ended.

You should see me in Siege, she said brightly, and got no answer. *Chase?*

Are we clear, Cal? Chase asked.

For the present, Caliban answered. *I am attempting to determine the source of the attack, but I have had no luck so far.*

I should have been doing that, Cammie thought. *Let me try.* She reached for a screen, calling up a handful of trackers, but to her surprise, Chase shook his head.

Let Cal do it.

But why? Cammie started. *I'm better than he is. No offense, Cal.*

None taken, though possibly I should, Caliban answered. *I have tracked the infiltration to an internal node that acts as an exchange between the base and the Ether.*

But did it come in from the Ether or was it local? Cammie bounced, wishing she could get her hands on the code herself.

If I could be certain which it was, I would have said so, Caliban answered.

Maybe I can tell—

Cammie, Chase said again.

What? Cammie glared at him. *Do you not want me to find out?*

Has it occurred to you that it might have gotten in by hacking you? Chase asked. *I don't think it's a coincidence that we get attacked now, after you ran into something nasty in the shadows.*

It wasn't me. Cammie shook her head in frustration. *Look, this is the thing I know, yeah? I've been doing this since I was tiny. They didn't get anything off me.*

Then why now? Chase's voice was gentle, which somehow made it worse.

Because they've shown their hand, Cammie said. *Because they were hoping all the parties would slow down security. Because they were working their day job until just now. It could be anything!*

You were attacked, Chase said again. *Migas. How're you doing?*

Everything's green here. His voice seemed to echo in the empty space. *Good thing you came when you did; we were starting to have some problems. But the hardware and the software are all safe. Nice work, by the way.*

At least someone appreciates me, Cammie muttered, and let the flames die away.

I appreciate you, Chase said. *You did a great job stopping this attack. I couldn't have done it without you. But we need to look a little deeper at this.*

Cammie took a breath, the lack of sleep tugging at her as the adrenaline receded. He wasn't wrong—that was the problem; they *did* need to figure out who was doing this and deal with them, and she could see why he thought maybe they'd gotten something from her. But she knew they hadn't gotten the codes from her, which meant it was more likely that this was coming from inside the base. And that meant the refugees. *I agree, let's look deeper. Because I still think it's one of the refugees.*

Colonel Varden says they've checked out, Chase said. *But, yeah, I'll tell him what happened, and I'll tell him what you think. Right now, what I need you to do is lock down all our systems. We have to protect gen:LOCK and the Holons. That has to be our first priority.*

Makes sense, Cammie said. *Yeah, I can do that.*

"I'd be glad of the help," Migas interjected, and Cammie heard Caliban make a sound that was almost a sniff.

Chase nodded. *I'm going to let Colonel Varden know what just happened. Run a quick check, and if nothing turns up, try to get some more sleep.*

Yeah, Cammie said. *I'll do that.*

She sat up in her bunk, lighting her tablet and slipping in an earpiece before she pulled a secondary screen into existence.

"Hey," Migas said in her ear. "Nice job. Things were starting to look hairy."

"They were not looking 'hairy,'" Caliban interjected, his voice sounding sharper than ever over the network. "There was some risk of intrusion, that is all."

"Whatever it was," Cammie said, "it's five in the f—five in the ridiculous morning." She made an effort to keep her voice down, but even so she heard Kazu stir in his bunk. "Let's lock this down and then we can look at the details tomorrow."

"Copy that," Migas said, and she bent her attention to her screens.

It didn't actually take as long as she had feared to make sure that gen:LOCK's systems hadn't been compromised, and that their access points were all clean.

"It would have taken longer if it hadn't been for me," Caliban pointed out, and Cammie groaned.

"Oh, stuff it, Cal. We all did our part." The android didn't answer, and she hurried on before he thought of something that contradicted her. "Migas, everything's good in real space?"

"Everything's quiet," Migas answered. "Everything's been quiet. Though I've set up a couple of screamers to wake me if anything comes near the Holons, so I'd say we can go to bed."

"I will keep watch," Caliban said. "Since I don't need sleep."

"And a very good thing you don't," Migas said cheerfully. "Cammie, you're coming by in the morning for a postmortem?"

"I'll be there," Cammie said, and she closed her screen and tablet, dragging her blanket back over her shoulders.

Nugget whirred and settled, a familiar weight against her shoulder, and this time, at least, she didn't dream.

Valentina shook her awake a little before nine, and she rolled out of bed feeling sluggish and irritable. The others had already eaten, and somehow it was more annoying that they'd saved some of her favorites than it would have been if they'd eaten them all. And that was seriously unreasonable, a sign that she definitely needed more sleep. She spooned sugar into her tea, ignoring Kazu's inadvertent shudder, and slurped at it loudly.

"I could cook you an egg," he offered.

She considered for a moment. She wasn't all that hungry, but it probably made sense to eat, get enough calories into her to make up for the exhaustion. "Yeah, thanks."

"Were you up again last night?" Yaz asked, her voice carefully neutral, and Cammie frowned.

"Somebody tried to hack us. I had to deal with that."

Valentina looked up from her tablet. "What sort of someone?"

"I don't know. I'm going to check into it after breakfast—Chase's orders, before you tell me not to."

"I am not telling you anything," Valentina answered, and looked back at her tablet. "The storm is winding down, it seems. The base has resumed drone patrols."

"That's good," Yaz said.

"I thought you were not worried about an attack," Valentina said.

"I still like knowing all the security is working," Yaz answered.

"Egg," Kazu said, sliding a fried egg neatly onto Cammie's plate. "More tea?"

"Yeah, thanks." She slid her mug across the table and let him fill it, took another long drink of the steaming liquid. It wasn't Gran's tea, black and bitter until you cut it with milk and sugar, but it was good enough. "When can we get out of here? Can you tell?"

"Not yet," Kazu answered.

Valentina sighed. "The winds are supposed to die down this afternoon. Or at least enough that *Renegade* should be able to handle them."

"That would be good," Kazu said. "I'll be glad to get back to RTASA."

"We need some other base," Yaz said fretfully.

"Yes, but no one is offering us one," Valentina said.

It was an old argument, and Cammie was abruptly sick of it. She swallowed the last bite of egg and toast and grabbed her mug of tea. "I've got to go."

"You don't want anything more?" Kazu asked.

"I'm good, thanks," she answered, and slipped out the door before anyone else could say something.

She hurried toward the hangar, but as she got closer, she found her steps lagging. Suppose Migas didn't want her help—suppose Caliban didn't? Suppose they agreed with Chase that her connections were too dangerous, that she should only watch from the outside while they did the real work? The worst of it was, she couldn't entirely blame them. She had taken a risk, visiting the nonhuman quarter. She probably wouldn't have been attacked if she hadn't tried to find out just a little more. The last thing they needed was to draw attention, especially when they were stuck at De Soto Base—and isolated from RTASA—until the hurricane ended.

Maybe she should stop in the mess hall and get some more tea. Or something else to eat. But the thought of more food turned her stomach, and she knew perfectly well that she was just delaying joining the others. She'd screwed up, and not for the first time. Maybe she was too young, too inexperienced, to be part of gen:LOCK. Probably she should just do what she was told, and not try to do more. She wasn't exactly making a good job of it, between the stupid nightmares and getting herself jumped on the Ether.

And she still wasn't as good a fighter as she needed to be, for all that she'd tweaked her targeting drones to the limits of the current hardware. She still froze when she was faced with something new, or with something that reminded her of a nightmare, and that was something she absolutely couldn't afford. When they got back to RTASA, she needed to upgrade the drones, and spend as much time as she could with RTASA's soldiers—and with Kazu. He could teach her as well as anyone. And she had to learn, had to get better, or she was just going to be a liability.

But. She could do that. Surely. It wouldn't be easy, and it wouldn't be fun, but she'd never yet found anything she couldn't handle if she just put her mind to it. And if this was that thing . . . She shoved the thought away because she didn't have an answer. She would have to do it, that was all.

Renegade's rear ramp was still closed tight, but when she came around to the side, she found Migas sitting in the open hatch. He scrambled to his feet at her approach, and she climbed the short stairs to join him.

"Any more trouble?"

"No, thank God." Migas waved her into the main compartment. "Did you get breakfast? That was a weird late night."

"Yeah. And I ate, thanks."

"I got us doughnuts." Migas held out the open box, and she hesitated, tempted.

"Okay, maybe one."

"And there's tea." Migas closed the box and nodded toward the nearest console, where a tall thermos stood waiting.

"I'm fine." Cammie finished her doughnut, letting the sugar rush course through her.

"Good," Caliban said. "Then we can get started on the analysis."

"Hey, I needed breakfast," Migas protested, but pulled a display out of the air. "What have you got?"

"So far, I have retrieved one hundred thirty-eight code

fragments from nine hundred sixty-eight blocked intrusion attempts," Caliban said.

Cammie settled herself cross-legged on the nearest seat, pulling up her own screen. "That's not so bad."

"Those are routines that penetrated primary and secondary ICE," Caliban answered. "Also, my analysis is not yet complete. There may be some incursions of a more subtle nature."

"So you're saying we need to do better," Migas said.

"I think that would be advisable," Caliban answered.

Cammie scowled. "You might give us credit for what we did do."

"I do," Caliban answered, "but the fact remains that the attack very nearly got through."

That was inarguable, not to mention depressing, and Cammie curled herself into a more comfortable position, frowning at her display. Caliban was right: She had to do better, and she pulled up the building blocks of gen:LOCK's primary ICE, separating them into their various components. "Caliban, can you tell where we were targeted?"

"Across the spectrum," Caliban answered. "The most successful incursions occurred here and here."

Lights flared gold on her screens. She nodded slowly, her ears flicking forward as she began to make sense of the pattern. The successful attacks had all been against a piece of code she recognized from her time with Pol Cy, an older module that supposedly had been updated. But if you didn't also update Watchman 2—her fingers flew over the virtual controls, summoning new windows and highlighting sections—then there was a point where a targeted attack could overwrite the buffer and gain access. She expanded that screen and checked. Yes, that led directly to the point of attack, though she'd added a second checkpoint that had stopped the invader. "Got it."

"Yeah?" Migas looked up, half-hidden by the layers of screens, and Cammie balled up the relevant screen and tossed it to him. "Oh, hey, yeah."

"That seems to be the problem, indeed," Caliban said.

"That I can fix," Cammie said, and Migas nodded.

"It's all yours. I'll keep checking the hardware, then."

"Sounds good to me." Cammie bent over her virtual controls, ignoring Caliban's plaintive *So I'm doing nothing here?* She could see what needed to be done; better, she could see a more efficient way to do it. If she reworked the trapper subroutine in Watchman 2, rather than just doing the update, she'd tighten the parameters even further, make it impossible to override from this location. She isolated the section and began typing, excising the redundant bits of code and weaving in her own. She lost herself in the work, the code growing under her fingertips, until at last she had an entirely new version, and fed it into the test environment.

Migas was pinching most of his screens into standby mode, and she grinned at him. "All done?"

"So far, so good. I've got a couple of disinfectors running, but they're going to take a while."

"Yeah. I'm testing a new trapper myself." She glanced over at the console where Caliban was standing. "Any progress with the analysis?"

"I have not so far found any other indications of a successful incursion," Caliban answered. "Also, I believe I will be able to reconstruct part of one of the attacking programs."

"Oh, that's helpful," Cammie said.

"Is it?" Migas looked doubtful. "I mean, that's your business and all that, but is that going to tell us anything we didn't already know?"

"If we're lucky, it'll give us a line on who attacked us."

Migas ran his hand through his hair. "I mean, it was the Union, right? Wasn't it?"

"Probably," Cammie said. "But I may be able to say what part of the Union, or whether they hired black hats on our side of the line to do the work for them. How long is the reconstruction going to take, Cal?"

"It will take more time if you keep asking," Caliban said.

Cammie rolled her eyes. "Right. Well, we'll just sit here and finish the doughnuts, then."

"Not a bad idea," Migas said. He brought over the box, and Cammie poured herself another mug of lukewarm tea.

"So everything's good with the Holons?"

"Should be," Migas said. He brushed crumbs off his shirt. "Like I said, I'm still running disinfectant, but I'm not expecting them to find anything. The Holons' systems are pretty well insulated from the rest of gen:LOCK. They'd have to have hacked Mindshare to get real access."

Cammie nodded. "Not easy, that."

"It had better not be," Caliban interjected. "That's unique to gen:LOCK."

"Yeah." Cammie expanded that screen again, checking the tests she'd embedded in the code. None of them had been activated, which should mean they were clean, but she'd feel better when Caliban's reconstruction was finished, and she could be sure she understood how the program had gotten in.

"How long have you been doing this?" Migas asked.

"If that's saying I'm too young—" Cammie began, and Migas held up both hands.

"No, no, not at all! I just wondered. They start us in fourth grade here."

"My dad bought me some code space when I was six," Cammie said. "On ElwysNet. He taught me the basics and pretty much turned me loose."

"ElwysNet!" Migas said. "I remember them! My sister and her friends had a whole MyBrownDog amusement park set up there."

"Yeah?" Cammie couldn't decide if it felt good to know that Migas's sister had shared space with her garden, so she just said, "But you weren't on it?"

Migas shook his head. "I was always better with things I could get my hands on—literally, I mean. My dad had a garage; he and my uncles did some amateur racing."

"Oh, yeah? My dad raced motorcycles."

"We mostly raced drones," Migas answered. "One of my uncles used to race dragsters, before the fuel got too expensive. Where'd your dad race?"

"European Tier 3, before the Union attacked." Cammie hesitated, but she'd learned the hard way that it was better to get it out in the open. "He broke his back in a wreck and had to quit." She braced herself for pity, for the questions that always followed, but Migas only nodded.

"That sucks. But he taught you to program?"

"Yeah." She nodded, trying to put the gratitude she couldn't express into her tone of voice. "Yeah, he was good at it. Taught me a lot." She pointed an ear in his direction. "He and Gran helped me make my first set of ears."

"Those are seriously cool," Migas said.

"Want to see the specs?" Cammie pulled the design out of memory and set it dancing in the air between them. It was the public copy. There were still a few tweaks that she wasn't sharing with anyone just yet, but Migas's eager nod was gratifying.

"Wow, yeah." He pulled the image closer. "Oh, that's nice."

Cammie scooted over so that she could see what he was looking at, the tension finally easing from her gut. She could trust Migas—she *did* trust Migas; he'd given her programs she wasn't supposed to have, and she'd helped him with the Holons. If he thought she'd done good work, she could believe him. And that mattered, that respect. She'd earn it from the others, too.

They had moved on from the ears to some ideas for further

Holon modifications when the alarm popped up in the corner of Cammie's vision, warning her that it was time to meet XPNSV. She hesitated, still sure she would find out what she needed to know, but she'd promised Chase. And he was right: She had put gen:LOCK in danger. She couldn't risk doing that again. She pinched the alarm down to the absolute minimum, just a pinprick of light at the very corner of her eye, and made herself focus on the Holons instead.

"Ahem," Caliban said. "I've completed reconstruction of the attacking program, and done a very good job of it, if I do say so myself."

"And you do," Migas murmured. "Back to work, I guess."

Cammie nodded, tucking away her notes, and reached for the files Caliban slid their way. She didn't recognize the hand as she flicked through the code. A lot of it looked to be prebuilt modules strung together, though Caliban had already highlighted areas that it thought were unusual and noteworthy. A couple of those pieces had a Union flavor to them, but that didn't mean anything. Despite Pol Cy's best efforts, Union code circulated in the shadows, and the black hats would use anything that got the effect they wanted.

She separated the various segments, looking at each one individually, then fit them back together to look at the whole. It was competent work, not particularly clever or innovative; they just used familiar code in slightly different ways. Slightly more like the Union that way than the Polity, but there were plenty of black hats who relied on scripts roaming the Ether.

Maybe she was looking at it the wrong way. Maybe if she looked at what it was supposed to do . . . She rubbed her eyes as though that would clear her brain, and searched for the payload. There was something familiar about it, a shape to the result, and she closed her eyes, trying to imagine what the code would do. *A swarm of spiders*, she realized, just like the code that had been hidden behind the image of Nemesis. Like that program, this one had been designed to distract regular ICE while a smaller, sneakier subroutine burrowed between the layers of ICE and tried to chew through the inner firewalls to gain access to the secure data.

So how did it get into what should be a super-secure Vanguard base? She could hack the gatekeeper, but she had been going outbound, and she knew the Vanguard codes. Someone from the Union wouldn't have that advantage. *Well, probably not*, she amended, her hands busy on the screens. But even if they did, there was always extra security on the inbound data channels . . . There, that was where the attack had entered, through a backup Ether link—except that made no sense. The backups were an obvious attack point; she'd written monitor and alarm code for them, and what she could scrape up of the lockpick should have triggered at least one of the alarms. Unless—she shifted screens, calling up a new set of images—unless someone inside the base had launched the attack, and was trying to make it look as though it had come from outside. She scrolled down the records of the attack, looking for any indication that someone had spoofed the attack point. She couldn't prove it, but it felt right. Someone on the base had triggered the attack on *Renegade*'s systems.

That was definitely Union work, not black hat, and probably meant she was right about the refugees. She'd only been attacked after she'd made contact with XPNSV, which meant the attacker was trying to keep her from getting XPNSV's answers, and again, that meant it was someone among the refugees. This had the four-square, major-chord solidity of good code, and that meant she had to make the meeting with XPNSV.

Except she'd promised Chase she'd stay off the Ether. Maybe she could find him, ask him first, but it would take time to convince him, and she could see the timer ticking down. If she didn't make the connection, XPNSV was going to assume something had gone wrong, and it would take days—weeks— to convince them to talk to her again. That was how they'd stayed in the business, being cautious like that. She pinged Chase anyway, felt the query fall into null-space: Chase wasn't taking contact at the moment. She tried Mindshare instead, got nothing, and switched back to the gen:LOCK network.

"Kazu, Yaz, Valentina—do you guys know where Chase is? I need him—it's an emergency!"

There was a confused babble in answer, Yaz's voice overriding the others. "He is with Colonel Varden—"

Cammie reached for Mindshare again, but the space was empty. *Chase! Chase, I need you . . .*

"Cammie?" Migas said.

She pulled up the timer again, wincing at how late it was, and batted away the hovering screens. It was now or never. She'd just have to explain later. "I'm taking Caliban. I have to go out on the Ether; there's somebody I've got to meet—"

"Didn't Chase say you weren't supposed to do that?" Migas asked warily, putting aside his own screens.

"Yes, but I didn't know this was the same hand." Cammie shook her head impatiently. "Look, whoever jumped me was behind the attack on *Renegade* and the Holon systems. And while that still could be black hats, it feels like the Union. And I asked XPNSV to look for Union connections from the refugees. I have to get their answer before they get into trouble."

"Call Chase first," Migas said.

"I tried! I can't get him." Cammie grabbed her goggles. "Caliban can back me up, make sure I'm not compromised."

"This is a bad idea," Migas said.

"No time to argue," she answered. "Caliban, you're with me."

"But—"

She dropped onto the Ether without waiting for an answer. A moment later, Caliban mixed in beside her. "I don't think this is a good idea, Cammie."

"F— Too bad," she answered, and opened a portal into the underworld.

She took a roundabout path, even though she could feel the seconds ticking down, doubling back twice to be sure nothing was following her, and emerged at last into the darkness of the nonhuman quarter, only the golden bricks glowing beneath her feet. The timer was ticking down the last two minutes, and she pinged XPNSV directly, the packet flaring like a lit match before it disappeared. She held her breath, and then, abruptly, she was in a private space, not the same one they'd used before, she could see that the address was different, but the fittings were entirely the same: white walls, white windows, white furniture. Caliban was missing, excluded from the space; she sent a reassuring message via gen:LOCK, and looked around.

Diamonds fell from the ceiling, formed a loose spiral. "You didn't mention a friend."

"It's all right. He can wait," Cammie answered.

"It's not like I was going to let him in. Not even for you." XPNSV paused. "You're late. I wasn't going to wait much longer."

"Yeah, sorry." She hesitated, then decided there was no harm letting them know she'd been attacked. "I had a little trouble after I left you last time."

"Oh?" XPNSV sounded genuinely surprised. "That's . . . interesting. As it happens, I had some trouble myself."

"What sort of trouble?"

The swirl shifted, suggesting a shrug. "Someone came banging on my doors. My ICE held, but I didn't manage to get a good look at them. I assumed it was Union, given your job, but if you know otherwise . . ."

"I think what came after me was Union," Cammie said.

"You know, messing with them is usually a bad bet," XPNSV said. "They don't play nice."

"Tell me about it," Cammie muttered, and felt XPNSV's attention sharpen.

"Just what *are* you doing these days, Cammie?"

"Can't tell you." That had always been her answer, even when she was freelancing as a black hat, and XPNSV sketched a smiling face in answer.

"No, seriously."

"Seriously. Did you find anything?"

"I did." A coil of diamonds detached itself from the main swirl, then resolved into a standard data packet. Cammie took it warily, letting her sniffers check it first.

"How about a summary?"

XPNSV made the shrugging movement again. "The woman from Gum Neck checks out clean as far as Union connections go, though she's a known broker for bootleg biofuel."

"That's not so bad." Cammie could feel the sniffer working under her fingers, testing the code for traps and tricks. So far, there was nothing, but then, XPNSV was very good.

"The man's a factory hand, got a record for petty offenses, mostly juvenile, real-world theft. He was employed up until nine days ago, when he went missing and was fired—in that order, by the way."

"Which would be when he made a run for it," Cammie mumbled. "And?"

"Ah, there's the prize at the bottom of the box," XPNSV said. "Nothing absolute, but *she* smells, Cammie. Her work history doesn't check out, she's got a few too many nice things for her pay grade, and her record's just a little too neat. Someone's edited it. If you're looking for a Union plant, my money's on her."

"Yes." Cammie pumped a fist.

"You were betting on her, too?" XPNSV asked.

"I was hoping it was her," Cammie said, more honestly than she'd meant. "I don't like her at all."

"Convenient."

"That's not the point." Cammie's sniffer pulsed under her fingers, and dissolved: It had found nothing dangerous in the data. "How deep did you go?"

"Outer layers only," XPNSV answered. "I don't do more than that unless you pay me the serious bucks. Too many people end up dead that way. But what I have is reliable. And I'd say so even if someone hadn't jumped me."

"Thanks. This is helpful."

"Remember, you owe me," XPNSV answered.

"Like I said, I'm not with Pol Cy anymore," Cammie explained. "But I'll put in a good word."

"Do that," XPNSV said. "And deal with this . . . person. I don't like the Union, and I especially don't like being threatened."

"No fear," Cammie said, and the space dissolved around her.

She was abruptly back in the shadows of the nonhuman quarter, though this time the bricks and the drifting fog looked ordinary enough. Caliban was waiting, dodging tendrils that stretched up from between the bricks to clutch at his avatar's ankles.

"This was not a good idea," he said. "Also, I am inclined to consider this an attack."

"Sorry." Cammie reached into her tool kit, found the routine she wanted, and hooked it into Caliban's icon.

"What is that?"

"Visitor's pass. Kind of. I should have given it to you before I talked to my contact."

"Yes, I think you should have." Caliban shook his foot, and the last of the tendrils dropped away.

"I was in a hurry. I didn't want to miss them." Cammie turned toward the invisible exit, the bricks leading her without trouble this time, and Caliban trailed after her.

"You promised Chase you wouldn't do this," he said.

"I have the information we need," Cammie answered, and hoped it would be enough.

There was no pursuit as she wound her way back to the bright-lights sections of the Ether, but she ducked in and out of several popular Ethertainment spaces just to be sure. Only then did she mix out, lifting the Ether goggles from her face, to find both Migas and Chase waiting in *Renegade*'s cabin. "Um . . . hi?"

CHASE FOLDED HIS arms. "You promised you wouldn't go on the Ether."

"I tried to ask you," Cammie protested.

"I replied and you were already gone," Chase answered.

"There wasn't time. If I hadn't made this meeting, XPNSV would have gone to ground, and it would have taken me weeks to convince them to talk to me, and by then we'd be gone and the refugees would be scattered God knows where."

"You should have asked," Chase said. "Cammie, how can I go to bat for you when you break your word?"

"I wouldn't have done it if I hadn't had to!" Cammie pulled up her screens, spreading and turning them so that Chase could see what they'd found. "I only put it together at the last minute—literally the last minute. XPNSV was about to close me out. And I took Caliban; he's entirely capable of watching my back. But look! This is the program that was used to hack *Renegade*. What it does is exactly the same thing that the Nemesis-spider-thing did: distracts on one plane and sends in some sneaky little bots to try to chew through your firewalls. It's the same hand, the same person—it can't be anyone else."

Chase frowned at the displays. "I'll take your word for it—"

"I would," Migas said, and in the same moment, Caliban said, "I believe Cammie is entirely correct."

"Okay, okay, I said I believed it." Chase shook his head. "But that still doesn't change our agreement."

"There's more," Cammie said. "I'm pretty sure that the attack on *Renegade* came from inside the base systems, and you know what that means. I asked XPNSV to check out three of the refugees, and the clock was ticking." She stopped. "I tried to reach you, but I didn't figure it out in time. I'm sorry—sorry that I wasn't quicker, and sorry that I couldn't ask."

"You're sure the attack came from inside?" Chase asked.

"Yes—well, seventy-five percent. Seventy."

"And you got something on the refugees?"

Cammie nodded. "Aris Webb. This is the data XPNSV pulled out of main records. It matches what the Vanguard was looking at, or some version of it, but XPNSV went deeper." She pulled up that screen as well, let it unroll in the air in front of Chase. "And when you do, it's too neat. Too clean. And then you start seeing the seams."

Chase scrolled through the file, his avatar distorting slightly as the images shifted in front of him. "Okay, yeah, I see what you mean. She just steps right up the ladder, runner to line worker to machine boss, never gets a reprimand or a commendation. You're right; that's weird. Nobody does that."

"She also isn't making enough money to have a bike like that," Cammie said. "She's using high-pressure fuel injectors, which are super expensive, and hard to maintain unless you have access to a proper garage. All the parts are brand-new, and she's hooked them up like she expects to be able to replace them, not rebuild them. That's not conclusive—there are lots of off-the-records things she could be doing, but that doesn't go with her work record."

"Yeah." Chase nodded. "We need to take this to Colonel Varden."

Varden was willing to see them, though to Cammie's eyes, he was starting to look a little frayed around the edges. Probably he hadn't slept much since the storm started, she thought, and with the weather improving, the patrols would be starting up again. Their news wasn't going to make his life any easier, either.

"It's about the attack on Cammie," Chase said, "and the refugees. We've got some solid evidence this time." He went through it in detail, layering window on top of window so that Varden's face was almost hidden by the cascading data.

Varden paged through it quickly, then went back and read several of the files more carefully, his frown increasing.

"Major Rountree said you were banned from accessing the Ether, Ms. MacCloud."

"She tried to contact me first," Chase said. "And I would have given permission. This is vital information, and it was time sensitive."

Cammie blinked at him. She hadn't expected him to defend her that wholeheartedly, considering that she'd gone against his orders.

"The main thing is," Chase went on, "the attack came from inside, and we've got one refugee whose profile doesn't add up."

Varden nodded slowly. "If you're certain—"

"We are," Chase said firmly.

"Right." Varden crooked a finger, opening an internal communications channel. "Major Rountree."

10

Yaz stirred sugar into her mug of tea as though that would make it taste more familiar, aware of Valentina's wry smile.

"I know," Valentina said. "When I was little, we put jam in our tea to sweeten it. But here?"

"They look at you strangely," Yaz said.

Valentina shrugged. "Also, the water is never hot enough to melt it."

"I miss cardamom," Yaz said, "and rose petals." She remembered her mother swirling the china pot to mix the flavors, then pouring the dark liquid into the narrow-waisted glasses. There was a bowl of sugar cubes on the table, and a plate of dates . . . and she would not think any more about home, lost through her own terrible choices. "Did you have a samovar?"

"We did not," Valentina said. "Though my grandmother did." She stopped abruptly, her eyes traveling to something over Yaz's shoulder, so that Yaz turned herself, frowning.

Several Vanguard security officers were moving quickly through the mess hall, and a brief glance to either side revealed more of them blocking the exits and posted on the mezzanine level where they had a clear field of fire. "Trouble."

"But not for us," Valentina noted.

Yaz nodded, watching the team fan out to surround a knot of refugees sitting at a back table. Someday, she thought, someday she'd get over her instinctive assumption that Security was coming for her. The leader of the team spoke to a group at one table, and then put her hand on the shoulder of a fair-haired woman in a leather jacket. Valentina whistled softly.

"So. It seems our Cammie may have been right after all."

"That's the one she suspected?"

The fair-haired woman was on her feet now, protesting, but Security was insistent, and finally she threw up her hands and walked away with them. Yaz looked up to see the agents on the mezzanine still covering them: They were taking this very seriously indeed.

Valentina nodded. "I think so. Cammie didn't like her."

"That doesn't mean she's a Union agent," Yaz said. *People don't always like me, and I gave up everything to join the Polity.* That was too much, too revealing, and she shut her mouth tight over the words.

"No," Valentina said. "But Cammie is very . . . easy. Not quick to be annoyed, not seriously. And the woman treated her like a child."

"She's not a child," Yaz said, and in spite of herself heard the note of sorrow in her voice. Valentina cocked her head in question, and Yaz sighed. "She's young. I wish she could enjoy it, that's all."

"When I was Cammie's age, I was already in the fight, too," Valentina said. "And I wanted nothing better than to be there. There was no time, no place to be a child."

"And I was a cadet pilot," Yaz admitted. She shook her head. "That doesn't mean it's right."

"Oh, certainly." Valentina gave her crooked smile. "And if we are talking about right, then probably neither one of us should have been where we were, either. But I am talking about what is necessary."

Yaz nodded, sighing. "We should see if we're needed."

De Soto Base's security team had any number of observation suites, Cammie discovered, and an equal variety of interrogation rooms. The one where they'd taken Aris was more austere than the ones where the refugees were debriefed—those had sofas and comfortable-looking armchairs and no central table—but it was still a lot more comfortable than she thought the woman deserved. There was the table and chairs, a wall screen, and a side table with a coffee machine; the walls were painted a soothing cream, and the floor was covered in the same all-weather carpet as the barracks room. The main sign that the Vanguard was taking this seriously was the armed guard at the door, and Cammie looked over her shoulder at Lieutenant Herrera.

"So when are they going to get started, then?"

"Major Rountree and Lieutenant Chase are putting together a few questions," Herrera said. He nodded to another screen, where Rountree and Chase's avatar were conferring over a tablet. "That was nice work, putting the pieces together like that."

"Were you able to confirm that the attack came from inside the base?" Cammie asked.

Herrera nodded again. "Yeah. You were right. The incursion was spoofed—and a very neat job they did of it. I don't know if I'd have spotted it if you hadn't told me. We're generally looking for attacks from outside, not from within." He paused. "And the refugees shouldn't have been able to access the main systems; they're supposed to be restricted to an internal network and the Ether, but the system's never been tested before. We're going to have to rebuild it."

"Yeah." Cammie felt her ears twitch as Chase waved away his displays, and Rountree picked up her tablet. "All right. Here we go."

In the screen, Chase turned, looking up into the camera. "Cammie. Can you hear me?"

"Loud and clear," Cammie called. "Can you hear me?"

"Perfectly," Chase said, and Rountree nodded. "Remember the plan. If you spot her lying about technical things—well, about anything—let us know. And if you see questions we should ask, pass them along."

Cammie bounced in her seat, then made herself sit still. "Got it. We're ready to go."

"Right," Rountree said. "Let's get on with it."

They disappeared from the screen, appeared a moment later on the main screen as they walked into the room where Aris waited. She rose to her feet as the door opened.

"Hey, can you tell me what's going on? I just got dragged out of the mess hall like I was under arrest, and nobody will tell me what I'm supposed to have done—"

"We have some questions for you, Ms. Webb," Rountree said. "Shouldn't take long."

"I've already answered a lot of questions." Aris attempted a smile. "I've told you everything I know."

"Shouldn't take long," Rountree said again. "Please, sit down."

Aris hesitated, but did as she was told. Rountree seated herself opposite the woman and pulled out her tablet, deliberately taking her time to swipe through the pages. Cammie thought Aris looked nervous, watching her clasp her hands under the table, but her voice sounded perfectly normal.

"Really, if there's anything more, I'd be glad to help you."

"We appreciate that," Rountree said. She started on a round of questions, mostly ones that Cammie was sure Aris had already answered, and Cammie glanced down at her console instead.

"You don't have, like, a lie detector?"

Herrera gave her an apologetic smile. "The Union trains

its people to beat them, so mostly we don't bother. I've got the pickups running, but I'm not getting anything useful."

He detached a screen and slid it in her direction. It showed Aris in silhouette, various monitors flickering along the bottom of the screen, vertical columns of green and gold that rose and fell like the stacks of an audio monitor. Cammie eyed them dubiously. "I'm guessing green means good?"

"Green means no stress," Herrera answered. "But, as I said, the Union trains its agents to cover stress with biofeedback."

"Right."

"I've told you all this before," Aris said. She didn't even sound annoyed, just as though she was pointing out something obvious.

"We'd like to go over it again," Chase said.

Aris shrugged. "Sure. Whatever you want."

"What I'd like," Cammie said, "is to connect her to the internal attack."

"Me, too," Herrera said. "I'm still working on it, but here's what I've got so far." He copied another screen, and passed it across. "I haven't been able to identify the original user, or the node they used."

Cammie expanded the screen, digging down into the traffic logs laid out before her. "Okay, yeah, I see where she spoofed it—"

"Neat work."

Cammie nodded. "But she left some threads hanging."

"If it was her," Herrera said scrupulously. "But I think

you're right, it has to be someone hiding among the refugees. Any of our people would have used shortcuts."

"Unless they wanted you to think it was a refugee," Cammie said reluctantly, then shook her head. "No, that doesn't make sense. The shortcuts would be easier to hide in the regular traffic."

"Exactly." Herrera paused. "Hey, look at this."

A new packet bloomed on her screen, and Cammie couldn't hide a grin. "Is that what she used to get in?"

"Looks like it to me. Standard unit, but definitely civilian make."

Cammie reached for the file that gave the list of the refugees' belongings, and she slumped as it unscrolled before her eyes. "Most of them have devices that run that OS. Or the mailbox itself."

"Yeah." Herrera nodded.

Cammie frowned at the screen, Aris's voice echoing from the speaker.

"I told you, Jake was the one who knew about that project."

"Can you be a bit more specific about what he said?" Rountree asked.

"The phrase he used was 'stolen brains.'" Aris shrugged. "I don't know what he meant."

"If you had to guess?" Chase asked, with a smile.

An answering smile flickered over Aris's face. "I guess I thought maybe he was talking about scientists? There was some story about some of them being snatched across the Eighty-Eighth a few months back."

Cammie suppressed the desire to roll her eyes, though she knew her ears were twitching, and turned her attention back to the screen. Aris wasn't going to tell them anything useful, not if she could help it; it was up to Cammie to find some key, some missed bit of data, that would let them prove her guilt and maybe compel her to tell the truth.

She turned back to the list of belongings, flipping through the screens until she found the photos of Aris's gear. The mini-pac was standard, the sort of thing that everyone had had before the Union attacked New York; a note at the bottom of the screen said that Security had done a forensic scan and picked up nothing. She drew out that file, expanding the ghostly image until she could see the shapes of chips and clips and tiny wires. If she had the actual device, it would be easy to dissect it, but she might be able to get some information out of the scans.

She frowned at the image, tracing familiar pathways, isolating internal systems. Everything looked normal—except, no, that wasn't the standard chip, and that certainly wasn't the usual I/O port. "Extra pins," she said, and spun the image so that Herrera could see. "And what do you think those are good for?"

"Lockpicks," Herrera answered instantly, drawing up his own screen. "I'm sending someone to collect that right away."

"Yeah." Cammie reached for her board, switching to the

gen:LOCK network. *Chase. I've got something. Her tablet, her mini-pac, it's got nonstandard rigging.*

Copy that. In the screen, she saw Chase put his finger to his ear, as though accessing an earbud. Rountree flicked him a glance, but finished her question, and Aris sighed.

"I wish I could help you, I really do. I just don't know."

"You're a technician?" Chase asked, and for the first time several of the columns showed yellow tips.

"I work in a factory."

"Doing what, exactly?"

Again the flicker of yellow. "Installing fixed-system chip sets."

"So you have a working knowledge of computer systems," Rountree said.

"Not on your side of the Eighty-Eighth," Aris answered, and Cammie thought the hint of bitterness in her tone was probably real.

"How about the Ether?" Chase asked.

"We haven't had Ether access since New York," Aris answered. "I was on the other night, for the hurricane party. Things have changed."

Cammie kept prying at the images, expanding one section as far as it would go, separating the levels of screen and chips to get a better look at each one. *Definitely not standard*, she said in Chase's ear. *The chips are overpowered, and . . . they look like our hardware, but I don't think they actually are.*

In the screen, Chase nodded. "You wouldn't mind if we

took another look at your gear, then," he said, to Aris, who shrugged one shoulder.

"Sure, but I don't have it with me—"

"You don't carry your tablet?" Rountree asked, mildly enough, but the readouts below Aris's image flickered yellow again.

"Oh, you want my tablet? Yeah, I've got that." Aris started to reach for her pocket, then stopped, fingers on the tab of the zipper. "You want it now?"

"Please," Rountree said.

"Sure." Aris fumbled with the zipper one-handed, frowning as though it was stuck, and pushed back her chair to work at it with both hands. Then she surged to her feet, the tab coming apart in her hands to release a cloud of purple smoke.

"Chase!" Cammie screamed, and in the screen Chase's avatar blinked out, to reappear behind Aris.

"Don't you dare," Aris said, "or I'll smoke the major."

Chase stepped back, lifting his hands, and the nanites coiled around Aris's shoulders, rising above her head like a cobra's hood.

"Nice guess," Aris said. "But now you're going to let me walk to the hangar and fly out of here, or I'll set this loose in your systems, and that'll bring down this base."

"You'll be dead if you do," Rountree said. She had a pistol in her left hand, but was holding it flat against her thigh, as though that could win her the chance at a shot.

"The Union doesn't care," Aris answered. "They'll probably give me a posthumous medal and send a bonus to my mother. Now. Tell them to let me out."

Rountree moved toward the door, lifting her hands in surrender. "Herrera. Unlock the door."

"Yes, Major." Herrera's voice was tight and controlled as he shifted boards. "The door is unlocked." His hands were busy on a second set of controls, Cammie saw, spreading the alarm silently and clearing Vanguard staff and civilians out of the corridors. Security doors slid shut, closing off sections of the base, and a light began to flash, warning that the environmental systems had shut down. That was to contain the nanites, Cammie knew, and felt her throat tighten.

"Open the door," Aris said.

Rountree complied, pulling it back, and Aris stepped cautiously around the table, the nanites swirling about her in a cloud darker than the worst of the hurricane.

Aris raised her voice. "I'm coming out! Anyone attacks me, I loose the smoke."

There was no answer, and she slipped out of the room.

"Armor Team Two to corridor Juliet Seven," Herrera said quietly, and Cammie saw Rountree shake her head. In the same moment, another voice came from the speakers.

"Negative, we have civilians in Juliet Seven—"

"Security, Armor Team Three. We're at November Nine, heading for the hangar—"

Cammie closed her ears to all of that and let herself slide

into the security monitors. Aris was easy to find, a cloud of static flashing from camera to camera, weaving through the corridors as though she could see Rountree's security. "Migas! Caliban! Lock down *Renegade,* Union smoke coming your way—"

"On it," Migas said, and she felt the gen:LOCK network activate.

Cammie. Hangar controls. That was Chase's voice, mixing in to the hangar.

On them. Cammie overrode local security without thinking, accessing the base's systems the way she would access the Ether. *Where's the rest of us?*

Barracks, Kazu answered. *Trying to get through.*

Mess hall, Yaz came in, and Valentina added an epithet that Cammie's systems didn't translate. *We are trying to persuade them to let us out—*

There wasn't time. Aris was in the main corridor now, still protected by her nanite cloud. Base Security hung back, not daring to get too close, and as Cammie watched, Aris sent a tendril of the smoke into the controls of a locked door, then wrenched it open. A young woman in a Vanguard uniform stumbled out, pistol drawn, and Aris waved her hand. The smoke circled the Vanguard woman, and she froze. Aris said something, and the other woman dropped her pistol and raised her hands. The smoke pressed closer, and she flattened herself against the wall, her eyes closing, bracing herself for the attack. Cammie ran her hands over the control surfaces, searching for something, anything, that might stop them, and then Aris laughed and ducked through the door, the smoke whisking behind her.

Cammie leaped after her, flowing through the base's systems, flashing from node to node as the security cameras tracked Aris's progress. She could feel Herrera working with her, dropping firewalls for her, tagging her as safe, and she leaped ahead, reaching into the hangar's automation just as the door rolled back.

"Smoke! Evacuate, evacuate—"

Someone tried to get off a shot, but Aris waved her hand, and a swirl of smoke wrapped around his head, dropping him in his tracks. A moment later, it rejoined the rest of the cloud, leaving a heap of uniform pieces and gear, one boot pointing forlornly toward the door.

Tell me what to do, Chase said. *I'm in, I can stop her—*

No! Cammie could see it all, see what would happen, how it would go wrong, but there was no time to explain. *Let her take a ship—*

What?!

Let her take it, let her get in. Cammie's hands moved over the controls, unlocking security on the nearest Vanguard fighter, inserting her own program into its internal systems.

"Wait," Herrera exclaimed, his voice distant, but she ignored him, marshaling the autosystems under her hands.

You're sure, Cammie? Chase asked. *I can take her—*

The smoke will get loose, Cammie said. *Can't risk it.*

Aris was moving more slowly now, scanning the ships lined up to either side, the smoke spreading out as though she was using it to check for something. Cammie risked releasing the last lock on the nearest fighter, and Aris's head snapped around. She started for the fighter, the smoke roiled ahead of her to infiltrate the systems and lift the canopy.

Cammie, Chase said again.

Cammie ignored him, watching Aris swing herself up into the cockpit, the smoke tucking itself in around her. She could see the nanites infiltrating the fighter's systems, and shut down all connections to the outside. Aris's head moved from side to side as she scanned the controls and began flipping switches to start the engines. The fans whined up to speed, and the fighter began to lift. Aris's voice cracked through the speakers. "Open the hangar doors, or I'll blast them open."

The fighter was six feet off the ground now, rotating to line up its missiles with the armored door.

"Open the doors!"

Now. Cammie activated her program. It was a simple thing, designed to do one thing: flip the kill switch on every system it could reach. She felt it fire, saw lights flash wildly inside the canopy, the smoke swirling as though it was trying to fight its way out, and then all the boards went dead. The engines cut out, and the fighter slipped sideways. It landed on the edge of its starboard wing, the metal crumpling, bounced, and crashed hard again, skidding a few yards over the hangar floor in a screech of metal.

Cammie switched to external speakers. "Don't touch it! Don't let the smoke out!"

Inside the fighter, Aris was banging on the canopy, trying to force it open. All around her, tendrils of smoke stabbed at the consoles, and recoiled, unable to find an active circuit.

She'll blow the hatch, Chase said. *There's an eject system—*

Nope. Cammie checked her board, saw everything steady red. *I locked that down, too.*

As if it had heard her, the smoke suddenly thickened, pulling back on itself like a first clenching. Aris looked up, her eyes suddenly wide and frightened, mouth opening as though to shout, and a strand of smoke drove into her throat. She fell backward, clawing at herself, and the nanites closed in around her.

"Suicide switch," Herrera said blankly.

They've got her, Chase said. *Damn.*

Cammie swallowed hard. It wasn't that she hadn't seen people killed before; she'd even seen people destroyed by Union nanites, but she hadn't expected them to turn on Aris so quickly. *What do we do now? The smoke's still in there.*

And very much alive. She could see it roiling behind the canopy, felt it pressing against the edges of her firewalls, trying to break through.

Self-destruct, Chase said. *That'll kill it.*

Right. Cammie reached into the system, found the pulsing node that was the self-destruct circuit, and isolated it. *I can—I've got it.*

"Clear the bay!" Chase's voice echoed from the speakers. "Clear hangar bay Bravo One! Clear the bay!" On the gen:LOCK network, he added, *Now, Cammie!*

Cammie activated the circuit. Light flared inside the fighter's canopy, hot white and blinding, turning instantly to rolling flame. She felt rather than heard the *crump* of the explosion, and the fighter came apart at the seams, leaking flame and black smoke that showed none of the dark purple glitter of the nanites. *Migas! Are you all right?*

Everything's fine. Migas's answer was reassuringly prompt. *Running diagnostics now, but she didn't even try to get into* Renegade.

Good. Cammie pulled back from the Vanguard systems, newly aware of the room around her.

"Seal Hangar Bravo One," Herrera was saying. "Repeat, hard seal, Hangar Bravo One. Hazmat Teams Two and Three, possible Union nanite contamination, Hangar Bravo One."

"We must have gotten them," Cammie said, and flushed as she realized she'd spoken aloud.

"High explosives have worked before," Herrera said. "But better safe than sorry."

"Yeah." Cammie shivered, thinking about the smoke, about the attack on the Anvil and a different self-destruct.

"Good call," Herrera said. "We totally missed her."

Cammie dragged her thoughts away from Dr. Weller. "The Union gave her good cover. And I had some connections you didn't."

"It's a good thing you did," Herrera said.

Cammie finished untangling herself from the base's systems, expecting any minute to be asked exactly how she'd managed to infiltrate them so thoroughly, but to her relief, Rountree and her staff were too busy separating the rest of the refugees from Tallahassee and taking them away for further questioning.

"Not that we'll find anything if you're right," Rountree said, mixing in from outside the holding cells, "but it's better to be sure."

"Agreed," Chase said. "Any chance we could look over her belongings? Especially that mini-pac."

Cammie nodded. "Yeah. I'd like to see what they did."

"We've taken everything we could identify as hers to a sealed lab," Rountree answered. "Just in case anything else had smoke in it. But you're welcome to take a look."

"Thanks," Chase said, and looked at Cammie. "Okay?"

"Yeah." She nodded again, more vigorously this time. "Yeah, that'd be good."

The base was still on high alert, live guard supplementing the security systems at the main junctions, doors kept closed and sealed until they had passed through. They were waved through, however, and finally reached a laboratory wing. One of the rooms was closed and sealed, hazard lights flashing above the door, and there was an armed guard outside as well. He came to attention as they approached.

"Lieutenant. The major said you wanted to take a look at what we found."

"Thanks."

"It's a double door," the guard went on, fingers busy on the control box that hung at his belt. "Air-lock style. I'll let you in and seal the door. The inner door won't open until the seal is tight."

"Got it," Chase said.

Cammie followed him into the lock, shivering as the door closed behind her. She understood the reasons for the precautions, but she couldn't say she liked them. Chase gave her a quick glance.

"You okay?"

"Yeah."

"You sure?"

"Really."

"All right." Chase still sounded doubtful, but the inner door slid back, cutting off anything else he might have said. Lights flashed on in the inner room, revealing a console against one wall, and a table in the center with a scatter of things on it. There was a pullover sweater, a pouch with a toothbrush spilling out of it, a crumpled pile of T-shirts and underwear, a bundle of cables, a battery pack, and a tablet. Cammie looked away from them, unaccountably embarrassed, and turned her attention to the console.

"No external connections," she announced, and Chase nodded.

"Good. Let's see what we've got."

Cammie nodded, still looking at the console, and Chase cleared his throat.

"That means you'll have to go through things."

"Oh. Right, yeah, sorry." Cammie turned her attention to the table and began sorting through the clothes. It was easy to get clothes that were rigged for hackers, either with internal wiring or hidden pockets and chargers, or even with RFID readers built into the cuffs or pockets, but everything here was perfectly vanilla. Maybe device-wear was harder to find in the Union. Cammie felt carefully along the seams and in the pockets, looking for spaces where something might have been removed, but there was nothing at all.

"Huh."

"Find something?" Chase asked.

Cammie shook her head. "No, and that's a bit odd. Given how she was getting into our systems, I'd have expected her to have at least some backup tools in her pockets. And it doesn't feel like she's ripped anything out."

Chase nodded. "Keep looking."

"Yeah." Cammie sorted through the rest of Aris's belongings. The pouch with the toothbrush held nothing but toiletries and a bottle of cheap over-the-counter painkillers.

"Do you think there might be another button in there?" Chase asked.

It was a logical place to hide another nanite source, and Cammie poured them all out onto the table's spotless surface.

They were little disks the size of a fingernail, and they all looked perfectly ordinary. She poked at them dubiously, but there were no odd-size pills, or pills with seams, or anything else that looked like it might conceal more smoke. "It's not a bad idea," she said, "but I'm not seeing anything. I'll leave them for the major, though."

"Good idea."

She swept the pills back into their bottle and set them aside, then turned her attention to the electronics. Those, at least, she knew. The bundle of cables was very similar to the one she kept for herself, the usual range of types and sizes, enough to access the Ether and most common systems. There was a needle tap, bigger than the ones she was used to seeing and she set it aside. "I don't know if that's to Union standard or if it's an industrial cable, but it's unusual."

"Okay."

She picked up the tablet next, unsurprised to find it a little heavier than it should be. The screen was retina-locked, and Chase sighed.

"Well, that's not going to be an option."

Cammie winced, thinking about why, and made herself answer calmly. "There's probably a password backup. Let me see if I can hack it." She turned to the console, wishing she had her own tool kit, but Herrera or someone had stocked the stand-alone machine with excellent programs. She selected a cable, connected the tablet, and turned the program loose.

"How long will that take?" Chase asked.

"Depends. A couple of hours, maybe more." Cammie shrugged. "We already know the chips are wrong, we can take it apart later. I'm more interested in this battery pack."

"Oh, yeah?"

"That's always a nice place to hide things," Cammie answered. She weighed the battery carefully in her hand. "And this one feels light. The tablet was heavy. Do you see any screwdrivers around here?"

"Looks like there's a kit over there," Chase said, pointing.

Cammie collected it and came back to the table, turning the battery over to find the access plate. She unfastened the tiny screws, setting them neatly to one side, then pried off the plate. A battery filled most of the space, complete with warning stickers, and a tangle of wires connected it to the plate that held the ports. She unfastened those, lifting away the ports—all normal—and then loosened the straps that held the battery itself. "Ah. Got it."

"Got what?" Chase drifted closer.

"That's not a battery," Cammie said. "It's data storage. Oh, it's nicely made, it's even got a chip here to spoof the scanners, but . . . definitely storage. If she got anything, it would be on here. Or maybe it's where she kept her tool kit; I don't know yet." Her hands were busy as she spoke, cracking the case and lifting out the various components. "See, there's the chip, and that's the actual data block."

"That looks like proof to me," Chase said.

"Oh, yeah." Cammie smiled. "I don't know what's on

there, and I sure wouldn't take it out of this room, but I'd say this proves that Aris Webb was a Union agent." She stopped, the pleasure going out of her as she remembered the nanites turning on Aris, the tendril of smoke diving into her open mouth before the fireball obliterated the cockpit. *Her* fireball, the one that she'd triggered. "Though we've pretty much got all the proof we needed already."

"Yeah." Chase nodded. "That wasn't a pretty sight."

Cammie shuddered. "No. But I'm fine. Really."

"You don't have to be," Chase said.

"I don't like seeing people blown up," Cammie said, trying to make a joke of it, but Chase nodded, unsmiling.

"Me neither. That was ugly."

Cammie hesitated. "Joe—Captain Herrera—said it was some kind of suicide switch. I just . . . I guess I didn't figure her for that type, somehow."

"The Union might have programmed the smoke to kill her rather than let her be captured," Chase said.

"Yeah." Cammie shivered. "Do you think that means she could have told us more?"

"Maybe. Or maybe the Union was just being thorough."

"Ugh." Cammie grimaced.

"Not nice." Chase gestured to the scattered components. "Do you think there's likely to be anything useful on those?"

"It's possible," Cammie answered, grateful for the change of subject. "It's worth taking a look." She glanced at the tablet. "And whatever's on that, too."

"I'd like you to leave that to Major Rountree," Chase said. "I want you to look over the Holons. Just in case."

"Migas said everything was all right," Cammie said. "Look, I can handle this—"

"I know you can," Chase said. "Major Rountree knows you can, or you wouldn't be in here in the first place. But our first responsibility is to gen:LOCK. I think you're right: We were lured here, and that means this Webb woman was supposed to get into the Holons. Migas and Caliban are good, but . . . you're better."

That was unexpectedly gratifying. Cammie blinked, feeling warmth spread through her body—blushing, she guessed. But also: She'd *earned* that, and she was proud of it. "All right," she said, and let Chase signal for the guard to let them out.

Firefighters had doused the wreck of the fighter in smothering foam, and now a mix of maintenance and security were busy clearing away the wreckage. Cammie averted her eyes as they passed it, and Chase said carefully, "There's nothing left."

"I'm not sure that makes it better." She glanced sideways to see Chase's wry smile.

"I'm not sure you're wrong." He paused as one of the security technicians detached herself from the group and came to join them. "Yes?"

"Lieutenant." The technician just barely stopped herself from saluting. "Just wanted to let you know that Ms. MacCloud completely destroyed the smoke. We're clean."

"That's good news," Chase said. Cammie nodded, though she hadn't expected anything else. If any of the nanites had survived, they'd be in the middle of a pitched battle right now.

Renegade was far enough away from the fighter line that it stood untouched, though Migas still had all the hatches closed tight. As they approached, however, the side hatch opened, the stairs unfurling, and Migas waved from the opening.

"Hey. That was exciting."

"Just a bit," Chase answered. "Everything okay here?"

"Still fine," Migas answered, and stood aside to let them climb aboard. "Caliban says someone tried to break in a couple of times, but they didn't get past the firewalls."

"There have been no more attempts since Aris Webb was killed," Caliban said, looming up out of the Holon compartment.

"That's a good thing," Chase said. "Isn't it?"

"If it had been me, I'd've left something running automatically," Cammie said. "But there are risks involved with that, too, so maybe she didn't."

"Check things out," Chase said, "and make sure that our security is all locked down."

"I assure you everything is in place," Caliban said.

"I'd like another set of eyes on the problem," Chase said, in a tone that brooked no argument, and Caliban sighed heavily.

Cammie ignored him and seated herself cross-legged at her usual console. She ran her hands over the controls, waking the various systems, then sorted the many layers of active and passive security into their own windows. It was fiddling, familiar work, the sort of thing she'd done a hundred times while she was freelancing for both sides of the law. She settled quickly into the rhythm of it, running the diagnostics once again, pulling up each of the layered firewalls to investigate the checksums and search for any other signs of tampering. In general, everything looked good, but as she dug further, she found a missed check, and as she followed that thread, she found a spot where the firewall might have been breached.

"I saw that," Caliban said. "I didn't see any indication that there was penetration."

"I don't, either," Cammie said, but called up a secondary screen anyway. The affected system was one of the ones that linked *Renegade* to the Holons' operating systems, and she pulled up another window. "But we ought to check anyway."

"What have you got?" Chase asked.

"Something tried to hack the Holons' OS," she answered. "Migas, did you check them out?"

"I checked the main systems," Migas answered, "and so did Cal. We didn't see any signs of infection."

"What about through the comm interface with *Renegade*?"

"I didn't check that," Migas admitted. "Want me to start diagnostics?"

"Yeah." Cammie stared at her screen, wondering if she was overreacting. Caliban hadn't seen any sign that the attack had gotten through, and she didn't, either, but it was better to be sure, given everything else that had gone on. "Please."

"Is this a problem?" Chase asked.

Cammie leaned back, minimizing her screens. "I don't know yet. I don't think so . . . Caliban didn't find anything, but I'd like to be sure." She tapped her fingers on the edge of the console, and called up another set of diagnostics. "I'd better check out gen:LOCK, too."

Caliban shifted suddenly, and the hatch slid back, allowing the rest of the team to climb into the cabin.

"So," Kazu said. "You shut her down properly, Cammie. Good job."

"It was," Yaz said. She looked at Chase. "We couldn't get out of the mess hall in time to do anything. We need to make contingency plans for next time."

"Hopefully, we won't be dealing with anything like this in the near future," Chase said. "But I take your point."

Valentina looked from Migas to Cammie, frowning at the screens surrounding both of them. "Has there been a problem here?"

"Not so far," Migas answered. "Unless . . . did you find something, Cammie?"

"The diagnostics are still running," Cammie answered. "Nothing so far."

"Great news!" Kazu flung himself into his favorite chair,

cocking one leg over the arm. "And the storm's just about over, so we should be getting out of here soon, right?"

"Haven't looked at the weather in a while," Chase admitted. "Yaz, have you been keeping track?"

"I'll check," Yaz answered, but before she could reach for a screen, lights flashed in the hangar, a klaxon blaring.

"Attention, attention! Scramble Interceptor Wing One, Interceptor Wing Two, Strider Teams One, Two, and Five. Defense Condition Red. Union forces inbound. This is not a drill. Repeat, Defense Condition Red. This is not a drill."

11

"CALIBAN!" CHASE SAID. "Patch me through to Colonel Varden—"

Before he could finish the sentence, a patch of static appeared, then opened to reveal Varden, the lights of a battle map flashing behind him. "Lieutenant. We have a significant Union force inbound. I'm requesting gen:LOCK assistance."

Chase looked at Cammie, who looked at her screens. "Diagnostics are still running. I can't promise we're clean—"

In the same moment, Caliban said, "You mustn't risk the Holons. That's what the Union is after."

"We don't know that," Chase said.

"It's the only logical inference," Caliban said. "Keeping the gen:LOCK technology out of Union hands is our first priority."

"What's the situation?" Chase said to Varden, who raised a hand to allow a tactical map to unfold.

"We picked them up on our side of the river," Varden said. "Not sure how they got across, given the flooding, but they did.

And they got past our ground alarms and the outer drone patrols—we don't yet know how, but we'll worry about that later."

Aris? Cammie wondered. Could she have burrowed further into the base's security systems? Her tool kit didn't look like she was prepared for that, though. Varden was still talking, and she dragged her attention back to him.

"I've got more drones out, but I'm not sure it matters at this point. We make it two detachments of Spider Tanks, plus air cover. They're definitely heading for us: They've bypassed some of our fortified settlements where they've attacked before. Currently, they're on the old highway and making good time, but they'll slow down once they have to move cross-country." Lights rippled across the map as he spoke, sketching out the movements. "We're hoping to intercept them here, before they enter the forest."

"How's the weather?" Kazu asked.

"Still windy and raining, but the winds have dropped enough to let us get fighters up," Varden answered. "Of course, that means they've got air support, too."

"Flooding?" Chase frowned at the map.

"Unknown," Varden said. "We've marked areas that usually flood—" A set of orange patches flared on the map and then faded back into the background. "But we don't have confirmation. We had reconnaissance drones out, but the fighters have already picked off several of them."

"Does this mean they know where the base is?" Yaz asked.

"More important," Valentina said, "did they know that before?"

"To answer Ms. Romanyszyn, we don't know," Varden said. "The Union knew our general position, but it looks as though they have a lock on us now. Whether that's thanks to their spy . . ." He shrugged. "Your guess is as good as mine. I don't think it matters at this point."

"They are after the Holons," Caliban said again. "Clearly, this entire operation—the mention of stolen brains, the timing, everything—was intended to lure gen:LOCK into a position where they had a chance to capture one of the machines. We can't risk that."

"I hate to say it," Cammie said, "but Cal's right. That's the only thing that makes sense."

"They couldn't have relied on the weather," Kazu said.

"We all knew this storm was building," Yaz said.

Cammie checked her screens again, watching the codes flicker past as the diagnostics did their work, then looked at Chase. Varden was right, gen:LOCK would make all the difference; the problem was, Caliban was also right. The only thing that made sense was if this was an attempt to capture a Holon. The Union had tried that before, and Nemesis had proven that they could make terrible and effective use of anything they did capture.

"It's just Spider Tanks with air cover?" Chase asked.

"That's all we've seen," Varden answered.

Chase put his hand to the back of his neck. "We can

handle that. Colonel, we're still checking things out after the incursion, but as soon as we're sure we're clean, we'll back you up."

"Thanks." Varden nodded. "Let me know when you're certain."

"Will do, Colonel," Chase answered, and Vaden's image winked out. "Cammie?"

"So far, so good." She adjusted the screen as though that would make the program run faster. Another bar turned from gold to green, but there were still half a dozen more to go.

"This is a terrible idea," Caliban said. "We know this is what the Union wants. They are attacking to draw us out. We shouldn't give them what they want."

"If we don't appear," Valentina said, "they will start attacking civilian communities."

Yaz nodded, her face somber. "Standard tactics."

"Yep," Chase said. "Not to mention that we can handle tanks a lot better than the Striders can. And we owe the colonel any help we can give him. If we hit them hard now, we'll save a lot of trouble down the road."

"I still don't approve," Caliban muttered, but his voice was low enough that Chase could pretend not to hear.

Cammie focused on her screens, trying not to think about what would happen if they didn't join the attack. A lot of towns close to the border had been abandoned in the aftermath of the Union victories, but there were still a few that clung stubbornly to their roots. Some of them had been for-tified, but none of them was in any shape to stand against a full-on Union assault.

Caliban was right, this was the entire purpose of the Union plan, but she couldn't see any way out of the trap. The last of the bars flipped to green, and she scrolled quickly through the results. "Everything checks out. I don't see any problems with the Holons. We should be all right."

"Let's go," Chase said.

Cammie gave her screens a final look, wondering if she'd missed anything. The diagnostics weren't perfect; she had programs in her own tool kit that were designed to spoil or evade those checks. But the fact was, she couldn't see any-thing to indicate that the hack had gotten past the firewall. At some point, she had to trust her own system. She shut down the last screen and followed the others into the next compartment. They were all in their pods before her, and she hurried to join them, Nugget hopping out of the pod and onto Caliban's shoulder. Caliban looked down at her, metal head tilted to one side, and she made herself nod. "I'm ready," she said, and hoped it was true.

It was still raining as Kazu released the wheels in his Holon's feet and ducked out of the hangar, but at least the punishing wind was gone. He fell in behind Yaz, calling up internal guidance as they crossed the base perimeter to steer him toward the fighting. Fifty yards ahead, Chase spread wings and leaped into the air. A moment later, Yaz followed, yellow metal vivid against the dark sky, and Kazu lifted his hand.

"This way." He pointed down the nearest road that seemed to be going in the right direction, and slid forward, feeling pistons engage to push him to greater speed. Val and Cammie followed, the sound of their wheels loud even over the noise of his own Holon. He checked his displays, locating the Vanguard forces and the oncoming Union Spider Tanks, and upped his speed again, reveling in the feeling of the Holon surrounding him.

"Do we have a plan?" Val's voice sounded in his ears. "Or should we perhaps be a little more cautious?"

Kazu wanted to roll his eyes, but Chase spoke first. "Interceptors are engaging Union air support. Yaz and I are going in. Kazu, see if you can break the line of Spider Tanks, make some gaps for the Striders to work with. Val, Cammie, cover him."

About time, Kazu thought. Finally, he could take down some of the Union—a nice, simple job, no smoke, no computers, nothing but machine against machine. It was time they got to do that.

"I will hang back at the tree line to start, and cover you," Val said. "Cammie, see what you can do when we get there."

"My drones can handle the weather," Cammie answered.

Kazu closed his mind to everything but the need for

speed, the rush of wheels and the thrust of legs against the pavement. It wasn't in great shape, but he'd had plenty of practice on uneven surfaces. He could handle it. Then the road bent to the left, and he saw a break in the pavement, water frothing nearly to the top of the bank, a sixteen-foot gap where a bridge had been. He gathered himself without thinking, crouched, and leaped, and landed easily on the far side without losing stride. Behind him, he saw Val slow slightly, his cape flaring to balance him. He landed safely, but paused for Cammie. Cammie didn't slow but missed a step and shrieked a curse as she jumped, arms flailing. Val caught her elbow, steadying her, and Cammie straightened.

"For f-freak's sake!"

"You still owe for the first one," Val said, picking up speed again.

"S-stupid," Cammie said. "That was a stupid idea."

Kazu grinned to himself, focusing on the road before them. Overhead, in the distance, he saw the flash of rocket fire, and then the glow of Yaz's heat beams. The Vanguard chatter flowed past him, familiar and currently unimportant; he gave it just enough attention to know where the Union Spider Tanks were massing, and pumped his arms to get even better speed.

He burst out of the trees into what had obviously once been farmland, now left fallow. The Spider Tanks were advancing in a wedge formation, firing into the trees where the Striders had taken shelter; overhead, Interceptors and Union craft wove patterns against the clouds. Chase and Yaz were up there somewhere, but that wasn't Kazu's job. He picked his spot, and let his momentum carry him into the Union line.

Two tanks immediately fired at him, shrapnel rattling off his armor. He drew his sword and sliced at the nearest one, grinning as he sheared off two of the legs. The tank tipped sideways, blocking the shot of the tank behind it, and Kazu brought his sword down on the top canopy, crushing it and knocking the tank to the ground. He stepped up onto it, a few last sparks flaring around his foot, and leaped for the next tank, swinging for its belly as it reared back to fire at him. A missile sizzled past him, narrowly missing the tank; in his rearview screen he saw another tank explode as Valentina got in a shot.

Cammie's drones were in the air, swooping and dodging Union fire as they guided her shots. He caught a glimpse of her behind a group of Striders, clearing a path for their attack, and then another Spider Tank fired at him at point-blank range. He dodged, but the explosion caught him mid-body, enough to stagger him momentarily. Instantly, Val laid down covering fire, and he straightened, swinging his sword in great sweeping arcs to clear some room to maneuver. He felt it connect, saw a Spider Tank pitch sideways, and grabbed the uplifted leg to swing the tank into its neighbor. The shock of impact reverberated up his arm, and he let the spin pull him around to take another shot at the next tank.

Out of the corner of his eye, he saw Cammie edging sideways, trying to lay down covering fire, and abruptly, there was movement in the woods behind her. A second, smaller detachment of Spider Tanks emerged, and Kazu missed his next shot. *Cammie! Behind you!*

The nearest Spider Tank exploded: Val's work. Kazu swung at the next tank, but his blade rebounded from the tank's armor. It pivoted, machine guns flashing, and he saw sparks, felt the impact as the shots stitched dents across his thighs and belly. He reached for the tank's front leg, swinging it into another machine. *Cammie!*

Cammie, look out! Val took up the call. *Kazu, cover her—*

Kazu started to turn, and a Spider Tank loosed a pair of missiles into his back. The armor held, but the explosion overbalanced him, sent him stumbling to one knee. Instantly, a pair of Spider Tanks charged him, trying to bowl him over. He turned his shoulder to take the first rush on his pauldron, and heaved himself upright as the second tank fired another missile at point-blank range. It hit just below the knee, and warning lights flared across his vision. He slashed with his sword, knocking the tank aside, but two more were closing in. *I can't; I'm fully engaged here—*

He managed to wrench his head around, hoping Val would be free to make a move, but he was falling back under the combined assault of Spider Tanks and aircraft. For the moment, at least, Cammie was on her own.

Cammie heard the warning, and swung around, pistol clutched in both hands, to see a dozen Spider Tanks rushing at her, machine guns blazing. She felt the bullets ping off her armor, called her drones to find new targets among the onrushing tanks. A blast from Val's heavy rifle ripped past her, knocking a tank off its legs and into the path of another, nearly tipping it over. Cammie's drones picked up the weakness, and she poured fire into the second tank. It collapsed, spewing thick smoke, and she turned to look for a new target. A Spider Tank was closing on her left, and she aimed at it, the drones cycling, feeding data to her gun, but the trigger stuck as she pulled it. She pulled again, harder, and the pistol fired, but her aim was off, and the tank sidled closer, while another fired a missile over its back. Cammie ducked, but the Holon didn't move with her, and the missile caught her in the shoulder, knocked her back on her heels. She flailed her arms, managed to regain her balance, but the movements were weak, and increasingly uncoordinated.

Cammie! That was Val again. *What's wrong?*

Cammie scanned her readouts, seeing nothing out of line, but it was taking all her strength to lift her pistol. *The system's slow—it's like pushing through mud.*

Get out of there, Val said. *Fall back.*

He was right. Cammie let off a last fusillade of shots, not caring if the drones aimed them accurately or not, and tried to turn back toward the Vanguard lines. There were a couple of Spider Tanks in her way, but she could push past them—if she could make herself move. Her legs were ridiculously heavy, her arms stiff and awkward, the gyros failing to balance her. Her heads-up display claimed that everything was running fine, but she could barely keep herself upright.

Something slammed into her leg just below the knee, and she looked down to see a Spider Tank grappling with her armor. *I've been hacked! I'm so stupid—this is what they were after* . . .

Fall back! Val shouted again. *Kazu, help her!*

I'm trying, Kazu answered, but the heads-up display showed him tangled among another gang of Spider Tanks.

Chase, Yaz! Val called. *Cammie's in trouble. She can't move—*

Copy that, Chase said. *We're fully engaged. Do what you can to help her.*

We'll do what we can, Val said. He fired again, a Spider Tank collapsing as the shot tore off half its legs. *Cammie, what's happening to you?*

Cammie forced herself to concentrate on her Holon, on the deceptively positive displays. *Think, Cammie. If you were going to hack a Holon . . . oh.* The pattern spun, resolved itself into a plan, obvious and elegant: If you were going to hack a Holon, you'd want to insert the virus invisibly, then lure it out into a fight and trigger the virus there. That's the only chance you'd have to grab the electronic brain, while the Holon itself was incapacitated. *They're after my eBrain,* she said aloud, and was proud that her voice didn't waver. *Again.*

Download. Chase barked the order. *Bail out. Now!*

But they'll still get the eBrain—

They'll get an empty eBrain, Chase said. *They've already got that. Go!*

Right. Cammie reached for the escape, bracing herself for the jolting drop back into her body—and nothing happened. She tried again, and a third time, but the system refused the download command. She hit the emergency escape, and nothing happened. *I can't! It won't let me!*

Kazu, Val said.

Negative, I can't get to her.

Chase, can you? Val kept firing, driving back the Spider Tanks. On her heads-up, Cammie could see the Striders trying to move in, but they were still too far back to help.

Negative, Chase said. *We're trying to break off—* There was a flash of light within the clouds, and a fighter arrowed down into the open land beyond the Union forces. Cammie's heads-up painted it as Union, but she no longer trusted her displays. *No luck so far.*

I copy. Val's voice was grim.

It was up to her, Cammie thought. No one was coming to save her, she was going to have to save herself. If she could. She'd never been able to do it before. And somewhere Nemesis was lurking—

No. Nemesis is dead. You know he's dead, she told herself. *You know what to do. You know how to sanitize an infected system, and you know where to do it.* She felt her Holon sway, and swiped ineffectually at the Spider Tank clinging to her leg. *They've hacked Mindshare,* she said aloud. *I'm going in.*

There was no answer, and she leaped for the connection before she could change her mind.

Instead of the usual flat plane and geometric shapes, she was caught in a swirling fog that obscured all the usual landmarks. She tried to brush it aside, and it dodged, then swung back to enfold her even more tightly. Her feet were still caught in the dark blue ground, as though she was stuck ankle deep in mud, but that wasn't her biggest worry. The fog was cold and fizzing against her skin, and she recognized the technique from the Ether. She reached for her tool kit, activating the defensive program she'd used before. It sparked and died, and the fog pressed closer. She shoved down panic, reminding herself she had other tools. She grabbed a pair of programs that manifested as a burst of blue flame, sheeting down her body and off again. The fog recoiled, leaving her momentarily in a bubble of clear space, but her feet were sinking deeper, the system dragging her back into the Holon's systems.

She was in the center of an irregular patch where the ground had a faint oily sheen, the barest hint of iridescence to mark the breach in Mindspace. Her feet and legs were tingling, skin crawling as though she was covered in spiders, and she realized the attacking program was using her as a bridge to hack further into the gen:LOCK systems. *That's bad. That's really bad.*

She reached for her tool kit again, sent more of the blue fire sheeting down her legs to try to free herself. It flared satisfyingly along her calves, but hit the ground and immediately dimmed, the flames fading to weak flickers. Here and there, a stronger bit of fire ate a few inches into the breach, but each of them quickly fluttered out. But she was sinking more slowly, and that bought her time.

This called for her strongest ICE. She activated it, and a web of frozen crystals spread out from her trapped legs, pressing outward. The pressure eased, and she heaved herself a few inches out of the ground. *Yes!*

Something slammed against her legs, and she blinked hard before she realized that the blow had hit her Holon, not her avatar. She swore under her breath, and reached back to check her real-world status. The image popped up instantly, floating just to the side of her vision: Her Holon was under attack, one Spider Tank jolting back as Val blasted it.

Chase! Yaz! I cannot cover both Kazu and Cammie!

We're pinned, Yaz said, and in the same moment, Chase said, *Still trying to disengage.*

Cammie stood frozen, feeling a second Spider Tank bracing itself against her Holon's hip, her feet tingling again as the virtual attack re-formed. She knew what they wanted, to pull her down so that they could rip her head off and steal her eBrain, and a black cloud with glowing red eyes filled her vision, extending four clawed hands to rip and tear—

Dead! she screamed silently. *You're dead, dead, dead!* Nemesis was dead, and she'd beaten Spider Tanks before this, she could do it—but if she dropped out of Mindshare now, there was a good chance the hacker would lock her out entirely. She couldn't risk that. She'd have to protect both selves at once, Holon and avatar, and she had no idea how . . . She loosed another wave of ICE, saw it gnaw away a few more inches of the breach, but her skin still crawled with invisible spiders. *Breathe, Cammie*, she told herself. *Breathe.*

The drones. If she slaved the Holon to them, let the drones direct fire rather than just correcting her aim . . . She reached back into the Holon. It felt clumsy, unbalanced, like trying to reach for something on a too-high shelf while balancing on a teetering step stool, and she felt the attacking code press harder against her avatar. She released more ICE, and the Holon controls coalesced around her, ghostly shapes protected by the circle of her ICE. She adjusted the drone parameters, giving them fire control, and set her weapons to their highest power.

The fog swept back, tendrils reaching out for her so like arms that she couldn't hold back a shriek. She doused herself in the blue flame, driving them back, and grabbed for the Holon controls before they faded. Only a little more, only another second . . . The drone controls were done; she switched to the targeting system, giving the drones priority, then turned them loose and dropped fully into Mindshare again. In the back of her mind, she could feel the Holon jolting into motion, firing toward the Spider Tanks clustering at her feet. It wasn't pretty, but first one, then another, fell away.

She had sunk farther into the clinging surface while she worked on the Holon, all her previous gains erased. The color was fading from her avatar, dulled by the fog, and there was nothing solid, nothing not corrupted by the attack, that she could use to lever herself free. The fog darted in again, but this time she was ready, met it with an expanding wall of fire that drove it back beyond the edge of the breach. She followed that with her best ICE, setting it to work on the code at her feet, and the crawling sensation fell away at last. The ground around her was briefly normal; she hauled herself fully into Mindshare, and leaped away from the breach and into the fog, her favorite anti-bot weapon forming in her hand. The fog recoiled as she landed, and she swung the glowing ax, shredding the fog.

It retreated farther, writhing as though it was in pain, and she swung around to attack the breach. She deployed more ICE around the perimeter, freezing the attack and solidifying the surface, then lobbed another ball of flame to clear the area. The fog darted at her, and she swung her ax, cutting off tendrils that dissolved into nothing as they fell. She could feel the balance shifting, could suddenly see clearly just what she needed to do, where to attack to reinforce the work of the ICE. She had locked it out; all she had to do now was kill what already got in.

She pulled out a second bot-destroyer, a special, felt it shift to a flaming pickax as she deployed it, chopping at the edges of the breach. The bots screamed like tearing metal, retreating, and out of the corner of her eye she saw the fog shift. It thickened, curdled, became a sudden hail of poison-yellow spheres hurtling at her from all directions. She whirled and spun, the pickax shifting to a flaming staff, but a few of the spheres broke through, and she had to douse herself in flame again to remove them. She turned back to the breach, watching her ICE weave across the weakened spot, destroying the attacking programs and restoring the dark ground. She sliced out the last section of the attacker, and impaled it with the end of the pickax, and felt the link snap at last. The fog dissolved into nothing, and she was looking at Mindshare's familiar geometry.

Clear! she called, and Chase answered instantly.

Take over your Holon!

Right. Cammie made a final scan of Mindspace. There was nothing left to the attacker, no sign that it had done any permanent damage, and she let herself slide back into her Holon.

The automatic systems were in full effect, and she felt for a second as though she was rattling inside a big tin can before she reverted control. Her drones swooped and darted, signaling targets; she took three quick shots and realized that the Spider Tanks were retreating. Chase had landed next to her, clearing the ground around them, while Yaz swooped overhead, aiming heat beams at the fleeing tanks. *We've got them on the run!*

You're okay, Chase said. *Did you deal with . . . whatever that was?*

Got it, Cammie answered. *I'll need to figure out what happened, but—I got it.*

Good. Let's clean this up.

We'll teach them not to cross the Eighty-Eighth, Kazu said. *Let's go.*

I am ready, Val said.

"Striders," Chase said. "With us."

"Negative, gen:LOCK leader." The Strider captain's voice sounded deeply tired. "We've got an emergency call behind us. Town of Joyce reports flooding everywhere; we're needed to get people out."

"We can't just let them go," Yaz said. "There's no guarantee they *will* go."

"If I send Cammie and Kazu with the rescue group," Chase said, "will you let us keep some of the Striders?"

The Strider captain moved closer, looked up through the canopy at Chase. "I can give you ten. That enough?"

"It'll have to be," Chase said. He switched to gen:LOCK. *Okay. Cammie, Kazu, go with them and help with the rescue. Watch your uptime.*

We should have plenty, Cammie said.

Just keep an eye on it, Chase said.

I should go with you, Kazu protested.

Until we have a chance to check out Cammie's Holon, I want her out of combat, and you with her just in case.

I've got it locked down, Cammie said. *For f-freak's sake!*

Also, you're our worst shot, Chase said. *And you were good with the locals before. You're most useful there, Cammie.*

It stung, but Cammie had to admit he was right. She still didn't know *how* she'd been hacked, or by whom—Aris, surely—and until she had answers, she couldn't fully trust her machine. *I know, I know. I'll be good.*

"Right," Chase said. "Striders, with me. Let's make sure these guys go home."

———————————

Cammie followed the Striders back the way they'd come, and then turned off onto a secondary road that felt soggy under her feet. The gravel surface clogged her wheels, so she switched to walking, hearing Kazu grumble behind her as he did the same. According to her maps, they were heading back toward the base. That would help conserve uptime, she thought, and ran a search for the town. It didn't look like much, a cluster of houses on the edge of a small river with patches of cultivated land surrounding it, and she switched to the Vanguard frequency.

"Hey. Any idea what we're going into?"

"Just what we told you," a woman's voice answered. "The

whole town's flooded, is what we heard, and I know they took in some refugees from up by Portis Lake on top of the folks who live there." She sounded almost apologetic. "It's real flat around here, and when we get rain like this . . ."

She didn't need to finish the sentence. *That's one thing you could say for Scotland*, Cammie thought. The hills and valleys might only be good for growing oats and sheep and stubborn people, to quote her grandmother, but it didn't flood. Not like this. At least the storm seemed to be dying. The wind had dropped since they left the base, and when she looked up, she thought she caught scraps of blue sky through the scudding clouds.

"Here we go," one of the Striders said.

Ahead, the trees opened up into a clearing, and the road turned from gravel to concrete as it swung down a slight incline toward an enormous lake. Cammie blinked, and saw that there were buildings sticking up out of the water, and people huddled on the roofs and hanging out of attic windows. A couple of flat-bottomed boats were moving sluggishly between the houses, and Cammie realized that they were having trouble fighting the current. If there was a house in the settlement that wasn't mostly underwater, she couldn't see it.

"Are there any more boats?" someone said, echoing her thoughts.

"They say that's all they have—"

"We need some way to get them back to base."

"We've got a transport en route," the woman's voice said. "ETA thirty-five minutes. We need to get the people off the roofs so they can make the pickup."

Cammie looked around, but there were no other boats or wagons or anything that she could tow into the water. "Kazu and I can carry people out," she said.

"The current's pretty strong," someone warned.

Cammie braced herself as she waded in. She could feel it tugging at her, could feel things shifting underfoot, but it wasn't as strong as the river crossing. "I'm okay."

"So am I," Kazu reported. "Where do we start?"

"The house with the red roof," the woman's voice interjected. "There's a pregnant woman and kids."

"Right." Cammie waded farther into the flooded town, the water cold on the Holon's skin. By the time she reached the house, the water was halfway up her thighs and lapping at the edges of the roof. She could hear a strange creaking, and cupped her hand at the edge of the roof, not daring to touch it for fear of knocking the whole thing off its foundation. "Hi. I'm here to help," she said, through external speakers, and immediately felt silly. It sounded like something a waiter would say—*Hi, I'm Cammie, I'll be your rescuer today.* "If you can climb down into my hand, I'll carry you back to the road."

She saw the people on the roof exchange uneasy glances. There were seven of them, the pregnant woman, an old man and woman, a shirtless, shivering boy who looked to be in

273

his teens, and three little kids. The boy had a rope tied around the two bigger children, who looked to be about six or seven, and the old man had wrapped both arms around a toddler, holding the child tight to keep her from falling into the water.

"Come on," Cammie said. "There's a rescue transport on its way, but it can't pick you up off the roof. Just climb down into my hand, and I'll take you back."

The old woman looked up at her, shading her eyes. "Milla, you go first. How many of us can you carry?"

Cammie blinked, considering. She'd carried Miranda before, and could probably have held a second person. "Two in each hand? Two adults, I mean."

"We need rope," Kazu said, sounding annoyed with himself. "For them to hang on to."

"I got rope," the teenager said. "Mike, if you'll hold the kids, I'll slide down and then you can lower them to me."

Cammie waited while the pregnant woman inched her way down the roof and stepped gingerly into the palm of the Holon's hand. She wrapped her arms around Cammie's thumb, squeezing her eyes shut as Cammie shifted position to put her other hand out for the boy. He slid down, and the old man braced himself to lower the first child to him. He made the girl sit down in the middle of Cammie's palm, and the old man lowered the second child. This time, the old man let the rope go, and the boy reeled it in, looping it around Cammie's thumb before tying the ends around the children.

"I have the others," Kazu said, and Cammie moved carefully away.

That was how they spent the next few hours, wading from house to road and back again until everyone was accounted for. As they were checking the last house—empty—a cow drifted past, eyes rolling, legs churning as it fought the current. Kazu reached out and scooped it up, then deposited it on the nearest bank. It bellowed, all shock and surprise, and a couple of the locals leaped to secure it before it could escape again. Cammie suppressed a tired giggle. She wasn't sure who sounded more surprised, the cow or Kazu. The transport was there by then, as well as a medical team, and the lieutenant in charge waved them on as soon as Kazu raised the question of uptime.

"Go on back, you've done everything you can here. We wouldn't have gotten them in so quickly without you."

"Glad to help," Cammie said, and turned to follow a Strider unit that was also headed back to the base.

While she walked, she let her mind wander. She still didn't see how the attack had evaded her and Caliban's checks—well, they'd had to hurry, but even so, she thought she'd have picked up anything Aris could have done. Her own tool kit wasn't nearly sophisticated enough to get past gen:LOCK security.

She nearly tripped over her own feet as the ramifications of that struck home. If Aris didn't have the tools to hack gen:LOCK, who did? Could there be a second traitor? If there was—that would explain how the Union got so far inside Vanguard security before they were spotted, why the perimeter alarms and drones had failed to work. And it would certainly explain how Aris had known exactly how to bypass Base Security. She didn't have to be a top hacker, or to have a top-flight tool kit; she'd been given the weak spots, and was told how to exploit them.

That meant it was someone inside the base. She frowned, considering the programs she had encountered in Mindshare. They were familiar, certainly; they used the same swarming attack that she'd experienced on the Ether, only they'd been more resistant to her dispersal programs. It had taken her strongest ICE to knock them down. It was almost as if whoever had attacked her had known what was in her tool kit.

Herrera.

She had copied her tool kit to Herrera. She had given him everything Pol Cy knew she had, everything she was supposed to work with, and those were the programs that hadn't worked . . . But he was Base Security. It couldn't be him—could it? He'd been there when Aris was questioned, been the person monitoring her vital signs for indications that she was lying, and he hadn't found any. He'd said the Union trained their agents to use biofeedback, but suppose that was a lie . . . Her mind was racing, pulling bits and pieces out of memory, and she stumbled again. Kazu caught her elbow.

Hey. Are you okay?

Fine. Kind of. Cammie shook herself. *There's nothing*

wrong with my Holon, the system's all clear, but I think I know who did it.

Chase pulled up as the last of the Union fighters ducked into the clouds ahead and disappeared. Yaz started to follow it, then saw him and circled back.

Do we follow?

We're already past the Eighty-Eighth, Chase answered. *Head back.* He switched to the Vanguard frequency. "How're things looking on the ground?"

"The last of the Spider Tanks are running for home," the Vanguard captain said. "We're getting close to the Eighty-Eighth ourselves; I think it's time we shut this down."

"Copy that," Chase answered, and tipped into a lazy bank, setting himself to home in on the distant base. *Val, how are you doing on uptime?*

We should be back at De Soto Base in plenty of time, Val answered.

Chase—Chase! Cammie's voice cut in frantically over MindShare.

Cammie, are you hurt? Chase returned. *What's wrong?*

We need to get back to base—I know who did it!

Wasn't it Aris Webb? Chase cocked his head.

No. No, she didn't have the right tools, and she didn't know how to get into gen:LOCK, and it wasn't her tools anyway. Cammie took a breath. *It's somebody who knows the*

Base Security systems—Chase, it has to be Captain Herrera.

What?

It has to be, there's no one else who fits, who has all the connections. And I gave him my tool kit; he knew exactly how to bypass the programs he saw. Oh, that was stupid!

There was a moment of silence, the network seemingly empty, before Chase answered. *You sure about this?*

As sure as I can be, Cammie responded. *I'm putting the proof in Mindshare.*

Right. Chase's tone was grim. *I'll pass this on as soon as we're finished here.*

Yaz flew in beside him. *Did I hear Cammie say something about another agent?*

Yeah. I'm looking into that. Chase pulled up the file Cammie had left in Mindshare, scrolled quickly through her hasty notes. He frowned at the name—surely their spies came from outside—but by the time he finished, he had to admit she'd made a good case. *Damn. She says it's Herrera.*

Base Security? Yaz's tone was thoughtful. *Yes, that would be worth doing.*

And has been done before, Valentina said. *In other places.*

Yeah. Chase hesitated. What if Cammie was wrong? He, gen:LOCK, would lose all credibility with Colonel Varden. Worse, what if it was a false-flag operation, one last bomb in the system designed to screw up De Soto's security? But Cammie's files were all too convincing. *I'm contacting Colonel Varden directly.*

It took him some minutes to make the connection, and to ensure that they were speaking on the most secure frequency. Chase outlined what Cammie had found, transmitted her files, then waited, a part of his mind tracking the play of wind on his wings and the power from the massive fans, until at last he heard Varden swear.

"This," the colonel began. "This is pretty damning."

"I'm afraid so," Chase said.

"We'll get on it right away," Varden said. "Check in with me as soon as you get back to base."

"Copy that," Chase said.

Chase. Yaz swung closer. *You go ahead, deal with this. Val and I will come back with the Striders.*

For a moment, Chase wanted to protest, but it made sense. Yaz and Val could certainly protect the Striders if they ran into any trouble, and he wanted to be at the base to back up Cammie's accusations. *Good idea. I'll see you back at base.*

We will see you there, Yaz answered, and spiraled gracefully down to join Val.

He trailed the Interceptors back to De Soto Base, hovering while they made their landings, then followed them into the hangar. Caliban brought his Holon into the safety of *Renegade*'s hold, and Chase pinged the base systems. "I need to see Colonel Varden."

"In my office," Varden answered, and Chase mixed in to find the desk cleared of screens and virtual models. Rountree leaned against the back of the visitor's chair, her face set and angry; Varden had both elbows on the desktop and his head in his hands, but he looked up as Chase appeared. "Well. You were right, Lieutenant."

Chase looked from one to the other. "Then Herrera was a Union agent?"

"Yes," Varden said.

"He tried to run," Rountree said. "I'm not sure exactly what tipped him off—we're still analyzing what's left of his files, but maybe it was asking him about Ms. MacCloud's tool kit?"

"It doesn't matter," Varden said gently.

"It does, sir, because we might have taken him alive." Rountree shook her head. "But we didn't. He grabbed one of the refugees' bikes and made a run for it. An Interceptor caught him at old Highway 60, took him out with a single shot. We don't believe he made any last-minute transmissions. We've been going over his effects, real and virtual, and there's plenty of evidence that he was working for the Union."

"A sleeper agent, under deep cover," Varden said.

"This base is compromised," Rountree said. "I don't know what we can do to clean it up. Not to mention we'll have to look at everyone who's ever worked with him . . ." She shook her head. "Hell, I trusted him completely."

"They were after us," Chase said. "After gen:LOCK." The fact that the Union was still willing to go to these extremes to capture a Holon was a whole new level of alarming. They'd have to work with RTASA and the Vanguard to find some way of dealing with it—but that was for later. "I'm sorry we triggered it, but at least you stopped him."

"Better now than later," Varden said.

"There's no indication that anyone else was working with him," Rountree said. "But gen:LOCK needs to take this very seriously."

"We will," Chase promised. "Believe me, we will."

Cammie sat up, stretching, grateful to be back in *Renegade*'s familiar compartment. The others had downloaded ahead of her, and Valentina offered a hand. Cammie took it, hauling herself to her feet, and followed Valentina into the main compartment to find that the base had brought snacks and a cooler full of fizzy drinks to say thank you. Yaz waved for her to take a seat, but she dug into the cooler instead, not yet ready to face whatever conversation was going to happen. She pulled out a bottle with a familiar logo, and the label lit up, her favorite opening screen overwriting the logo. "Siege! You got the new Siege bottles!"

Chase mixed in just in time to hear that, and she saw him frown. Migas lifted his hands. "Hey, I didn't do anything. The commissary sent them."

"Still." Cammie turned the bottle, watching the logo transform to a quick scene, and then return to the opening. She twisted off the cap, and grinned as a second screen appeared.

"You were right about Herrera," Chase said. "He was a Union sleeper."

All the good feelings drained away. "I wish I'd been wrong."

"That's bad," Yaz said. "This base . . ."

"They're tightening their security and figuring out where to go from here," Chase said. "Herrera tried to run, but the Interceptors caught him before he could reach the Union. He's dead, and Major Rountree is pretty sure he didn't have time to send out any more information."

"What exactly happened?" Valentina asked. "Do we know?"

"It looks as though this was a setup to get their hands on a Holon," Chase said. "This would be the place to put a sleeper if you were going to use refugees as bait. De Soto processes more refugees than any of the other border stations. But if you're asking about the hacking . . ."

Cammie sat up, putting aside the flashing bottle. "Aris and the stolen brains, that was bait. And attacking me on the Ether, that was—well, it didn't matter if it didn't work, it got us looking at Aris. But Herrera snuck a virus through the firewalls while we were focused on her, and it lay dormant until one of the Spider Tanks hit me with an activation signal." She paused. "I gave him my tool kit. That's how he got in."

"It helped," Caliban said. "However, I am running additional diagnostics based on the new information, and I do not believe there was any further incursion. So it was not sufficient. And you didn't share everything."

Not the things I wasn't supposed to have. Cammie knew better than to say that aloud, and shrugged one shoulder instead.

"He asked," Chase said. "And if you hadn't done it, I would have ordered you to. He fooled all of us, Cammie. We're lucky you spotted him when you did."

"And they were after your eBrain," Valentina said.

"That would be my guess," Cammie answered.

"Or they were after any piece of the Holon technology," Chase said. "They've already got one eBrain."

"They *had* one eBrain," Yaz said. "Since Nemesis, we've seen no sign that they're trying to adapt gen:LOCK technology."

"Probably because they don't have enough of it," Cammie said.

"So now the question is, do they actually have a Holon program already, or was this story just bait?" Valentina tipped her head to one side in question.

"Bait," Chase said firmly. "It's got to be. If they had anything more than Nemesis, they'd have used it already."

Cammie hesitated. She wasn't entirely sure about that: Just because they'd defeated Nemesis didn't meant that there wasn't another copy somewhere, or that the Union had given up the idea of creating its own Holons, its own dark version of gen:LOCK, but she knew she didn't have proof. She could find it, maybe, if she went a little deeper into the Ether's black-hat spaces, but she knew what Chase would say to that. She reached for another drink, lining up the labels so that the scenes seemed to flow from one bottle to the next.

"So, did you get the rest of the Spider Tanks?" Kazu asked, sprawling in his usual chair.

"We took about a third of the remaining group," Chase said.

"Closer to half," Yaz interjected, with a quiet smile.

"And we chased them back across the Eighty-Eighth," Chase said. "I don't think they'll come back for a while."

"That's good," Kazu said.

"The weather is also improving rapidly," Yaz said. "We could even fly out tonight, but—"

"We've had a busy day," Chase said, with a grin. "Let's get a good night's sleep and leave in the morning."

"I still wish I'd gotten more of them," Kazu said.

"Can't have everything." Chase sobered abruptly. "We did well. All of you—all of us. And that means you, too, Kazu. We had to help get those people to safety, and you did it, you and Cammie."

Kazu shrugged one shoulder, but Cammie thought he was blushing.

"Kazu also rescued a cow," she said brightly, and saw the color deepen.

Kazu and Migas made a run to the mess hall around dinner-time, and returned with a box of more sandwiches and a multitude of sides. Cammie filled her plate, suddenly starving, and the others seemed equally hungry. Valentina and Kazu managed to get into an argument about cattle and swimming, or maybe it was about whether swimming was good for cattle? Cammie tuned it out, listening instead to Chase telling Migas about the fight to the 88th, and what repairs they might need.

Migas nodded. "Okay. You want me to do that tonight, or wait till we get back to RTASA?"

"Surely, it can wait," Yaz said, and yawned hugely. "Ugh. I'm glad not to be flying tonight."

"As long as Caliban says the system is clear, everything else can wait," Chase said.

"And I do say so," Caliban interjected. "I said so eighty-seven minutes ago, but no one was listening."

Cammie rolled her eyes. "Thanks, Cal."

"I'm tired, too," Kazu said, and sounded almost surprised. "I'm going back to the barracks."

"So am I," Valentina said. "Though I think I will spend some time on the Ether."

"You should sleep," Kazu said.

Valentina waved a hand. "I will sleep on the flight."

They were still bickering as they went down the stairs, and Yaz yawned again. "I think I'll join them. Coming, Cammie?"

"In a minute." Cammie lined up three Siege bottles on the edge of the console, adjusting them so that the characters seemed to jump from one to the next.

"I'm going to go see what Caliban's doing," Migas said, and ducked into the aft compartment.

"Mind if we talk?" Chase perched on the chair next to Cammie's, his avatar matching the cushion's contours perfectly.

"You're getting good at that," Cammie said, and winced. "Sorry. That wasn't tactful."

"I've been practicing," Chase said. "Did you give any more thought to what we talked about?"

Cammie looked away, twisting the last bottle until it was just right. An armored knight lumbered across the bottles, followed by a pointy-eared elf with a bow and arrows. Behind them, a dragon swept from bottle to bottle, trailing clouds of smoke. For a moment, she thought about pretending she didn't know what he was talking about, but she owed him better than that. "A little. Maybe. I'm still thinking."

"Okay," Chase said. "It's just . . . we need you, Cammie."

Cammie felt warmth spread through her, pinking her cheeks and settling in her chest. "Och, you'd manage."

"Not today, we wouldn't," Chase said. "There was nothing we could do right then to help you, but you saved yourself. And then you figured out about Herrera. That was well done."

The warmth abruptly vanished. She'd saved herself, yeah, but she'd put herself into that position in the first place because she'd trusted Herrera. She'd *liked* him. But that wasn't something she could say—or maybe it was. She reached for her Ether goggles. "Look, maybe—yeah, maybe I'd like to talk, if you've got the time. But not here."

"I've got time," Chase said. "Lead the way."

Cammie dropped onto the Ether before she could change her mind. Chase mixed in beside her, and she looked up at him, scowling. "I'm going to take you somewhere—not shadowspace, nothing black-hat, just . . . private."

"Okay." Chase nodded.

"I don't want you to say anything," Cammie said. "I'm just taking us there because it's secure."

"I won't say a word."

She threaded her way through the intervening volumes, Chase keeping up easily, and finished at last at the pink-and-green entrance to her garden space. She gave him a suspicious glance as she reached for the magic key, but his expression was thoughtful.

"Is this ElwysNet?"

"Yeah."

"I had a game space here, when I was a kid," Chase said. "Me and some friends." He shook his head. "Sorry. You said not to talk."

"It's okay." Cammie manipulated her key, and the gray tunnel opened in front of them, gate gleaming at the end. She led them through and out into the garden. Menus flared, warning her of failed updates and systems conflicts, but the light was brighter than it had been, and the grass was more like her original model. The message tree held a few leaves again, and a note popped up to signal that the system had recovered more messages and was waiting to convert them to the current format. She told it to go ahead, dealt with two more high-priority warnings, and turned to glance at Chase. To her surprise, he was looking around with what must have been genuine curiosity, the space's sunlight bright on the vivid blue of his avatar. "Sorry. I'm trying to get caught up here."

"What is this?" Chase waved a hand. "Did you make it?"

"Yeah. My dad bought me the space when I was six, said I could do what I wanted with it." She watched him fiercely for any sign of amusement or contempt. "I've been keeping it up ever since, only—after Mam died, and then Dad, and I got arrested, I wasn't able to maintain it, right? So it's not what it was. But it's private, and that's why I brought us here."

Chase nodded. "Polity Cybersecurity wouldn't let you take care of it?"

"I didn't tell them about it," Cammie said. "It wasn't their business. This is mine, my space, my family—" She broke off then, shaking her head.

"I didn't know you'd lost both your parents," Chase said tentatively. "I thought—"

"I lived with my grandmother," Cammie said. "She's still living, not that I get much chance to contact her. Mam was killed when the Union attacked the last of the old North Sea oil rigs—she was a decommissioning engineer. And Dad died of complications from a motorcycle wreck. But that's not what I wanted to talk about."

Chase nodded again. "Okay."

"Captain Herrera." Cammie felt her eyes prickling behind the Ether goggles. "He was nice to me, and I gave him my whole damn tool kit—most of it, anyway—and he turned around and tried to kill us. I *liked* him."

"He had everybody fooled," Chase said. "Major Rountree said pretty much the same thing. She trusted him completely."

"That's something," Cammie said, but felt some of the tightness ease. If Rountree had trusted him—and she'd worked with him, side by side; she knew him as well as anyone could—maybe she wasn't unbearably naive to have trusted him as well. "Do we know why?"

"No." Chase didn't pretend to misunderstand. "At least Rountree hadn't found anything so far. He was born this side of the Eighty-Eighth, too."

"I don't understand," Cammie said. "I just don't get it! Why would he help the Union?"

"You're asking the wrong person," Chase began, then sighed. "No, I owe you a better answer than that. I think—the Union feeds on fear, fear of the smoke, fear of the behemoths and the Spider Tanks and the troops who can take you away, and they promise that they won't take *you* as long as you do exactly what you're told. It'll only take those other people, and those other people have to be bad, or the Union wouldn't take them. For a lot of people, that's the smart thing, the easy thing—the *safe* thing."

"Until it isn't," Cammie said.

Chase nodded. "Some people think only force and fear can win. For them it's the smart bet. And some people want to frighten other people, either because it's better to be on top or because they like hurting people. What Herrera thought—I don't know. We probably won't ever know."

"And if we did know," Cammie said slowly, "I don't know if it would help much, really."

"Yeah."

They stood for a moment in silence. Another set of menus appeared, but Cammie compressed them without even looking, her nerves too raw to concentrate on the code. She was full of grief for things she couldn't even name, wanted to dig up some schematics and fling herself into them so she wouldn't have to think . . .

"Cammie," Chase said.

"I can't talk to you," she said. "It's no fair, not when you've been through so much more than I have. Nothing's *happened* to me, I just have bad dreams about something I actually got away from."

"Oh, Cammie." Chase's tone was rueful. "That's not how it works."

"But it isn't fair," she insisted. "You lost half your body, and then you put yourself permanently onto the Ether—"

"I chose to do that, Cammie," Chase said. "Never forget that. I made that decision."

"Did you have a choice?"

"Yeah." Chase nodded. "Never believe I didn't. Maybe they weren't great choices, but they were choices, and—I chose." She stared at him, not quite sure whether she believed him or not, and he gave her a crooked smile. "Besides . . . It's not a competition. We don't have to add up points and the person with the most damage gets the help. We're a team. We take care of each other. Nobody understands what gen:LOCK can do to us any better than we can."

"Nobody else has nightmares," Cammie said.

"One, we don't know that," Chase said. "Two—two, the only reason I don't have nightmares anymore is that I don't have a body. There's no downtime on the Ether, so, no dreams."

"I just want them to stop," Cammie admitted. "I mean, I've done the reading, I understand how this all works, and all the books say it'll go away eventually. But I want it gone *now*." Just saying it out loud made her feel a little better, and she slanted a glance and a smile at Chase. "I mean, I know you've got an answer, but I'm not sure it's entirely practical."

To her relief, Chase grinned. "It's kind of a drastic solution. We can find you something better."

"Time." Cammie sighed.

"Time," Chase agreed. "Talking helped me—Dr. Weller listened to a lot of me moaning and complaining those first couple of years. I'm here if you want an ear."

"Thanks."

"The others—"

Cammie interrupted. "They think I'm a kid."

"They wish you could *be* a kid," Chase said. "*I* wish you could be a kid. But you're not, and you're doing an adult's job, and doing it extremely well. But nobody who's seen what you can do thinks you're a kid."

"They think I'm off on the Ether gaming all night."

"Because you haven't said you're not," Chase pointed out. "What do you think would happen if you said *I'm having nightmares, and I go on the Ether to calm down from them*?"

Cammie paused. "I—don't think I'm ready for that."

"Give it some thought," Chase said.

"Yeah." Cammie worked her shoulders, the muscles feeling as tight as if she'd been working. "Kazu was right: It's been a long day."

Chase nodded, accepting the change of subject. "It has. But, like I said, you did really well."

"Yeah, well, I'm glad to get some credit." Cammie looked sideways again. "Maybe I could get a break on the swearing for a day or two?"

"You were the one who wanted people to listen to you," Chase pointed out.

She sighed. "I know. Right. Maybe some extra credits for the Ether?"

"Maybe," Chase said with a grin, and she smiled back.

"Right. But now, I should take everyone's good advice and try to get some sleep."

"Good idea," Chase said, and mixed out ahead of her. She swept her gaze around the garden, prioritizing the update list and setting them to run. This was where she'd started, after all, where she'd first learned what code could do, and it was all the more special because Dad had given it to her. That was worth keeping. Maybe she could make it her haven against all the nightmares. But that would take time, time to update and rebuild, and she couldn't do it all at once. She took a last look around, then dropped off the Ether into *Renegade*'s familiar cabin. Tonight she would see if she was tired enough to dodge the nightmares. And if she couldn't, well, she could check the garden again. She collected Nugget and headed for the barracks.

about the author

MELISSA SCOTT is from Little Rock, Arkansas, and studied history at Harvard College and Brandeis University, where she earned her PhD in the Comparative History program. She is the author of more than thirty original science fiction and fantasy novels as well as authorized tie-ins for *Star Trek: DS9*, *Star Trek: Voyager*, *Stargate SG-1*, *Stargate Atlantis*, and *Star Wars Rebels*. She has won Lambda Literary Awards for *Trouble and Her Friends*, *Shadow Man*, *Point of Dreams* (written with her late partner, Lisa A. Barnett), and *Death By Silver*, with Amy Griswold. She has also won Spectrum Awards for *Shadow Man*, *Fairs' Point*, *Death By Silver*, and for the short story "The Rocky Side of the Sky" (*Periphery*, Lethe Press) as well as the John W. Campbell Award for Best New Writer. Her most recent solo novel, *Finders*, was published at the end of 2018, and she is currently at work on the next book in the sequence.